THE
FLUTE
ACROSS
THE POND

THE FLUTE ACROSS THE POND

FREDERIC WAKEMAN

THE WORLD PUBLISHING COMPANY
CLEVELAND AND NEW YORK

PUBLISHED BY The World Publishing Company
2231 West 110th Street, Cleveland, Ohio 44102
Published simultaneously in Canada
by Nelson, Foster & Scott Ltd.

First Printing 1966

PROLOGUE

The conductor, pale and bitter, looked over his shoulder at the muttering audience, and began the slow movement.

In Row J, Andrew Alberg glared over his shoulder and went "Sssst!"

Why do they bother to cross oceans, deserts, prairies, *and* the Alps to mix their tourist chatter with Mozart? Why did they queue up to buy expensive tickets *not* to hear Herbert von Karajan?

And why don't I stop chasing these music festivals all over the place and admit the truth? That I get more real listening pleasure out of my own hi-fi. No goons gossiping in six languages around me, or, worse, sighing *schön* at the pauses and applauding *between* movements.

Andrew Alberg shifted away from the elbow of the fat lady on his left.

Less body interference, too, theirs and mine. No hot squeezed feet, no chafed knees, no coat or necktie—just sloppy old me lolling at the crossroads of stereo, maybe listening to The Man's piano concertos, One to Five in order, as taped by Richter, Horowitz, sweet old Artur, and . . .

Between him and the elegant Von Karajan, mind's picture-tube projected an image of Laney abandoning her algebra lesson to loll and listen on the sofa beside him; and on mind's soundtrack, overriding present music and mutter, Laney's voice shouted at Stan upstairs: "Pleeease, Bunny, close your door on that TV gunfight"—and Betty on the landing warning both kids about lessons and bedtime, and . . .

Yes, time to face it: hi-fi is better.

On his right, the boy with the new beard leaned over and tapped the shoulder of the girl who was looking at the music through blue-colored glasses. She turned.

New-Beard said, "Great, huh?"

"The greatest."

"Where you from?"

"Stanford. You?"

"Princeton."

"I'm impressed."

"Enough to have a drink?"

"Well . . ."

And so, no doubt, to bed. In New-Beard's case. In my case it would be, "Well, nice talkin' to you." And her curtain line would be, "Nice talking to *you*." Whatever it takes to make out with strangers I just ain't got.

Von Karajan finished the *Haffner* and turned contemptuously to the audience, which applauded better than it listened.

All hands insisted on an encore, and the maestro brilliantly expressed his loathing by giving them "The Blue Danube," triple-fortissimo.

Just what they so richly deserve. Jesus-Joseph-and-Martin-Luther, how I hate secondary music about primary cities: the Vienna of Strauss, the London of Elgar, the St. Petersburg of Moussorgsky, the Rome of Respighi, the Paris–New York of Gershwin.

Now, the audience went wild. Bravos were a pfennig a dozen. The pale, icy conductor didn't even bow; the applause, like a bumptious busybody, slowly got the idea it wasn't welcome.

Andrew Alberg rubbed his chafed knees, stood himself up, and drifted with the crowd toward the Salzburg streets.

Back of him, New-Beard was saying to Blue-Glasses, "Okay, so your hostel is cheaper than my hostel, but I bet my water is colder."

Mind's Atlas flipped to a map of the U.S. Mind's pencil drew a straight line from Princeton to Stanford—bisected it.

Yep, all their kids should go to college in my home town. Nebraska U.

Hi-fi is better.

On the way out, he checked his ticket for tomorrow: *Così Fan Tutte*, Row H.

And there she was, tucking her program into her purse as she beautifully paused on the steps of the Festival Hall. Still alone, just as in Bayreuth, just as in Prades.

Seeing her again is not *that* much of a miracle, hundreds of us are making this same music festival circuit; the miracle is a girl like that *alone*. All the time, *alone*.

He hurried several steps below her, then turned, not looking at her but farther up the steps as if in search of some other music-lover, though with eyes alert to receive the signal from her eyes if such shock of recognition happened to happen.

Her face was pale ivory framed in brown hair, straight and shining, shoulder length.

Chances are she doesn't even speak English. Might try out my Swedish on her. Fat chance. She's about as Scandinavian as . . .

Then it hit him: she reminded him of Da Vinci's Saint Anne. All that sadness, loneliness, compassion. Not least or last, all that beauty, too. Here and not here, just as she had seemed there and not exactly there in Bayreuth and Prades.

A person dislocated from the present tense.

The girl—woman, rather; she was in her late twenties—walked past him, and he tried to force himself to speak or at least nod in cheerful recognition, but of course he did neither, and she walked down the steps and across the street and around a corner, and again he was alone.

Back in his hotel, he wrote a letter which began *Dearest Betty and Laney and Bunny, in case you haven't yet got the flare I*

vii

sent up from the Casals Festival, I am now at Salzburg. Laney, you should have been with me yesterday to . . .

And so on. When he reread the letter, he felt it was rather unsatisfactory but couldn't understand why.

As he was dropping it into the box outside the hotel, the reason came to him.

I wrote it to Laney, just to her, and completely forgot to include Betty and Bunny in it.

But it was too late, this time; the letter was out of his hands.

He went to American Express and checked the train schedule for Verona and Callas and *Medea*-under-the-stars.

PART 1

CHAPTER 1

~~~~~~~~~~~~~~~
~~~~~~~~~~~~~~~
~~~~~~~~~~~~~~~

Tape knocked, got croaked at, and entered Nelly Finch's bedroom.

"You Swedes are never late," she complained. "Being on time is no way to treat an old pal. How's Sonya?"

The hour was noon and Nelly was still in bed, breakfasting on her usual Bloody Mary and Pall Mall. She had gone to bed drunk, it was clear, with all her bracelets on, and her arms were bruised and nicked.

The diamonds, rubies, emeralds, and sapphires winked and blinked maliciously at the damage they had wrought.

Tape offered her the latest scatological story, accepted coffee, and then unwrapped his drawings, for Nelly was building an even bigger house on an even higher mountain and he had brought the plans for her new garden.

His watercolors were rendered with love, skill, and imagination from every point of view: ocean, valley, canyon, and mountain, as seen from the terrace and entering the gate, with stately trees, rolling lawns, flowering shrubs, and strategic hedges artfully natural, for Tape's ideal was the English park made semitropical with California-loving plants.

Nelly, a raucous blonde widow of great wealth, bent her head

3

over the pretty paintings, spreading them around her on the bed. Tape looked down on Nelly's slept-in hair, mostly straw-colored but with roots so embarrassingly gray that he lowered his gaze discreetly and counted the bracelets on her bruised, flabby arms, six *à gauche* and five *à droit*.

Suddenly she leaned back and sipped Bloody Mary, suspending him in that helpless, frightening, yet thrilling moment before Yes or No, the bravo or the Bronx cheer, the . . .

"Some pal you are. Hell, man, you left out my swimming pool."

Tape winced, recovered, and said, more impertinently than he felt, "Hell, Nelly old pal, this is just a test run so's you can visualize it without the pool, just in case you . . ."

"I want my swimming pool," she pouted, like a sixty-two-year-old toddler, and he quickly added:

"You'll get a revised plan first thing tomorrow."

And how the hell could I forget that garden-ulcer, Olympic-sized? Probably because I hate the goddamn things.

He got out of there as fast as he politely could, turning at the door to plead for an extra day of Nelly's grace, because he and Sonya were giving a party that night to introduce another rich widow, Katie-from-Chicago, to the Best People in Pobrecito.

"Tape? Like in worm? Who hung that cutie-pie on you, Mr. Alberg?"

"I've been labeled and relabeled four times in forty-four years, Mrs. Jordan. My mamma . . ."

"Oh, call me Katie." . . ."It's a deal, if you'll reciprocate." . . . "Hi, Tape." . . . "Hi, Katie." . . . "That's settled."

"As I was saying, Katie, my mamma dubbed me Andrew, the schoolkids cut it to Andy, New York preferred Swede, but my wife wanted none of those guys in *her* bed, so at the delicate age of forty, I got taped."

"But how come she picked tape, Tape?"

The answer came from behind his shoulder, in Sonya's party voice; he smelled hot melted cheese and turned as his wife, offering canapés, said,

4

"Isn't it obvious, Mrs. Jordan? Take his measure, please. So thin, so narrow, and only five inches longer than the one in my sewing basket."

Katie plucked, nibbled, and said, "Delicious. What on earth are they?"

"Sun-dried fish eggs and stop exaggerating, wife. I'm only six-four."

White teeth gleaming in bronzed face said, "When slumped, he means."

"But I'm always slumped."

"Also, to make his name even more fitting, Mrs. Jordan . . ."

"Katie to you." . . . "Sonya me first." . . . "Shake, Sonya, now do tell me, what makes Tape tapier? Whatever you call him, he's a real cutie-pie."

"His mind, Katie, is exactly like a tape-recorder. Click, and he records, every syllable. Click, click, and he plays back, months or years later. No hiss, no hum."

"But plenty of wow and flutter, Katie. My tweeter woofs and my woofer tweets."

"You're a crazy couple. Real crazy."

As young wife smilingly smalltalked to old widow, husband looked at her the same way he listened to Mozart, with the humble adoration accorded only the masterworks.

Saint Anne had a suntan now, and her face and body were the *exact* old-bronze shade of her shining silky old-bronze hair. That bronze hair, smooth as a shield and almost shoulder length, framed the bronze face in a way that would have driven Botticelli crazy to get it all down on canvas.

"His playback is very disconcerting to a wife who can't remember what's been said from one minute to the next, although I often suspect him of doctoring the tape to fit his own propaganda line."

"Where'd ya get that dress, Sonya? Gorgeous. Saks?"

"Magnin's. Thank you. Excuse me; Nelly Finch looks hungry."

She bore her canapés to the crowded bar-room, husband's eyes

5

following. Tonight, the white teeth and the white coral necklace matched, too.

Katie said, "I'm old enough to enjoy her, too. Tell me, Tape, does she tint the hair to the skin, or . . . ?"

"It's just one of those California sunkist deals," he said. "When I first met her, in Europe, she had what the boys back in Lincoln used to call a pool-hall pallor."

The bright orange dress was fabulous on her, no joke.

Katie said, "She sure is a lady with real quality. What part of Yurrop is she from?"

"Sonya? Why, she's as American as caviar and truffles. Me, I'm as American as smörgasbord."

"Oh, so you *are* a Swede. I was wondering."

"My mother was a Dane. My dad is a squarehead. I used to pretend I was all Dane. Hamlet-envy."

"When you said Yurrop I thought Sonya . . ."

"We both happened to be wandering from music festival to music festival, and after the fourth coincidence, at Verona, I finally worked up the courage to say Beg your pardon, Miss, but what say let's go to the fifth one together?"

"Well, your tag sure fits. Caviar and truffles."

"Yeah. But I was speaking antecedently. Her mother was the daughter of a French diplomat stationed in Washington in the twenties. Her father came from Petrograd—Sonya's maiden name is Osinoff—and he was a fugitive from those Ten Days that are still shaking the back teeth out of the world. In New York he met Sikorsky, who got him started in aeronautical engineering. They're both dead, by the way, and she is all alone, except for me. Just me and her inheritance. Yes, Katie, I'm a dirty low-down Scandinavian gigolo from Lincoln, Nebraska; and my pore ol' Grandpa Alberg, who on Sundays when he wasn't farming was the Lutheran pastor in Beaver Crossing— that's about ten miles up from the West Fork crick before it runs into the Big Blue river, case you didn't know. Anyhow, pore ol' Grandpa must be yumpin' in his coffin for shame, by yiminy."

"Cute," said Katie.

6

"In fact, Katie" . . . am I talking too much? Probably. Martinis affect me same as laughing gas. But Katie is basically shy, she needs two more drinks before I expose her to all those snobby Native Sons in there, and, besides, she's interested in People, she said. Especially rich, social, or glamorous ones, in that order. So roll on, Tape.

"Without Sonya's inheritance I wouldn't be here. 'Sa fact, Katie. Before she changed my life, I was an art director in a New York ad agency. House in Oldtown, Connecticut, one Dufy, one Maize Goddess, all that. An art director, case you don't know, is a buggered artist who doodles layouts. New York always bugged me, all that building material, and like the man said Nature I love and next to Nature, Art. Besides . . ."

He mixed her a drink and steered her to the quiet, far end of the huge room.

Take it easy, Tape. It's too early for the hard sell. But time for the soft one.

"Besides, I grew up in the landscaping business. My dad ran a nursery in Lincoln. I could force a poinsettia to turn red in time for Christmas when I was eight. And by ten I was grafting gardenias. You wanta know the real secret of gardens, Katie dear? Don't treat plants like human beings or they'll get all tensed up, just like us. Anyway, there I was, suffocating in New York and sick of being a sensitive art director. Then I married Sonya. Four years ago."

"That long? You two cutie-pies act like you're still on your honeymoon. Gosh, you mixed me a strong one."

"We are. Anyway, her legacy and my lack of prejudice against living off women gave me the courage to break loose, so I quit my job and came out here to be a sensitive landscape architect. But we keep everything fifty-fifty. I buy the groceries, and she pays my alimony . . ."

Whoa, boy. Better change that tune or you'll hate yourself tomorrow.

He said, "Did you finally okay the house plans?"

"Not yet. I still don't think it's real Ranch."

"May I be permitted to correct a term, dear Katie? It's not

7

Ranch. In Pobrecito, there are ranch houses, like the Brewsters' next door, and *rawnch* houses, such as yours will be."

Flattered, her mauved eyelids fluttered and she looked around the living room. "This must be rawnch."

"Oh, no, this is a pre-rawnch, early-Palladian garage. According to the oldest gardener up at the big place, this selfsame living room once housed two Rolls Royces, one plain, the other wicker-work, and . . ."

"Shucks, I only got one measly Rolls."

"But this was back in 1928. Plus a white Cord roadster, a Hispano-Suiza, and a Duesenberg covered in alligator leather both inside and *out*."

Katie pretended not to be impressed. "I like to conceal wealth. That's why I bought all forty acres up there on top of Rattle-snake Canyon. I'm the shut-in type."

"Ol' Doc Alberg'll shut you in so"—the hard sell—"so tight the milkman'll need radar to find your kitchen door."

Katie looked out the window at the surrounding privet hedges, ten feet high. "You got beautiful privacy here."

"Except on the north, where ruthless subdividers dozed down a forty-year-old acacia hedge. We're planting hysterically to defend ourselves, but—for the moment, we're bare-assed to the Brewsters."

Katie said, "I think my architect is falling in love with your wife. Let's go break it up before we lose both of them."

Tape laughed heartily, for his Sonya had eyes for no one.

8

CHAPTER 2

~~~~~~~~~~~~~~~
~~~~~~~~~~~~~~~

A strange, expensive cigarette lighter was on the TV set. Probably Katie's-from-Chicago, whose loud cheerful voice now came on strong in his mind's hi-fi:

"Tape? Like in worm? Who hung that cutie-pie on you?"

He put the lighter in his pocket and poked the ON switch.

TV, our household barometer, only looked at in times of atmospheric depression, like now.

"Ah, a Drama," he said, adjusting the BRITE knob.

She wouldn't call me Swede because that's my New York name; and she couldn't call me Andy because that's my Oldtown name. So she minted herself a new one.

He turned out the sofa lights. Sonya was looking out the north window and he mock-snarled, "Drop them blinds, quick. If the Brewsters see us looking at TV again they'll think our marriage has gone thataway. It'll be all over town by morning."

"What?" She moved toward the sofa.

"Nothing. Just globbling." He went to the window and peered out.

"Imagine," he said, "outdoor lighting before the grass has had time to grow, those bulldozing barbarians. Did you remember to water the brush cherries?"

"Of course."

Of course I'm only trying to force some conversation out of her. Her passion to make that hedge grow taller is even greater than mine.

Tape dropped the blind, closed it tight, and sat down on the sofa beside her.

On Channel 3, some colored people were moving into their neat new suburban cottage. Next door to it, the white neighbor was peering balefully through his Venetian blind and muttering about property values. The white neighbor was a heavy he'd seen in many a late, late movie, but the name escaped him.

Tape threw a leg across Sonya's lap. "Contact."

But there wasn't any. TV had won the battle for her attention. She's depressed. Again. Probably the time of the month.

And then, just testing Sonya's click-click playback remark of yesterday, he became fascinated with the sound of his own thought-voice. It was coming in clear but not loud through and over the TV voices, with no confusion, no overlapping. Perfect fidelity, the highest.

If a Period problem, it would be the middle time of the month, her ovu—

"Hey," he said, "is your thinking voice the same as your speaking voice? In sound, I mean."

He'd won this round from TV; she looked away, considering the matter, then said, "Yes. I think so. Sort of. But a bit disembodied."

"Mine's much faster. Of course, when I think of something somebody else said, I hear *their* voice. Like right now, Nelly Finch. Miaaa!"

Then, tapping head and lips, he said, "I sound lots smarter up here than I do down here, to you outsiders."

Shouldn't have said that. *Outsiders* is one of her words when she's . . .

"My mind refuses to stay put," she said, interested for perhaps the first time that evening. "A phrase peeps out here. An image pops up there. A word rolls down a long, black alley."

10

"Strike or spare? But what phrases, what words? As of now, I mean?"

He never found out, for TV recaptured her eyes, her face went dead with melancholy, and he was alone and lonely in the corpsey glare of the picture tube.

"Git them brats a yours off my property, nigger."

Your leg just told my leg, "Git off my property, you too damn heavy."

Tape removed his chastened leg and Nelly Finch floated into focus on his memory-screen, as the white sadist and the colored masochist, both armed with, or rather handed with, dispatch cases, simultaneously opened their front doors, for the inevitable eyeball-to-eyeball confrontation at the curb.

"Hell, pal, you left out my swimming pool!"

Tape winced again at the memory.

My first big mistake since opening shop out here. The worst kind, too, that turns an easygoing client into . . . the kind that *could* turn a client like Nelly into a nonclient like Nelly.

He said, "Gotta get going on Nelly's garden. Man, she was raspy yesterday."

The Negro was at the curb, side-glancing. The white guy sneered and licked his lips. Wincing wives at windows.

Nelly Finch faded from Tape's thought-screen. Not entirely: she became one of many unguided missiles hurtling across Rattlesnake Canyon. Then everything fragmented into a meteorite shower of past experience and present concern and future fantasy.

Mind—he thought, dispelling the myriad swarm by a simple twist of the topic under consideration—is like the Universe, with visibly glittering and invisibly transmitting objects in Space, and deeper mysteries like Time as yet unfathomed. It even has its own God, the Thinker. In my case, me. *Cogito ergo sum deus.* Therefore, God is God and Mind is Mind and never the twain shall agree.

Sonya opened the old rococo silver casket which bore the Osinoff arms and took a cigarette.

Did I remember to show that to Katie? I did. Was she impressed? She was.

He made a fast draw, aimed and fired a jet of Katie's gas at the cigarette; Sonya murmured thanks. He kicked off a moccasin and put his bare foot on the coffee table, carefully avoiding the Tang horse (Tangish horse, for who can trust the devious Chinese?) with the broken tail, kicked off by—what else?—a too impulsive moccasin on a less prudent evening.

We live and learn to respect the bric-a-brac.

Uninhaled cigarette smoke trickled out of Saint Anne's mouth.

Yes, even in the bronze, she still looks like the Da Vinci beauty I saw on the steps at Salzburg. The same great sad beautiful eyes, half-hooded, with their enigmatic side glances. The same untamed mouth . . . flawless skin pulled tight over a broad Slavic skull, but made exotic with Mediterranean eyes and ripe southern lips.

But when you marry Saint Anne and get to know her over-lapping little toes, and the three coarse hairs around her left nipple, and the wart on her shoulder blade, and especially the way her nostrils splay and flare rhythmically when she's passionate, is it still Saint Anne?

If Nelly drops the boom, I'm in trouble again. Alimony. Alimoney-Honey-Bunny. Unless Katie . . . at least she called me cutie-pie. Was I bragging, or protesting too much, about Sonya's inheritance? And did I conceal the amount because ten thousand, six hundred dollars a year is not enough to impress Katie, or . . . ? Yes, it's half a protest, as befits half a Hamlet.

The white racist was creeping toward his neighbor's house, gallon can in hand. A TV owl hooted.

"Nelly wants her swimming pool on the leeward side of that eucalyptus grove," he said. "I keep telling her about prevailing winds and dead leaves and all she answers is 'Mack'll fish 'em out.' "

"Nelly will put that pool where she wants it," Sonya said, "and later she'll dispose of the leaf problem by cutting down the trees."

"I'll kill her first. I believe in all forms of individualism except letting idiots cut down trees. You know, some fine noon Nelly's going to wake up and find both of her arms chopped off. She's taken to sleeping in her bracelets."

With his bare foot he stroked her bare knee. Her noncommittal knee. Her uncommitted knee.

Depressed. Again. Is it estrogens? Or me?

Another Quick Relief commercial interrupted the Drama, and he said, "That's the seventh one in less than a half hour. Definitely, America is the most commercial country in the world."

But this is mid-month, so it must be her ovulation day. Better not get too . . . come to think of it, I'm not getting very much these days. But this is no time to bring *that* up. We got rhythm. She keeps saying she doesn't want a child but maybe she's just saying it because she knows I don't. I've never said so, flat out, but she knows. Maybe she wants one. Maybe I'd better try to make her believe I do too. But dammit, my point of view *has* to be different from hers. I'm pretty damned old to take on the burden of another family. Still, if I thought she really and truly wanted one, then of course I could whip up my . . .

Funny, I usually see Stan and Laney in bed. Honey and Bunny. Sleeping. Always thirteen and sixteen, the way they were then. Sweet Laney, so good about writing, so apologetic because Stan won't. My other self. Once. Maybe in time, he . . .

Sleeping. Like two young— why I didn't wake them up to say goodbye I'll never know —corpses. Stan laid out flat on back and mouth open, Laney spreadeagled face down like killed in battle. Two young corpses.

Maybe Stan would agree to come out here this summer. Maybe that would make him . . . change. I'll mention it to Sonya. Not now of course. Later. I know it would cure her. All *she* needs is to break the ice. Fifteen minutes with either one of those kids and all that stuff she tortures herself with would disappear. Melt away.

Break the ice and melt the guilt. You'd think time would make

13

her less sensitive, less . . . like in my case. All their cases. Time heals and continues to do so. Of course. After all, everybody lives engrossed with the Now, nobody got maimed. They eat, drink, date, go to school, struggle toward their own version of independence, all that.

The white neighbor poured the liquid from the can, backed away, and touched off a match.

But maybe it's more than that. She's not happy enough. At least sometimes. Like now. The prize slips out of my reach, my touch, my . . . Sonya the Rare. The Beauty. Physically, intellectually, artistically, every way. There's none of this disbalance of interest, this boredom, this need to have the marriage held up by things outside it, like most couples. When we're going okay, we like to sit around gassing about Wittgenstein, listening to Pergolesi though Telemann is better. We balance each other in most of the important ways. Now, even our incomes just about match, thank God. Although, sometimes I think our first two years out here, when I was such a load, were our best times. Even when she had to pay my alimony it made her feel good. I could tell. Yes, that was our best time, in every room, living, kitchen, especially bed, and of course, bath. Me in there watching her bathe, or stand in the water shaving her legs, all that joking, sexing . . .

Now the Negro's house was fully aflame and he in desperate retaliation was creeping toward the white's house, cigarette lighter in one hand, bottle of lighter fluid in the other.

There was a far-off wail of sirens, a distant clang of bells.

A fire on both your houses, Tape thought, and said, "Wish I knew where that scriptwriter lived. I'd set *his* house on fire. Mind if I turn it off?"

"Prefer it."

"The best thing on TV," he said, enjoying it, "is that momentary little plane of light receding into the blackness. An instant diamond."

The first diamond is forever—maybe she's just a victim of De Beers advertising.

He turned on the living-room lights, reacting with pleasure, as

14

always, to the rich stuff Sonya had saved from her mother's house in East Hampton. It should have been out of place in this otherwise rustic room, but it wasn't. Nymphs and fauns Dresden and Meissen, camels and nags Mingish and Tangish, Thomas Sheraton and Marie Laurencin . . . somehow, all were very amiable with the walk-in fireplace of rough-hewn stone and the hunting-lodge walls of crude knotty pine.

"Yesterday," he said, "Katie Jordan asked me for the name of our Interior Decorator. Want a job?"

It was half a joke and half a suggestion, for Sonya had been a professional decorator with many dazzling jobs to her credit between Hampton Bays and Montauk Point.

So here I am—he passed behind her and ran his fingers through her shining brown hair—cruising around somebody else's bric-a-brac. Kicking the tail off other people's Tang horse. This particular collection of loot happened to reach me through the death of a mother-in-law, but it could just as easily have been the original setting for a previous husband. After all, Sonya was twenty-nine when we met and why there hadn't been a previous husband is one of those mysteries I'll never understand.

Not one saucer did I contribute to this menage. Ashtrayless I came—just as Ashtrayless I left Oldtown. The family possessions are supposed to be split fifty-fifty at crack-up time, but I have yet to meet a husband who even retrieved his fishing rods. And if my ex-wife ever remarries—God, the relief if that happened— her new husband, cleaned probably as was I, will be prowling among my treasures, stroking my Cambodian head, no doubt kicking over my Maize Goddess—the bastard will probably even go bird-watching with my binoculars, fish with my fly-rod.

"You want a Coke or a beer or a coffee or something?" he said, smoothing her thick hair, again marveling at the match it made with her clear brown skin.

"No, thanks."

"Care for a little music?"

"If you do."

"Gad," he said. "You're cryptic tonight. Is anything the

15

matter, sweetheart? And when I say sweetheart, I really mean sweetheart. You know that, don't you, sweetheart?"

"I'm a little tired."

"You're more than a little depressed. Jesus, I hope it's not me."

"Never you, Tape. You know how I feel about you. It's just . . ."

"Maybe," he said, "I should put you to work."

"Doing what?"

"Interior Décor, what else? Our business cards could read: Contact Sonya and Tape for Gracious Living Inside and Out. Let's do it, Sonya. We'll hire a maid to take the house off your back and soak the rich together. Teammates."

"No more maids for me. Never."

"Oh, some of them are okay."

"All of them enslave me. They start long conversations and I haven't the courage to shut them up. I hate such daily proof of my cowardice."

Then she added, "But of course, if we need the money. Do we?"

"If Nelly Finch recovers from her shock and Katie Jordan comes through, I'll outbracket you for a change. Not to mention His Honor, the Mayor. On the other hand, I sort of enjoy having you support me. I guess your inheritance and I have one of those love-love relationships."

She rose suddenly and left his hand stroking air. She went to the far end of the room and studied titles in the bookcase.

She is going to start reading to avoid talking. No other reason. Rejection. If I called it that she'd say Silly and accuse me of having a rejection neurosis. Which it probably is. But knowing it doesn't change it.

He crossed to the hi-fi complex; old but not forgotten cartoons signed *Alberg* flew across Rattlesnake Canyon, on their journey back from *The New Yorker*. Sorry, but . . .

Rejections. He turned on the Scott solid-state amplifier, her Third Anniversary gift to him; he set on Playback the Ampex tape-deck, his Fourth Anniversary gift to her, for he had given

16

up discs and now all his music was on tape. Indeed, all his discs were back in Connecticut with the Maize Goddess.

So here we are on our feet, at opposite ends of the room, she with her books, me with my tapes. Which book she? Which tape me? My mess. Really must catalog it. Into things like centuries, or better ROMANTIC, CLASSIC, ATONAL, FOLK, OPERA, DRAMA, JAZZ, and all that BAROQUE.

As usual, the very *bulk* of the collection thrilled him—once he'd estimated there were over three million feet of what the stereo mags called Glorious Sound. Which it mostly was.

Now, what would best undepress her? Mendelssohn's *Italian* was gay and so was Offenbach's *Gaîté Parisienne,* but me no like. Haydn's *Clock?* Boyce's Symphony Number Zero? A real clown, that Boyce. Britten's great *War Requiem?* Jesus, no. Sweet old Artur and his sweeter Mozart? Those slow movements kill her, even in the good times. Gluck? Don't be selfish. Something different. Homage to Sonya. Music hath . . . Ahhhh. The fabulous Ives' Concord Sonata, magically played by another great man of music. Not exactly gay, but . . . inspiring.

"If you had just one more hour to live," he said, threading the tape on the spool, "and your executioners let you listen to any piece you wanted, what would it be?"

"Anything," she said, rising slightly to the lure, "so long as it's Beethoven."

"Them's tall words, pardner. Don't forget Wellington's Victory."

"Oh, the Thirteenth Quartet, I'd say." She turned back to the bookcase, disappearing from the topic.

"Personally," he said loudly, trying to mend the broken connection, "I'd take one of the Mozart piano concerti. Probably the Twentieth. But maybe the Twenty-first. No. Both. I don't know why the piano gets me the most. Probably because my mother played. When I was ten I thought her 'Anitra's Dance' the supreme achievement of the instrument. I wonder how it really sounded? But I guess all mothers are talented. Didn't you tell me once your mother claimed she had been a prodigy at six, but in your whole life you never once saw her open the piano?"

17

"Um huh," Sonya mumbled, suddenly finding what she wanted, *The Oxford Book of English Verse.*

"Since you've got more than one hour to live," he said, "you're gonna get the only insurance salesman I ever loved. Mister Charles Ives."

He turned the switch and the tape began to slither from reel to reel at a steady seven and one-half inches per second.

At the other end of the room, Sonya stiffened and held onto the bookcase; she turned her face away from him and bent her head, trembling, as she awaited the blow.

CHAPTER 3

Ives. Please let it be one of the symphonies and not the Concord Sonata. Never the Concord Sonata. I won't have it, and I can't bear it.

The piano started and she did have it, so the remaining question was Could she bear it?

Over four hundred tapes on those shelves of his, thousands of titles, and it has to be *this*.

White knuckled brown hands clutched *The Oxford Book of English Verse*. Tape sat in his listening chair, strategically placed for total stereo.

"For years," he said, "this piece was considered unplayable. Not merely unlistenable, technically impossible. Now hear how easily this guy tosses it off. No more trouble than the Minute Waltz. Dazzling."

Now there was a fortissimo. Sixty decibels of anguish. The room became dense with all those favorite Ives sounds, gleaned from picnic and marching band and forest and music hall; harmony changed to tone cluster, each one an unbearable pain.

I cannot bear it. But I must not run, or even close my ears, or run, or run.

There was something cowardly about leaving the room. More

than cowardly: ignominious. No, more than that. Leaving the room would be making a statement she did not care to make, even to herself. It would tell her more about herself than she cared to know.

She dropped into a chair, sitting sideways, still facing the books.

As the Emerson movement disappeared into the Hawthorne movement, Tape said, "Yeah, there's that Beethoven-Fifth theme again. The guy who wrote the blurb claims the whole sonata is tied together by those three Churchillian notes. Glad to hear it, although personally I think what ties it all together is talent."

Stop shivering. Stop listening. Stop thinking. Stop feeling. And have I stayed long enough not to call it running?

Sonya rose; pretending casual business elsewhere, she out-flanked her husband and slipped into the hall. Pausing a moment as if trying to decide which way to go, she escaped into the bedroom and closed the door, reducing Ives by two-thirds, but not nearly enough.

She tossed her book on the bed and blindly found the chair in front of her dressing table. Although the room was not air-conditioned, she shivered, and clutched her shoulders.

Now there was a viola and a piano.

Now a surprised, stretched-out tinkle, and the music stopped. Instantaneous death.

She inhaled so sharply that her nostrils snorted, horselike. The speakers rumbled, as he cut the amplifier. Deadest silence.

She exhaled, half sigh, half moan.

If you're not going to have music, please work on Nelly's swimming pool. Or the Mayor's Expressway. Or water the brush cherries again—do anything, but don't come in here.

Please.

Please don't try to console me, to help me. Above all, don't try to understand me. You must never try to understand me. I cannot bear your trying to understand me.

Back of her, the bedroom door opened.

Please don't say I blame you or reject you. I don't blame

20

anybody but me. I don't reject anybody but me. And don't say I don't love you. I don't not love you. I just . . .

The light went on. He was back of her.

I am begging you not to stroke my hair, or pat my cheek, or squeeze my shoulder. If you touch me, my skin will scream.

"Remember old Togo, that Jap gardener used to work for me?"

She raised her eyelids for one quick furtive glance into the mirror. He was standing well back, with *both* hands in his pockets.

"Laziest bastard in the business, bar none. One day when I was remodeling the old McCormack estate, I ordered him to cut back the bougainvillaea and hibiscus—all that tropical junk goes to pith and bramble unless you keep pruning it without mercy, as Togo well knew. Anyhow, days went by and nothing happened, as usual. So one morning I got fed up and screamed, 'I want those hedges pruned immediately.' Well, old Togo pasted a crafty look on that innocent baby face of his, a hurt look like he was highly distressed at my lack of esthetic sensibility, and he protested, 'But they're still in bloom, Mistle Albell. Watsa matter, don't you like flowers?' "

Tape unpocketed a hand, reached out a long thin knobby arm that exactly fit his long thin knobby body, and stroked her hair.

A breeze rattled the date palm outside the window, producing a sound that used to make her think it had started to rain.

"Watsa matter, Missy Albell, don't you like music? That's the first, and still the greatest, piece of modern music. And what a pianist! For my dough, this guy Werner Grunwald is the new Schnabel, the greatest living philosopher of the keyboard. Also the best technician. Why, Grunwald just shakes his hands and the notes roll out of his sleeves."

She shivered. He moved in to pick up a cashmere cardigan which he draped over her shoulders.

"The nights," he murmured, "are still a little cool."

Long pause. He added thoughtfully, "For April, that is."

The sweater had covered her opened jewel box. He reached over and closed the lid.

"Of all the things you inherited from your mother, this is my favorite. A beauty, inside and out. Like its present owner."

Of all the things I did not inherit from my mother.

Tape switched on the dressing-table lamp, a severe and prim little Chinese matron in white jade shaded in bedragoned silk, and bent over the box to enjoy the Watteauish oval miniature of the high-breasted beauty in the high white wig who graced the ivory-inlaid, brass-fretted ebony cover.

"Madame Pompadour's Jewel Box," he said. "Well, it could have been, at that. Sure does look like her."

He raised the lid of the elegant little casket and marveled at the workmanship inside. "They don't make stuff like this any more," he said. "But of course they don't make Madame Pompadours any more, either."

He closed the box and looked at Sonya in the mirror.

"Please don't cry, sweetheart," he said. "You know you can't stop once you start. Please try to hold it. You can, if you'll just use your will, sweetheart. Please."

He went to the bathroom and returned with a wet towel. He held it against her eyes. She nodded her appreciation and took the towel, dabbing its coolness against her forehead.

Yes, yes. I must control it. With my will. What will? I must not start crying for his sake. Poor thing. What have I done to him? What am I doing to him? What will I do? To him?

She put down the towel and said, "I'm all right."

"It's probably just your ovulation day," he said. "A period problem. Doc Hart explained it to me. Lots of women get this hormone disbalance and the body won't slough off its liquids, so it literally swells up with water, including of course the brain cells. And the ensuing mere mechanical pressure of the swollen brain pressing against the skull produces, in millions of women apparently, terrible periodic depressions. Temporary ones, thank God. You really should take those pills he gave you, sweetheart, even if they do keep you up all night going to the can. He says it's the only way to get rid of the excess water in a hurry, and . . ."

Periods. You blame everything on periods. Just pee-pee-pee

22

your problems away. Well, I can't piss away mine. Forgive me. My ugly thoughts. Ugly uglier ugliest thoughts. You're too nice to suffer me. So nice and blind. So nice and full of hopeless desperate optimism. Periods. Pills. Pee-pee.

Countering hopefully, flinging his activity against her lethargy, again he hustled himself into the bathroom, calling cheerfully:

"Where are they, sweetheart? I'll get them for you."

Speak. Squeeze out the civilized words through the throat's sluggish torpor. Speak.

"No," she said. "Never again. I lost twelve pounds in one day. I felt like death."

"You probably took too many."

"I took one."

"Then try a half."

"No." She could not bear the lady in the white wig and covered the jewel box with her sweater. She rose blindly from the chair and flung herself across the bed.

Help! Will-power, where are you? Come and help me.

The hunter gave up his pill-hunt and stalked her to the bed. There *is* no escape. There never is. There never will be.

"Christ, I want to help you," he said. "It's awful, loving you and wanting so desperately to make you happy with me, and not . . . succeeding. The terrible thing is, I can't find any reasons. Unless it's me, personally. Sure you ain't developed an allergy to Sensitive Landscape Architects, sweetheart?"

Oh, the probing. Oh, the well-meant torture. Two vices have we. The vice of talking too much and the vice of not talking enough.

"Is that our problem, sweetheart? Is it? Because, if it is, then I . . ."

Turning away from the excruciating probe, she rolled over the book; its edges pressed sharply into her side but she didn't change position, just lay there on the book. The poem she had been reminded of, which she had looked for because she had forgotten all but the first two lines, suddenly appeared in clear,

23

well-lighted print against the surrounding mists of—no, the
black, the terrible black fog of memory:

> I am! yet what I am, who cares, or knows,
> My friends forsake me like a memory lost.
> I am the self-consumer of my woes;
> They rise and vanish, an oblivious host,
> Shadows of life, whose very soul is lost.
> And yet I am—I live—though I am toss'd
> Into the nothingness of scorn and noise,

Scorn at least does not fit my case. Mister Clare was much
worse off than I, poor fellow.

Rejection, Tape thought miserably, now afraid to touch her.
Again.

> Into the living sea of waking dream,
> Where there is neither sense of life, nor joys,
> But the huge shipwreck of my own esteem
> And all that's dear. Even those I loved the best
> Are strange. Nay, they are stranger than the rest.

"If I only knew how to buck it," he said.

The swirling fog around the poem had cleared and the words
were now chiseled in gray on a black marble wall:

> I long for scenes where man has never trod—
> For scenes where woman never smiled or wept—
> There to abide with my Creator, God.

Oh no sir, Mister Clare, you don't fool me with that solution . . .

> And sleep as I in childhood sweetly slept,
> Full of high thoughts, unborn. So let me lie,—
> The grass below; above, the vaulted sky.

Oh, if I only could . . . the sweet sleep, the high thoughts
unborn, as I too in childhood sweetly . . .

"But that's what it is," Tape said. "Definitely. Rejection."

She twisted her body off the thick blue book and said, "It's
not rejection."

24

"Written in Northampton County Asylum"—poor mad poet. Yes, he was much worse off than I. Mine is not madness. Just misery. I'm a petty miserable person. I should have lived in some other century, when I could have romanticized and glossed over my miseries. Once-upon-a-time my guilts, my griefs could have been made to seem poetic. Therefore bearable. Now there's too much psychology around even for that low-cost relief. Self-pity is a pleasure only the ignorant can afford. Knowledge has made it too ugly, so . . .

I am—I live—though I am toss'd . . .

"I'm only trying to help you, us," he said, "find another basis for life. A happier solution."

Rip. Twist. Gouge. He finally succeeded. He pried and probed and drilled into my misery until he uncovered the mother lode. The meanness and the badness. My ugliness. Here goes. Play ball.

It was a relief for her to say, "Don't ask for the impossible."

"What's so impossible about trying to find a happier basis for life?" he asked. "Please try to take a good, clear-eyed look at us, Sonya. We've been married four years last January, and they've been on the whole wonderful years. Speaking personally, the best years of my life, the greatest, except for these occasional . . ."

"Four years last February," she corrected, secretly pleased with the knife he had just put into her hand. "Four years last January was when you were divorced."

Is badness preferable to misery? At least it's a change.

"A forgivable error," he cried, frustrated and stung. "Naturally, I associate the one with the other."

"Please let me try to sleep," she said, "and you go finish your work on Nelly Finch's garden, before . . ."

Before we start saying the unsayable, speaking the unspeakable, remembering the . . .

"Rejection," he repeated, and it was a sigh in three syllables. "Can't we be . . .? What's wrong with us, Sonya, that a little understanding, a little give-and-take, a little confiding in each other won't cure?"

25

There was another silence, which he fractured with, "The truth is . . ."

Ah, we have finally reached the truth. Let us now with ruthless compassion strip away our muscles, membranes, nerves, and tissues until the bare bone of Unspeakable Truth gleams whitely in its raw red bed.

"Nothing will cure us," she said, "because we lead flawed lives."

Of course, truth produced anger and hurt, which in his case, as usual, came out as sarcasm.

"Flawed Lives?" he countered. "Never heard of that cat. Who he? A folksy singer maybe? You ain't never lived less you heard ol' Flawed render them 'Lard-assed Blues.' How Flawed clawed his lil ol' 'lectric *gee*tar."

She sat up and angrily flung her version of the truth into his truth-twisting and truth-twisted face.

"Oh, stop it," she cried. "Just ask yourself once, as I ask myself a thousand times a day: What are we doing together? Why are we here? Me. You. Why aren't you back in Connecticut with your wife and children where you be— . . ."

"My ex-wife."

"You can't call them ex-children. Who am I to make you abandon your family? That needs you. And making you give up a well-paid job that was beautifully taking care of your perfectly fine wife and marvelous children, that you were perfectly happy with until I . . ."

"I was not. I told you a thousand times. I was not."

"So you think because you have to think it. If you didn't have to convince yourself a thousand times a day that you were dying of unhappiness with them, you couldn't justify what we did. But try to take a closer look at that poor lonely woman back there, with her . . ."

"Lonely? Betty? She's the most social character in Oldtown. The very epitome of the gay divorcee."

"Those two children growing up without a father while we went off to . . . play games. And why? Because I wanted my pleasure."

26

He looked into her anguished self-incriminating face and tried to catch her glance, which refused to be caught, and he said softly, leaning forward from his bed, on which he was sitting, to be nearer her bed, on which she was lying,

"Pleasure? Is that all? I wanted love. Which in my case is another name for life. Companionship with a real mate—glorious days and nights together, touching, always touching, with word and act and thought and feeling, living to its best each day that goes, each never-returning day. Until the day they are all gone but that final one, and I can look back on all the days and say, 'I didn't miss life. It never passed me by.' If that's what you call playing games, then . . ."

It was as if he had never spoken, for she said, more bitterly than ever, "And so I cut you loose from them—slash-slash—for of course I had to have my pleasure. Who cares how much other people get hurt so long as I have my pleasure?"

"That's just too melo— You're getting carried away, Sonya. Oh, I admit I had my guilts, especially at first, but . . ."

"At first? You'll be buried with them. As will I."

My pointless attack. His hopeless defense. I the hopeless attacker pointlessly attacking; he the hopeless defender hopelessly defending the indefensible.

She added, "If they don't bury me first."

"Games," he repeated, bitterly, hopelessly, defensively. "If the past is the one and only measure of the present, then we'd all be so hopelessly bogged down in guilts and recriminations that life would be impossible. But the present and how best to live with it *must* take precedence over the past. Let's look at us from another point of view, sweetheart. I was thirty-nine that night we met in Verona. A lone wanderer whose marriage had gotten, not terrible, but just so tired that I'd started taking holidays alone. And you were ten years younger. Twenty-nine. And we found joy and vitality and spirit in just being together, and finally, we fell in love. At least, I think you fell in love and I know I did. The kind of love with the kind of person I'd never even had the nerve to dream about. Sure, I had my past, such as it was. And you probably had yours . . ."

27

Verona. Verona and Tall Boy saying "It's nothing but a suburb of Stratford-on-Avon." Verona and Callas, and in the intermission Tall Boy introducing himself and offering me a ride to Spoleto in the rented Fiat he had not yet rented, poor thing. And my No, No, No, and meaning it, and thinking but not saying, He must be the tallest Romeo in Romeo's home town. And parting in the hotel lobby and saying Goodnight and Goodbye, naturally Goodbye and certainly not *Au revoir* or any thought of *Au revoir*, and the next morning sitting in the square drinking *capuccino* and reading the London *Times* in the hot bright sun. And then I saw the news about . . .

Flawed Lives . . .

. . . Married. Just like that. So this was why the frantic phone calls, the storm of cables, had stopped. Married.

In mind's eye, the rust-red palace across the square was weaving and trembling, turning bright, then dim, as Self, rising, pays and walks.

And walking—for who knows how long?—brought me consolation: his marriage promised relief, for him, for me. It should scab the suppurating wound; perhaps, in time, scar it.

Perhaps.

And *CUT*—to the hotel lobby and Tall Boy checking out and saying, "Sure you don't want that lift to Spoleto?"

And Self suddenly suddenly *suddenly* answering, "Yes. Why not?"

Why not, indeed? He had a crew cut then, which I loathe above the teen-age level, and he decided to show me the mosaics at Ravenna and Classe en route, and while I was checking out, he ran like a boy to rent the rented Fiat.

And it *was* a relief; he assuaged me with all that talk of music and philosophy, those bright-clever and bright-blue eyes set deep under that jutting forehead and the great lantern jaw light-bearded, and my first thought was Scandinavian *manqué* but later I changed it to crewcut Kierkegaard, and

CUT—to the weedy churchyard in Classe, and Kierkegaard turning into the world's tallest proudest little boy promising to show me the world's loveliest flock of sheep.

"I'm not probing into your past, sweetheart," he was now saying earnestly, one long leg bridging the gap between his bed and her bed.

Still, mind was a tomb until we entered the church and then all that black marble melted away in the heavenly Byzantine glow. For there it was, the Mosaic of the Apse, the lyric sheep, six on each side of the saint, grazing like Keatsian odes to sheep on the pale jade slopes dotted with singing flowers and trees and birds, the heavens and Cross heaven-high above.

Truly a scene where man had never trod, a scene where woman never smiled or wept. And

CUT—to the Fiat grinding up the steep fairytale road to San Marino, and the sound of Tall Boy on her soundtrack mumbling ashamedly, "Sonya, it's no use pretending I'm not married."

Three nights later in Spoleto, Fonteyn and Nureyev danced me into another state of *Yes, why not?*—but crewcut Kierkegaard didn't mention his children until the next morning when we were having our breakfast in bed, the cunning man—that's not fair, the discreet diffident embarrassed sweet cunning Tall Boy.

"And any two pasts are bound to have their collision points," he presently said. "Wherever my previous history touches you, it hurts. As yours would mine if . . . I knew, which I don't care to, if any. In my opinion, these full marital confessions are only good for the divorce lawyers. But everybody has to make a deal with the past, sweetheart, and learn how to absorb it into the present, which is all we've got to live with, come what may . . ."

Watch those tenses, Tall Boy. The past *is* the present. Trying to divorce them is like trying to divorce yourself from yourself.

"After all, sweetheart, divorce is not *that* tragic. You just get into these periodic black moods and make it seem so. Look at the millions of . . . why, half the people we know in this town have been divorced. And they . . ."

I wouldn't know about them. Just me. And to me, divorce when young children are involved is *that* tragic.

"Words," she said. "There's no point in talking about it."

But her poison was his therapy, and he went went went on on

on to say say say, "Sure, I've got a wife, ex-wife, and two kids. Your chief anguish, those two. Well, I got news for you about kids. All kids. Their lives are totally centered around themselves. Like always. As far as home goes, it's a place they want to bomb themselves out of as soon as possible, the quicker the better. But they like to have somebody back of them when they need money or other kinds of help. Like always. And I can and do offer them that kind of security, of course, within the limits of my own achievements. Admit it, wasn't your chief ambition when you were, say, Laney's age, twenty, or even younger, to fly the coop? That was my sole aim in life when I was exactly Stan's age, seventeen. And both my parents were boringly around me, every minute, at the time. And I flew. Never to return. Admit it, sweetheart, weren't you like that, too?"

A face in the lavender mist, a fugue with two voices: "You're so elegantly thin these days, Mother." . . . "Am I? Thanks. I'd take you to the airport, but . . . *bon voyage*, Sonya, my dear." . . . "*Au revoir*, Mother." . . . Oh yes, I flew the coop. I flew the coop even though in my deepest places I knew that it was not elegant thinness in her but relentless wasting. So out of the coop I flew, all the way to Europe, coddling my psychic aches and pains, choosing to ignore her physical ones. And the truth was not *au revoir* but *adieu*.

"And as to the present status," he said, said said said *said*, "Laney is definitely fully recovered from whatever shock she may have once suffered—her letters prove that, definitely. Stan of course is a maverick and always has been and always will be no matter what. Chances are he's just a typical teen-ager that nothing ever touches, and . . ."

Flawed Lives.

"And my ex-wife shows no psychic traumas whatever. The business aspect of our relationship is the only significant aspect that still exists for either of us."

She's the significant mother of your significant children. But Sonya merely said, "Please, Tape, let's stop this—whatever it is."

30

Unstoppably, the words poured out of him. "So, totting up the score, *you're* the only real sufferer, mentally or physically. Time in your case refuses to work its usual . . . even so, the score, therapeutically speaking, is four to one, and . . . Christ and Calvin, sweetheart, what would you have me do? If you could only accept things as they are. Unload your . . ."

"Whatever it is," she whispered, getting up to undress, the very act of standing a burden, of unbuttoning her blouse an ordeal.

"Why don't you take a Miltown?" he suggested. "To quiet your nerves. I really do have to show Nelly her goddamn garden ulcer tomorrow, no jokes."

"Go and do your work, Tape. Don't worry. I'll sleep. I'm sorry you have to bear me."

He rose and seized her by the shoulders and looked deeply into her eyes. "Don't forget," he said softly. "I love you. And I can bear anything—anything at all—but not having you. However you feel, please don't send me away, Sonya. Please."

She looked away and said, "I wouldn't do that, Tape. Not if you want to stay. I'm through with . . . hurting people."

His hands slid to her waist and, forestalling a more intimate caress, she twisted out of his grasp and stooped to unzip her skirt.

He left the room.

How can I be so sure that I know what it is, whatever it is? I know what I say. And don't say. What I think. And don't think. I know what it appears to be, to him on the outside, to me on the inside. But . . .?

She was twisting off her bracelet and dropping it into . . .

Madame Pompadour's jewel box that I did not inherit from my mother. Another gay divorcee. Poor gay things, divorcees. Lonely as death, all.

Poor pathetic optimist trying to erase the past the way he erases unwanted music from his precious tapes.

The indelible past.

Present despair becomes past despair in endless succession, as future despair hovers vulturelike over.

She was washing her teeth. The Observer observed herself; the Observer in the mirror was now an outsider, watching her with monumental contempt. "Now please tell me why," asked the observing Observer, "you so rudely tell him to stop talking to you when you won't even stop talking to yourself?"

She was taking a Doridene.

He wanted me to take a tranquilizer to depress my depression. For your information, Mr. Kierkegaard, Mr. Flawed Lives is not a folk singer.

She was sitting on the toilet.

And a little miracle pill to pee the past away. Just pee-pee-pee your tenses away-way-way.

And the guitar is not his instrument, either.

She was astride the bidet.

Bidet, my little post-horse, you are proving conclusively to me that I am not a manic depressive as one of the chief characteristics of manics whilst in the depressed state is not-washing themselves.

No, I cannot excuse my inexcusable behavior on the grounds of lunacy, unfortunately. Oh psychology, thou shouldst not be living at this hour; Sonya hath need of self-pity which thou deniest her.

She was turning out the light on the dressing table, obliterating for the present the sight though not the memory of the sight of Madame Pompadour's jewel box.

Nymph, in thy Doridene . . .

She was getting into bed . . .

Be all my sins forgotten.

She was pulling the covers over her and in the process knocking *The Oxford Book of English Verse* to the floor. Thump.

I am the self-consumer of my woes; they rise and . . . not woes, guilts, and although they rise they do not vanish. The guards have infiltrated the prisoner. As one, we skulk down the long black marble corridor, me and my shadows. Toward what? The Great . . . certainly not the Great Perhaps, Rabelais' hope and Nabokov's potato . . . in my case, the Great Escape.

The sooner the better. If I had fifty Dori—

What a century. Can't even discuss suicide with yourself. The certainty of its pathology, the cheapness of its motives, won't permit that harmless little form of self-abuse.

Out, poetry. *In,* pathology. Poor John Clare. At least he lived in a time when pathology was poetic.

Suicide. The ugliest form of revenge. The most disgusting threat, the hideous ultimate weapon. No one knows that better than I, or has better reason to know it. *Shut up!*

Shut up and stop pretending, Sonya, stop wishful hoping, you miserable creature shuffling down Guilt Alley? Black marble is for tombs and yours is a half-century off; nothing can induce suicide's victim to victimize others; I had that shoddy little trick played on me, and I'll not play it on . . .

No, misery loves longevity.

So stop you this sniveling. Pull down, I say, pull down. Find you the alternative. Light you up this tunnel.

Sonya said, Let there be light and there was not.

She closed her eyes tight and stared down the long black corridor. Try, Sonya, try. The treasures are there, but you must look hard, harder, hardest.

Success! Light! Bursting through the window of the Seville Cathedral, bathing all Goth in angel-glow, illuminating Primitive Italian Madonnas, Dutch Interiors, French Landscapes, Spanish Royalty, Greek Saints, and English Horses which had all this time been hanging unnoticed in the marbled darkness.

And the organ played Buxtehude.

See! It worked. You've been looking into blackness and counting guilts; relax now, and enjoy for a change your treasures; count now your bless—

But the organ turned into a piano, and Buxtehude into Ravel. "Oiseaux Triste." The cathedral glow faded, along with the pictures, and in the blackness sad little birds tinkled, and out of the blackness appeared the seignorial room on Central Park West, Apartment 901, where two pianos reigned in concert grandeur; and sitting at one of the pianos—the Bechstein, not the Steinway—was the man.

Flawed Lives.

33

But why am I hearing "Oiseaux Triste"? Why Ravel and not Ives?

Because, because, because . . .

The music stops. The pianist rises from the Bechstein. He comes to the huge white sofa. Looking down. Smiling. Touching my hair and stroking my cheek. He speaks.

Listen, listen, listen, and the words will say themselves again:

"Has her Royal Highness had enough music? My love. My madness."

"Never enough of your music, my darling."

"Then command. And I shall perform."

"If you're not too tired, Werner darling, please, the Concord Sonata."

Werner-darling smiling yes, and leaning down to kiss my cheek, and returning to his beloved piano, my beloved at his beloved piano playing for his beloved, and I wriggle and snuggle down on his sofa, then as now, in the tremulous thrill of waiting for the music, and snuggling down on his sofa in my bed listening for the first . . .

> So let me lie,
> The grass below; above, the vaulted sky.

Sonya slept.

34

CHAPTER 4

~~~~~~~~~~~~~~~~
~~~~~~~~~~~~~~~~
~~~~~~~~~~~~~~~~

"Forgive me, Tall Boy, sweet boy."

She was getting into bed with him. The sun made a Venetian blind on the carpet, golden strips before his eyes, a golden feeling at his back, what a way to wake up.

"Aw, sweetheart, there's nothing to forgive. Last night I was just too gabby for your mood, that's all. Me and my big lantern jaw swinging in the breeze. And thanks a lot for this joyous awakening. It's more than I deserve, but . . ."

"I should have let you sleep. Did you work late?"

"Until four."

"Oh, dear. And it's only nine. Please go back to sleep, Tape. I'll be quiet. Shhh."

"Sleep? And lose this? No sir, ma'am. And sorry, but silence is not requested."

He turned on his back and kissed her hand, like the rest of her a supremely beautiful object; Saint Anne on one elbow leaned over him; Saint Anne's hair covered one eye and both cheeks, the smaller eye, for Saint Anne's left eye was larger than her right.

Were Saint Anne's nostrils beginning to pulsate? He thought he detected the slightest hint, a certain widening perhaps, though not yet rhythmic.

"I've been watching you since seven. Two hours. Until I couldn't stand it any longer. Knowing your sleep was being poisoned by . . . my poison."

"Stop it. You're solid gold. A golden wife on a golden morning."

He turned back on his side, face away from her, as his mouth was fouled from the long night of drinking coffee and smoking and he feared for his breath.

She snuggled against him.

"Like two spoons. I'm the teaspoon and you're the tablespoon."

"Gold teaspoon," he said.

"Oh, why do I torture you so? A nice man like you. I'm so ugly. A despicable creature, really."

"I'll thank you to stop running down my woman," he said. "And I'm not a nice man. Besides."

"I hate liars," she said, caressing his stomach with one hand and clawing his shoulder with the other, for she was a rough type when it came to expressing her *tendresse*. "Hey. Oh-ho. What is this monster?"

"What else? Stone-aches don't grow on trees, you know."

"You must be the tallest and dirtiest-talking little boy in the whole world. Although of course I haven't the faintest idea what you mean. Nicely brought up ladies like me don't know words like stone-ache."

"Come to think of it," he complained, and he sounded very much like a complaining little boy, "I'm not getting too much these days. And when I say too much I really mean not very much. If any, if you know what I . . ."

"I know exactly what you mean. Your condition speaks louder than words."

"Hey, there's something I'd like to know. You're a woman, aren't you?"

"That's right, Mr. Petrified Forest in person. I am."

"Then tell me, does a guy get more if he comes right out and asks somebody for something he's not getting too much of these

36

days, or is it better not to ask anybody for anything and to . . . just sort of feel my way into the problem?''

"Well, I'm not a guy, so I really wouldn't know. Personally, I think we should just change the subject and take a nice shower *together,* and after we've had a nice shower *together,* then just sort of let things develop. Of course, if you disagree, then . . .''

He leapt from the bed, stripped off his pajamas, and hung them on the object under consideration.

"Show-off. Someday that trick is going to fail you.''

"When I'm eighty I'll switch to Kleenex,'' he said, stealing a hasty glance at her nostrils, which were now flaring rhythmically.

He ran to the bathroom happily crying, "Follow me, girls.''

"Yes, my lord,'' she said, obeying.

"I'm beginning to get the suspicion,'' he said as she was soaping his back, "that somebody around here is gonna get screwed. In case you never heard of that word either, it's a euphemism for . . . well, getting screwed.''

Like a cat she clawed him with her sharp nails. "You're much too young to use such a vulgar term, whatever it means. It's much more polite to do and not to say. I must wash your dirty mouth with soap.''

She slapped a handful of suds against his lips and ground it in.

"Eeeyach!''

"Let that be a lesson to you,'' she lectured, stepping out of the shower and getting towels for both of them. "Animals screw, but ladies and gentlemen fuck. Although of course I have no idea what that means, either.''

They were drying each other.

"Why you pore lil' ol' ignorant kid,'' he said, "it's mighty hard to say what that-there four-letter word means. It's one of them words mere words cain't describe. So I guess I jest gotta go to the trouble of demonstrating the deepest meaning of that-there word that jest come out of yore ignorant little ol' mouth.''

She said, "Shut up, mister, and get into that bed quick.''

Once started, Sonya's passion had no limits, and Tape was

always awed and inspired by her indescribable abandon, which he had never encountered in any other woman anywhere-time-or-place.

"Let's make this the longest one," she cried frantically. "The longest . . . in all . . . history."

"And the best," he said, as savage as he had ever been. "The very very very best best best."

"Longest. Best," she gasped, for it was moments like this and not what she had said last night that made her loathe having servants around, as any third person or slightest hint of any third person around froze her and made moments like this impossible.

"Good, better, best," he snarled, and in that wild moment she froze.

"Stop. That noise. Someone at the door."

"It's just the blind. It's no one. Just the blind. Fuck it."

"Fix it."

He ran to close the window, sealing the room.

He returned. She was almost normal again. "Good," she said. "It made it longer. The longest, you hear."

"And the best," he said. "I wouldn't trade this fucking partner for fifty harems, for a million . . ."

"I like it," she screamed, her voice hoarse, her eyes wild and floating, her nostrils in-and-out, in-and-out, in-and- . . .

The telephone on the bedside table started to ring.

She froze again, in her frenzy not really understanding that it was the telephone and not the doorbell.

"Let it ring," he rasped. "Fuck it."

And it rang again. To Sonya it was an obstacle that must be removed before the moment could again be seized, and she said, "No, answer it. It's probably Nelly Finch."

"At this hour? Maybe Katie though. She's an early riser."

He sat up and took the phone, pleased that, by the Sign of the Nostrils, things still looked promising.

"Get rid of her in a hurry, or I'll start without you," she threatened, cribbing the old joke about the orchestra leader.

"Hello," he said.

"Mr. Andrew Alberg, please."

"Speaking."

"One minute please. Long distance."

"It's long distance," he said to Sonya. "Sweetheart."

She froze in a different way.

"Go ahead please," the operator said.

"Hello, Mr. Alberg?"

"Yes."

"Dad."

"Laney! Honey!"

"Hi, Dad. It's Laney"

Sweetheart left the bed. Discreetly. Robed herself. Modestly. And slunk into the bathroom, closing the door, leaving him free to talk to Honey.

Dad—Tall Boy spoke louder than necessary, for the connection was perfect and Laney's voice was soft and sweet and perfectly clear; still, he spoke very loudly, as if wanting to make sure his voice not only reached Swarthmore but also penetrated the bathroom door.

"Is everything all right, honey?"

"I'm okay. Everybody's fine, Dad. I've got one more page and the bibliography to type on this paper on Sartre and then I'm through for the Easter holidays."

"Great. Happy Easter. You going home? How's everything?"

"Mom phoned last night. She says Stan is getting by okay at Beech Grove. You know Stan."

"Great. It sure is great to hear your sweet voice. Anything on your mind, honey?"

"Dad, I wrote you about Bark. This boy in pre-med."

"Who? Oh, yeah. Bark. So?"

"He's terribly nice, Dad. None of this . . . you know what I mean. Anyway, about a month ago, Bark started to pressure me about flying out over Easter to meet his folks—they live in Brentwood, near Los Angeles I think it is, and . . . "

"Yes, I know where it is. So . . . ?"

"So the funniest thing. Yesterday, his father and mother sent me a formal invitation . . . and they enclosed a round-trip plane ticket. Isn't it crazy? All that money, imagine.''

"Sounds like they really want to have you, all right.''

"Do you think I ought to accept, Dad?"

"Well . . . how crazy are you about this Bark guy?''

"Well, I'd sorta like to go because I'd like to see you, too, and I want you to meet Bark. You know.''

"Then by all means plan to come, honey. If it's that important. And as for the plane ticket, better let me take care of that for you.''

"But we've already made a reservation for tomorrow morning. We leave New York at nine-fifty.''

"In that case I think you ought to accept their invitation.''

"Oh, Dad." She giggled. He raised his voice to a shout.

"Give me your flight number, Laney, and all that so I can meet you at the Los Angeles airport, honey.''

"Since they'll be meeting us, Dad, why don't you wait till I get to their house and I'll call you and we'll arrange things?''

"Whatever you think best, honey. I'll be counting the split-seconds. It's only a couple of hours' drive from here to Brentwood, and . . . by the way, how's everything back there?''

"Oh, Dad. I already told you. You're wasting my money.''

"Next time reverse the charges, hear.''

Sonya came out of the bathroom. Her hair was brushed and she wore a batiste robe with pink flowers on it.

"Tape," she whispered, "invite her to stay with us.''

Tape said, "Hold it, Laney. Just one sec. Now don't you dare be a tightwad and hang up on me, hear.''

He covered the phone. "What'd you say, sweetheart?''

"Ask her to spend some time with us. The entire holiday, if she can manage it.''

"Uh. I uh . . .''

"I'd love to have her, Tape.''

"Well. If. Uh . . .''

"Hurry, Tape, or she'll think . . . go ahead and mention it to her, at least. I'd love to have her.''

His voice, soft with appreciation and tenderized with grati-

40

tude, said, "Laney honey. Sonya just came in with a great idea. The greatest. She . . . we want you to come up to Pobrecito and stay with us."

Pause. Then, "I'd love that, Dad. Really I would. I'm dying to meet Sonya. And I hate to spend all seven of the days in their house. You know. But I've got to spend *some* time with them. I'm supposed to be their guest and all. Look, Dad, today's Wednesday. I'll be out there tomorrow, and maybe I could come up to your place Friday afternoon and stay just for the weekend. They'd understand, won't they?"

"Sure they will. Sounds like a great plan. So you call me tomorrow night and arrange for me to drive down there and pick you up early Friday morning, see."

"Oh, Bark'll probably want to drive me up there. He's got a Corvette out there, and . . . Bark's so nice, Dad, really. You know."

"This is great, Laney. Wonderful, honey."

"Okay then. Bye now, Dad. See ya' Friday."

"Bye-bye, honey. Friday."

He hung up. Sonya said, "Tape, you should have invited her boy friend, too."

"Oh, if he wants to stay, he'll stay. He can sleep in the old chauffeur's room upstairs."

She took some clean panties from a drawer. He stood up, tossing away the sheet which had covered him, then, realizing he was nude, he modestly for some reason covered himself and went to the bathroom.

When he came out, she was gone. He dressed and went to the kitchen. She was pouring coffee. For two.

"Wonder if today's the day for that honeydew," he said.

Honey. Sweetheart.

She took the melon from its sunny sill and cut it open. He prepared cornflakes and coffee for two.

She sat down and began to eat with him.

This must be the most triumphant moment of his entire life, at least the part of it he's spent with me. But he doesn't exactly know how to handle it, and neither do I.

"We gambled and lost on the honeydew," she said, pushing it aside and going to the refrigerator for orange juice.

"Can't win 'em all," he consoled.

The breakthrough. At last. Fifteen minutes is all it's going to take those two to . . . thank God the first one was Laney and not . . . those two'll just *love* each other.

He lit another cigarette. "I'm smoking too much," he said.

Like dental work. One of those things that have to be done, sooner or later. His desire to bring those children back into his life is a . . . a Force I simply cannot stand up against. Poor thing.

"Did you finish Nelly's garden?"

"Just the south side where the swimming pool ought to be."

The breakthrough. Picking up the first broken piece and putting it back . . . the most important piece, because it's the first, the start.

"That's her only interest now," he said. "That goddamn swimming pool."

How will she feel? Just like me, probably. Yielding to her Dad's overwhelming pressure. Poor thing. I must manage to keep busy. Fade in, fade out, a moment of smiling hospitality with them here and there.

"More coffee?" she asked.

And if this works out okay, which it will of course, maybe this summer we can invite Stan out and . . . all the king's horses. Glue back the final piece. But this is not a Humpty-Dumpty operation, it's a Tang-horse project. Two little pieces. Two little shards.

Two dead . . . like two young corpses.

The phone rang. She jumped, but didn't rise.

My God, am I afraid to answer my own telephone?

"I'll get it, sweetheart."

He left the room.

If the boy friend comes, the meals will be easier to get through. I must empty the closet in the guest room. For her. And clean the room upstairs for the boy friend. Just in case. Thank

42

God I never yielded on our long-term bed argument. I couldn't bear to have her see one bed in our room.

He returned, knotting his tie. "It was Katie," he reported. "She wants me to come and see the new plans for her stable. I'd better get cracking. The signs are good. She's still calling me cutie-pie."

I wish I could say it now, but I'll keep it for later, sweetheart. You're going to love Laney. And she's going to love you. Laney has a beautiful soul, sweetheart. And so have you. You're two gentle people and I wish I could tell you how much I appreciate what you're doing, but . . .

Take it easy, Tape. Easy does it, boy. Don't force. The less gab, the . . .

He passed her, en route to the garage, then turned and stopped to kiss the top of her shining head. He pressed her shoulder fervently.

"Somebody around here loves somebody," he said gratefully.

She smiled and squeezed his hand on her shoulder.

And you do love me, from your point of view. But what about mine? What about mine? Have you ever thought of that?

He kissed her cheek. "Thanks for livin', sweetheart," he said huskily.

And left.

Sonya went to the guest room and started to empty drawers.

CHAPTER 5

~~~~~~~~~~~~~~~~~~~~~~
~~~~~~~~~~~~~~~~~~~~~~
~~~~~~~~~~~~~~~~~~~~~~

They were listening to the Mahler Fourth, and every time the triangle tinkled Tape twitched in the direction of the telephone. On the fifth false alarm, Sonya said, "Better turn it off before it gives you epilepsy. You're in no mood for Mahler or anybody else."

"She should have called by now," Tape said, crossing the room to stop the music. "Forgive me, Mr. Mahler," he apologized, and Sonya understood exactly how he felt, for it did seem rude to shut the Master up before he'd fully expressed himself.

But she said, "Give her time to get there and unpack. You started listening for that call at least two hours before her plane possibly could have arrived."

He sat down. She pinched his cheek. His gratitude was . . .

"Go out and water the brush cherries again," she ordered, but instead he went to the kitchen and admired the contents of the refrigerator, for Sonya had stuffed it with Laney's favorite foods, at least as many of them as he could remember to tell her.

"All that smoked salmon!" he exclaimed. "I guarantee you she'll want it for every meal, including breakfast."

Sonya came in and started arranging avocados on the window

44

sill. "Do you think she'd enjoy a picnic on the beach, Tape? It's still a bit cool, but we could grill fish shish-kebab or something, and . . ."

"Sounds great to me," Tape said, as everything else Sonya did or said sounded that particular evening.

"You know, I'm anxious to see her, too. She sounds delightful."

"She's exactly that. Wait and see. There's something so lyric about Laney. Like . . ."

You.

Me. I know, but please don't finish it.

He didn't.

"I've got peanut butter both crunchy and creamy," she said, "just in case she's reverted."

You sweet sweet sweetheart. All this shopping and cleaning and planning has worked the miracle even before Laney got here. See. You've tortured yourself four long years for nothing. You're cured. Already. By natural hospitality and native goodness.

The telephone rang. Tape galloped into the living room.

Yes, it is true; I am afraid to answer my own telephone.

She opened a bottle of Coke, poured it, and sat at the breakfast booth. Discreetly out of sound.

"False alarm," he said returning. "It was only that lazy old bastard Togo. He's stuck with about five hundred Natal plums and he wants me to buy them for Nelly Finch's upper hedge. I told him no dice."

"Watsa matter, Mistle Albell, don't you like flowers?"

That's my Sonya. What she heard in monstrous sadness she can repeat in fun.

"I got my heart set on dwarf myrtle for that hedge," he said. "Come, into the living room where a guy can sit in comfort."

She sat on the sofa and leafed through the new Mario Praz book. He watched the hot wire.

And it rang again.

"This has to be Laney," he said, and she was stuck on the sofa.

"Hi, Dad. I'm sorry about reversing the charges but I'm calling from a Brentwood drugstore and I don't have change."

"Shut up or I'll disinherit you. Laney. Honey. How's everything?"

"Oh, Dad, I already told you how everything was yesterday back in Swarthmore. Remember? Isn't California beautiful? I had no idea. And Dad, Bark's family is so *nice*. They're really nice people, Dad. The reason I didn't call earlier was Bark wanted me to have a swim in their pool as soon as we got there, and I didn't want to use their phone for long distance. You know. And . . ."

"Can't wait to see you, honey. Is Bark driving you up, or do you want me to come down for you, and if so when? And when I say *when*, I mean the sooner the best. Like right now."

"There's this big problem, Dad. The Scotts—that's Bark's last name—have planned a six-day cruise to Catalina and stuff on their yacht, and . . . Mrs. Scott was just sick that Bark hadn't mentioned you living out here and now they've already invited ten guests and it's only an eight-bunk yacht or is that a lot? And the worst thing is, we won't get back to the mainland until the day we have to catch the plane. Anyway, Dad, they've planned it especially for me and Bark, as a surprise, and . . . I just don't see how I can get out of it and come up there like we planned. I'd rather, you know that, Dad, don't you?"

She sounded so sweet and distraught and sincere that Tape tried to conceal his own sharp, sickening disappointment.

"Sure, honey," he said. "I know that. Gosh. That's bad news for me. Us. But not even your selfish old man can see how you could get out of a deal like that. When do you sail?"

"We leave—I think it's someplace called Newport—at six tomorrow afternoon. Mrs. Scott was so upset, Dad. If Bark had only thought to mention that you lived out here. Anyway, we can at least see each other tomorrow. That is, if you want to go to the trouble of driving down here. Bark's just too busy getting supplies for the cruise, and. You know."

"Trouble? I'd get down there to see you if I were a basket case and had to stub my way down."

46

"Oh, Dad. Hey, Bark just hollered Let's have lunch someplace down here tomorrow. You and us and Sonya. We can meet at some restaurant on the beach, he said, and save you the drive into the city."

"Fine. Great idea. We'll be there. What restaurant?"

"Wait. Here's Bark. Bark, this is my Dad."

"Hiya, Mr. Alberg. Nice to meet you."

"Hello, Bark. The same to you. I understand you and Laney are going to be my luncheon guests tomorrow. You name the place."

"Do you know the Seventh Wave? It's at Malibu."

"I've driven past it a jillion times."

"Then let's meet there at, say, twelve-thirty. I'll reserve a table."

"Twelve-thirty at the Seventh Wave. Fine, Bark. Be seeing you then, in person."

"Great, Mr. Alberg. Here's Laney."

"Then it's okay, Dad?"

"It certainly is."

"I'm dying to see you."

"Me, too, honey. You, I mean."

"I'm sorry I can't come up there and spend some time with you and Sonya."

"So are we, honey. Sonya was counting on it."

"Bye now."

And he hung up, saying "It's a dirty—" but when his back had been turned, Sonya had stolen off into the kitchen.

"Hey, Sonya, where are you?"

When he speaks to his daughter, or to me about his daughter, his voice is twice as loud as normal, poor thing.

"Here," she said.

"It's a dirty shame," he said, coming into the kitchen. "She can't come after all."

"So I gathered."

"They're yachty folk it seems, and they've planned a six-day cruise in her honor, leaving tomorrow evening."

"That should thrill her. But I'm sorry for you, Tape."

47

"So our one and only chance to see her is to drive down there tomorrow and have lunch, with her and the boy friend, who incidentally sounded very okay on the phone. Cultivated voice. Nice polite kid."

"Judging from everything I hear about Laney, she wouldn't be able to bear any other kind. What time are you leaving tomorrow?"

Oh, no. Just when I thought she . . .

He said, too off-handedly, "Oh, I'd say we oughta *frappé la rue* about . . . how's ten o'clock? That sound okay by you?"

The Force. Moving at me, through me. Pushing me, seizing and shaking me, twisting my nerves and brain and bones until I scream Uncle, Uncle. No! Not this time.

She started setting the table for dinner.

She said, "Tape, couldn't you please do me a very great favor and go alone?"

This is not fair. This . . . is . . . not . . . fair. To build me up these past two days with all this hope and joy and then . . . wham this at me. It is not fair.

He spoke pleadingly. "Sonya, sweetheart. That's not you talking. It's just your complex. And it's only for lunch, sweetheart. And we'd originally planned to entertain her for the whole weekend, remember? At your invitation, which you were sweet enough to make entirely on your own initiative. Not only did I not suggest it, I never even thought of it."

"If Laney could come here, to my own house, I'd still welcome her with honest pleasure. But going down there, can't you see it's different?"

"Different? It's not *that* different. In fact, it's a lot simpler and easier. That's the only difference."

Am I seizing on this change in her plans as an excuse, or is it really different? Yes, it is. Very different. *Here* she would be coming to visit her father in his house which also happened to contain me. *There* we would be two couples, a foursome of lovers, having a rendezvous.

Fortified, she said, "If it weren't different, then why were you so careful on that telephone with your *I*'s and *we*'s? *I'll* see you

48

tomorrow honey. *We'll* meet at twelve-thirty. Be *my* luncheon guests. Why were you so careful?"

Shall I pretend it was accidental, or shall I tell her the truth?

Carefully, he said, "Careful? No, sweetheart, just scared. Scared to death something like this was going to happen, and you'd refuse to go at the last minute, so to speak. So I tried to cover every possibility, including that. This. So as not to . . . lose face, I suppose. But you won't refuse me now, will you, sweetheart?"

"If you'd only go quietly alone and tell her I was sick or something and couldn't come. It'd be much the best thing. For both of us."

"For *both* of us? Oh no, you just simply cannot say that, honey."

I mean sweetheart but it's too late now, damn it.

"I meant for both Laney and me."

"Laney? Why that kid'll take to you like . . . and you to her. I know both you characters. The two most lovable people in the world. Oh, Sonya sweetheart, this problem'll only get worse if we don't grab it now we have the chance to do so and settle its hash once and for all. And what a painless solution. One little luncheon. A couple of hours. Remember how happy you were not ten minutes ago at the prospect of spending three days with her? This sudden switch is just not . . . logical."

The logic that three days is longer than two hours. The logic, the unbearable remorseless logic of *A* forcing *B* to do what *A* wishes when *B* does not wish. Oh, how can I tell you that logic does not enter my screaming swelling brain and if you try to cram one iota of logic into it, it is sure to burst? But if I told you that, you would answer something about Pills and Periods. Call me absurd. Unreasonable. Idiotic. Call me anything, but accept my fact. Please accept the condition of *me*. I will not even bother to put these feelings, these frenzied bitter feelings, into words because I know how utterly impossible it is for you to accept the condition and the fact of my existence. Anymore than you can accept yours. I live with a man who has been split in two—and all his possessions are split in two. You have Them. And you

49

have Me. You are welded to Them. And you are welded to Me. And you have this insatiable longing, born of guilt and love and anguish and ethics and all your yesterdays, to make the two separates into one. But separates we are, and a million luncheons can never change us. You think that my being friends with them will solve your problems. You even think it will solve my problems. Could you in your fantastic optimism also believe that it would solve their problems?

"It's different," she said.

"Please make the effort, Sonya. Give it one try. I'll stake my life on this one try. If it fails, I'll never ask you again. But I won't have to. Fifteen minutes of tension perhaps—no more— just to break the ice, and I guarantee you all will be just great from then on and forever. For both. For all. It's as much for your sake as it is for mine, sweetheart."

She opened the oven door and tested the meat with a fork.

"It's ready," she said. "Let's eat."

"That celery-onion-beef smell always reminds me of home," he said, adding too quickly, "My mother also put parsley in her pot roasts. It smells good, too."

Poor thing, he's afraid I'll think Home meant Them.

"I'll try it next time," she said.

Later, when she was putting the dirty dishes into the washer, she said, "Look, Tape, let's be practical. Treat this as just another social engagement. First of all, Laney doesn't even expect me. Especially after the way you put it. *I'll* be there, *I'll* see you tomorrow . . . can only mean you're coming alone. She won't even expect me to show up, after the way you put it. So . . ."

"I told you, I carefully covered both situations; I also said *We'll* meet at the Seventh Wave. At twelve-thirty. Remember? *We'll*, I said."

"That could apply to you and her and the boy."

"But she expects both of us, I tell you. And Bark clearly said I'll reserve a table for *four*. For *four*, he said."

"Who said four?"

"Bark."

50

"Laney never said four."

"But she was there. Listening. He was speaking for her. Let's face it, sweetheart, you're expected, whatever you decide."

Whatever I decide. Crucified on a table-reservation remark made by a strange youth I've never even seen.

"As a matter of fact, when Laney told me she couldn't come up here, she also added, I so wanted to meet Sonya. And she does. Of course."

She so wants to meet the bad woman who stole her father. The woman her mother calls Whore or Slut or That Woman. She so wants to meet the woman who changed her happy home into a morbid place to stay away from. Oh, Tall Boy, again you confuse the careful remarks made in the interests of amity with harsh and ugly truth.

"I have to launder some things," she said.

He followed her into the bathroom and sat on the edge of the tub, watching her.

If she doesn't intend to go, then why is she washing underwear? She probably plans to wear them tomorrow. Unless . . . she tortures herself. And, incidentally, me. I'm all snarled up, tangled . . .

Mind's eye saw a New Hampshire brook before sunup; the trout fisherman cast the one-pound nylon line badly and was fumbling in the semidarkness with the hopeless snarl, making it worse with each try, and finally in destructive frustration breaking the line and tossing the cobwebby tangle into the brook and watching it float away . . .

"Well," he said, "I guess the easiest way out is to go alone. I'd hoped this was going to be the big breakthrough. But. I'll tell Laney you're sick or something."

Does he really think he's yielding to me and my desperation, or does he know that he is just starting to apply the Force in another, crueler way?

"If you're going to wear your gray silk suit," she said, "I'd better press it for you"

"Oh, please don't bother, sweetheart. It's fine the way it is."

But she pressed it anyway, and then they went to bed.

But neither, it seemed, felt like sleeping. Tape studied some of the drawings with which he hoped to impress the Mayor, come Saturday, and Sonya looked at the new Mario Praz book of interiors.

She came to the nineteenth-century Russian rooms. A country house.

Chekhov must have slept there. That billiard room where poor dear Gayev played the fool. My father must have known houses like this. With paintings covered by gauze to keep out the flyspecks.

Suddenly, California became desperately foreign to her. A completely new kind of nostalgia deprived her of her citizenship, and a more powerful kind of birthright possessed her, making her feel that her true home was in a place she had never been, some great Slavic forest, some bleak palatial city—another place in another time. Was there anything to these theories of inheriting the ancestral past?

The feeling was accompanied by another feeling: that she was not even at home in this century, but belonged in an earlier one, a century when Mozart brought new elegance to elegant little music rooms, or when Chopin was danced to at ornate balls, as Vronsky and Anna forever wandered, forever pursued by Karenin's relentless wrath.

She studied the detail of the billiard room and listened to her father's advice:

"Don't waste emotions on that land back there, little girl; we were all living up to here in *merde,* that being just another name for boredom; and we were bored because we were worn-out machines that didn't function anymore. So we had to go, leaving our past behind us. And a wery good thing, too, for all concerned, them and us."

Very was the only English word he ever mispronounced. Perhaps he did it on purpose, as a way of hanging on to another world long gone. A world of desperate melancholy, of . . .

Am I my father's desperate daughter, lying here in my desperate bed, breathing this desperate California air?

But Thoreau was not Russian, and he, more than anyone else,

had felt this desperation, which Ives captured so hauntingly in . . .

The Concord Sonata.

The Praz book became unbearably heavy on her stomach. She could not withstand the Force and bear the burden of the book at one and the same time.

She put down the book and picked up the clock.

"When do you want to get up?"

"Oh, about nine. I should leave at ten."

She set the alarm, and because he too had put aside his burden, she turned out the light.

He had been lying on his side. But now he turned and was lying on his back.

He never goes to sleep lying on his back. When he's ready for sleep, he lies on his stomach, right shoulder bolstered by a pillow, feet hanging bare over the end. He needs a longer bed.

Her knees are up, her hands behind her head. Laney doth murder sleep.

Who is this murderess, and why do all who have been brushed by her gentle spirit love her with such pure deep pride?

"Be tender with that little fawn, Swede, lest she run back into the deep forest where she came from."

Who said that? Oh yes, the abstract poet next door. Sahlmann. Fawn is good, but brown thrush in the wild-plum thicket is better.

The murderess of sleep is also a nose freckled forever in one Nantucket Island summer; a hater of long boring auto journeys.

There was the sound of a small travel-weary voice piping hopefully:

"Daddy, is this Mexico where the sun shines bright?"

We were still on the wrong side of the Rio Grande, alas.

On my last visit to Swarthmore, she had discovered Appearance. In Philosophy 101. And nothing was Real anymore. At least that month. Of course it was the rainy season just before winter set in, and the smell of wet trees hung depressingly over the campus; no wonder the clothing dummies in the College Shop window had unnerved her.

"I swear, Dad, every time I pass that window those dummies grow more and more Real, in exact proportion to the way *I'm* getting less and less Real."

"It's just this smell of wet oak leaves, honey."

Once upon a time, Reality was a pair of missing tonsils, one hour past shearing time:

"Tell that doctor to put them right back," moaned the May Queen, the third-grade charmer.

The education of the Murderess was like the twelve Labors of Hercules; each one a terrifying failure until the arrival of the Fairy Prince, in the form of a report card stuttering *A-A-A-A-A* with never any variation.

Surprise, surprise. Years and years at the very top of her class never once convinced the Murderess that she wasn't completely stupid, an incapable dolt.

Ah, those knees just went down. Now the arms are creeping under the sheet. Maybe she'll sleep after all. Maybe a good night's sleep will . . . change her mind.

Honey and Bunny biked up the hill to fetch a pail of grammar; Honey fell down and broke her wrist, and Bunny came peeled-nose after.

Look Ma, no brakes.

"And isn't it stupid, Dad, my wrist is still weak, especially when I play the piano."

For many and many and many a day, she gave her soul to the black Steinway, bought secondhand from a want ad in the New Haven *Cour*—

"I do not like to play for people, just for myself, and no matter what Mr. Gregory says, Dad, I'm not *that* gifted. Besides."

And bringing my layout board down to the living room, just for the joy of hearing her practice; finally, being reduced to doodling, saying:

"Laney, for my sake, play the Mozart Rondo; my first fleeting fancy for 'Clair de Lune' has turned into bitter undying hate."

"Oh, Dad. Stop listening. How can anybody play nine-eight time? Debussy makes me furious."

54

Beethoven is better,
Late than never.

Ives. What was that, night before last? How could the Concord Sonata do that to anybody, especially her? She does not sleep. Her body is not even relaxed. Laney hath murdered . . .

He cleared his throat and turned, perhaps to let her know that nobody in that particular room was able to sleep.

The Murderess was six—no, seven—when we moved up from Manhattan to Oldtown. And the new house shamed her. Because her new friends had poorer ones. Ditto her school dresses. "Mom, please don't make them so beautiful."

Attention all Status-Symbolists: To be shamed by one's comparative grandeur is nobler in the mind than to be embarrassed by one's relative poverty. Face is not Grace.

Her fears. Her tears. Her worries about careers.

Be Somebody, I always said. "You're too defeatist, too negative. Be confident, positive."

And now, here in this sleepless room, I understand for the first time that she always was being Somebody, namely herself, which is to say, not negative but incorruptible.

Not even in the bad times, the predivorce times, the splituation times, the times of the nightmares.

"It was an old house, Dad, rickety, and I was alone in it. And scared. Of something nameless outside. And then I heard this frightening noise, this clawing sort of scratching drawn-out rasping noise. And it was outside of the house, first at the foundations, like rats gnawing, then it scratched its way up the walls, all the way to the window, and then I saw what it was, twisted ugly *human* fingers with long nails like animal claws, scratching at the shutters, opening them . . ."

And when she took me to that student discothèque on the last night, proud of me I could tell, full of Philosophy 101, loaded to the gills with an Identity Crisis, perhaps because she had just heard of that particular intellectual malady; anyway, she was Little Miss Nobody going Nowhere . . .

And the beer, the smoke, the spastic music, all those kids doing the Watusi, and honey with her beer and her cigarette, wrinkling the freckled nose and squinting the green honeyed eyes and saying oh so deliciously preciously earnestly:

"I mean I just don't believe in anything any more, Dad. Not education or marriage or family or even having babies; I mean there's not really any point, Dad, and since there's no point, why bother? Why keep pushing and shoving to get somewhere if there's nowhere to go? Oh sure, sometimes there seems to be a line, but what's the point in following it if it leads to Nowhere? Really, Dad."

Oh lyric girl, meandering through Time; the line you follow is so clear to everyone who knows you, everyone but you, who never understood that you were following anything. Perhaps that is your special magic, not knowing.

Will it upset me if the Sleep Murderess wants to marry this boy? Of course it won't, if he's good for her. But . . . do you *want* him to be good for her?

If they marry, I shall be relieved. Shame on me. I shall be relieved at this possibility of being relieved of my responsibility. Shame.

No, not exactly *that*. My greater relief is that it will help my situation. Her marriage should remove Sonya's guilt, at least fifty per cent of it, for then Laney will belong to somebody else. Shame on me.

In the desperate darkness, Sonya said, "I'll go with you."

He leapt from his bed and knelt on the carpet beside her. Fervently he squeezed her leg under the covers; he patted her bare shoulder.

"Thank you, Sonya," he whispered, moved almost to tears. "Thank you. I'll never . . ."

"Shhhh. I know. Back to your bed now. We both badly need sleep. It's very late."

But by the time another half-hour had passed it became apparent that insomnia for both of them was like a . . .

Contest? I am in the sleep-shattering grip of the Force, but my decision to go did not give him the catharsis, either.

Once he got up. Three-thirty.

On his return from the bathroom he whispered in the darkness

56

over her, "Sleep, you beauty. You lyric creature with the lyric line. I'll try to . . . pay you back for this. Sweetheart."

Honey.

Once she got up. Five minutes to five.

When she returned from the bathroom he was asleep.

At eight, she gave up, rose and had breakfast, then sat for a very long time in a very hot bath.

When he woke up at nine-thirty, she was at the dressing table fixing her eyes, getting ready to go.

"It's late," he said. "I thought you set the alarm for nine."

"I turned it off to give you an extra half-hour."

"Thanks, sweetheart. I sure needed it."

He shaved. She was polishing her nails.

"Had breakfast?"

"Yes. Yours is ready."

"Thanks. Thanks a lot." He was very appreciative.

He went to her lovingly, but her face in the mirror was terrible to see, deathlike except for the living eyes.

"Hurry," she said.

"I can't stand it," he cried, looking at the reflected anguished eyes. "You've tortured yourself all night. You're in no shape to go anywhere, sweetheart."

"So did you. Neither are you. But we'll survive. We always do."

"No," he said. "I cannot permit this. I'll go alone and tell them you're too beat to come. God knows I won't be telling them a lie."

"I'm going."

"No," he insisted, turning away from the deathlike beautiful face and putting on his gray shantung trousers. "You must not go. I didn't see it last night, but I see it now. I was wrong to insist. I thought that since you'd invited her up here for three whole days, then a mere couple of hours down there couldn't do any harm. I misjudged, I . . ."

I still can't see the difference, but . . . "so get yourself back into bed, sweetheart, and that's an order."

"Hurry," she said. "We must leave in ten minutes."

57

"I simply refuse to let you go, Sonya."

"It's too late."

"It's not. You exagger—"

"Listen, Tape, I've thought this through to the . . . end."

The bitter end.

". . . and I was wrong last night to pretend there was an escape clause in your talk with Laney. As we both know, you said 'We'll be there.' So . . . I can't escape. We'll be there."

"Don't crucify yourself on a casual phrase. Please."

"Casual? From the instant you said 'We'll be there,' Laney *expects* me. And if you go alone, muttering vague excuses, she will sense . . . this. She will understand she has created a . . . problem. And her father's house will forever become inaccessible because of it. That's why it's too late."

"Look, sweetheart, Laney's just a little girl."

"Of twenty."

"All wrapped up in her new boy friend. She won't think twice about whether you're there or not. We're the ones who are complicating this. Those kids couldn't care less. So you go back to bed, and I'll . . ."

Sonya rose and pulled on the new orange dress she had bought for Katie's party. Its color, like a tree-ripened blood orange, reminded her of azaleas.

And Charleston.

"No," he insisted. "I'm putting a stop to this funeral procession. I won't go either. I'll phone the restaurant and leave a message for them saying we can't make it."

He removed his gray silk jacket and tossed it on the bed; he unknotted his necktie.

She was spraying herself with Diorissimo, his favorite perfume.

"Then I'll go alone," she said. "The Seventh Wave, you said?"

"Sonya! You cannot mean that. It's just too . . ."

"Yes. I'll go now if I have to go alone. It's too late to do anything else. Now pull yourself together and put some Murine in your eyes"—he was crying—"and drink your coffee and we'll go. And you mustn't do me the dishonor of worrying about how I'll behave. I'll be as gay and friendly as any . . ."

. . . stepmother . . .

". . . any guest at any luncheon party."

She brought him coffee and his protests became feebler, and at last they were on the coastal highway headed south, making prosaic comments from time to time as they passed lemon groves and redwood houses, distant ships and careless drivers, ugly towns and other safe, visible objects along the way.

"Christ and Calvin," groaned Tape. "Here comes another Jaguar. Will he or won't he?"

The approaching E-type honked with egalitarian courtesy and its driver solemnly saluted the Mark 2. A Symbolic Status Act.

Tape courageously refused to return the honk, but he did lift one cowardly finger off the steering wheel.

"The goddamned pukka sahib," he griped, nervously keeping the speedometer needle at exactly sixty, for as the Club Members well know, Jags get tickets at sixty-two when Fords and Chevvies are whizzing by at seventy-five.

Usually I call it the Jag, or the Car, and often Our Car; but Sonya always carefully says Your Car, although it was Her Car when we picked it up in Coventry and brought it back with us. But when my wife ex-wife refused to relinquish either of my cars, Sonya gave it to me as a wedding present. That was a time. All my possessions expropriated, quitting my job, heading westward ho-ho-ha-ha with four thousand dollars cash and no visible prospects. And, God, it was September and I'd just gotten the tuition bill for Laney's school; and Stan decided to quit the public school and go to Beech Grove, and . . . what a time for a honeymoon. Money-money-money. I must have been a pathetic case by the time we got to Wichita, for that was the night Sonya decided to tell me about her inheritance. Sweet thing, doing her best to buck me up.

"Remember the trip out here, when our car was almost new?" he asked. "I insisted on using Castrol oil and couldn't find it after we left St. Louis, and finally when we hit Wichita we were three quarts low and I was forced to switch to Shell, certain it would ruin the engine. And now she's got four years and fifty-three thousand miles on her and running better than ever, give-take a valve clatter here and there.''

Wichita. The humiliating trek from motel to motel as he shopped for the cheapest one. The pretense of seeming to want to save money with my new husband as we honeymooned from supermarket to supermarket buying economy cuts for our portable charcoal grill. And that swimsuit in St. Louis. So much did I want it that I forgot the Hubby's-little-saver game I was playing and started inside the store to buy it. And he *stopped* me. Stopped his flighty extravagant bride. ''But you've already got *three* swimsuits in your suitcase, sweetheart.''

Oh, I knew his worries, his fears, and I respected them, but I was outside, incapable of sharing in or trying to help him with the centermost fear of all the fears, which was his fear that he wouldn't be able to provide for the ones he'd left back in Connecticut in order to be with me in California-here-we-came.

Now he thinks, or pretends to think, that California was his idea, but it was mine, the one time I used Force on him. And why? Because it's as far as possible from the scene of the crime, that's why. In every crisis of conscience, I get panicky and fly the c . . . ooo . . . p. But Distance is never Escape. Yet that's the history of my life, putting Distance between the spot where the *X* is and me. My folly.

That was the night I almost left him. In St. Louis. Over a silly little swimsuit. He'll never know how very close I was to leaving. Because if he couldn't stop fearing for Them enough to indulge me in that paltry item, why should I struggle trying to turn whatever it was I had for him into love?

And still I didn't mention the money from Mother's estate, who knows why? Until Wichita. That four-dollar motel where the road-workers lived was just too much. It was either leave or tell him we could afford to stay in seven-dollar motels.

So I displayed my wealth, poor thing. He pretended it didn't matter, but his relief was both touching and frightening. One money-spender off his back. Three dependents, not four.

The floorboard was hot under her feet, for Jaguars, with their many virtues, do not possess the one of running cool in tropic climes.

They stopped in Ventura for an oil check, as their Jag was getting old and somewhat addicted to the stuff.

While Tape was in the Guaranteed-Clean Restroom, Sonya bought a Coke and took a Miltown.

CHAPTER 6

~~~~~~~~~~~~~~~
~~~~~~~~~~~~~~~
~~~~~~~~~~~~~~~

And there was the Seventh Wave. And Laney shrieking Dad, Dad, teeter-tottering on high heels at high speed across the parking lot, the tall boy in Madras shorts slouching proudly after.

We've both got Tall Boys.

Sonya said, "How beautifully happy she is, Tape. And how beautiful."

"No," he said modestly. "Just pretty. But she has a beautiful soul."

Father and daughter kissed, wife and fiancé shook hands; then they went inside to the bar for a celebrative champagne cocktail, and Sonya said, "I'm so glad, Laney, that you don't have your father's height or lantern jaw; and I'm even gladder that Bark doesn't have a crew cut."

"Do you hate crew cuts, too?" Laney said in astonishment.

A young man passing through the bar hailed Bark—"You got two real pretty chicks there, man. Which one's yours?"

Which one indeed? A passing stranger has said it all. We are two chicks with proud dates. Does Dad, I wonder, now understand the difference between Home and Restaurant?

Probably not. Both our dates are bursting with pride to wear such pretty chicks on their arms.

Laney said, "Bark, could you get me an aspirin? I have a headache, sort of."

Poor thing. She is an anomaly, dressing well but with extreme modesty, indicating a shyness which does not show in her conversation, which is bird-free. She could improve her appearance enormously with eye makeup and a flashier mouth, but obviously wouldn't if you tortured her.

They were ordering lunch on the sunny outside terrace and looking at the Pacific, Laney for the first time and in awe.

"Seals," Bark said, going to the rail.

Laney ran to see.

Sonya whispered, "The crisis is over. I'm all right now. She's wonderful. Also, we're *sympathique*. So relax, Dad."

Dad relaxed. What a woman was his wife. What a girl his daughter.

"Man," he said, "it'd take a lot of this to kill me."

Across the albacore and rainbow trout, over the juice of Napa Valley, Tape said, "How's she doing at school, Bark? Still failing with honors, I presume."

"Mister Alberg," Bark said with deepest respect, "that's the best description of Laney I ever heard. Man, I sure am going to remember that one. Failing with Honors. In three years her name's never been off the top of the Dean's List, but to hear her talk you'd think she was Miss Stupidity from Ignorance, Mississippi, in person."

"With a Phi Bete Key," said Sonya.

"Now, Sonya," begged Laney, placing her hand (nails neatly bitten, no polish) on her stepmother's arm, "don't you join their conspiracy, please."

Her nose (small, freckled) twitched rabbitly, and her eyes (green-blue with honeyed specks) pleaded earnestly, girl to girl, indeed almost younger sister to older sister.

"I'm not smart, Sonya. And it makes me furious when people say I am. Oh, fathers and boy friends are expected to. You know. But professors ought to know better. I mean when a person has this very ordinary mind, well, that person knows it. I mean she's the first to know. And when other people, who should know better, start this big rave, it . . . you know.''

Bark and Tape mugged at each other. ''Here we go again,'' Bark said. ''Failing with Honors. I know you studied philosophy under Carnap at Chicago U., Mister Alberg, but where did you go to school, Sonya?''

Tape answered the question proudly. ''The Sorbonne. All four years.''

''I've got a friend over there,'' Laney said. ''On the Junior Year Abroad. She says it's maddening trying to learn conversational French because the French won't talk to Americans. Sherry wrote me this cute letter, clever actually, saying the French just rudely won't answer; they just walk off leaving you with *oeuf* on your *visage*.''

Laney giggled appreciatively at her friend's wit. ''Are they really like that?'' Bark said to Sonya.

''They are certainly Francocentric,'' she answered. ''For them *France* and *civilisation* are synonyms. So, naturally, the rest of us are hardly worth talking to.''

''Sonya's half French,'' Tape said. ''But they wouldn't even give her the time of day, until . . . tell them your Tashkent story, swee—it's a killer.''

''I went to Paris,'' Sonya said, performing dutifully, ''vowing to perfect my French and never to speak English, but with the same results as Laney's friend. So I turned to guile. I probed deeply into Sorbonnian Society, looking for a weak, entering point. The *bourgeoisie,* both *haute* and *basse,* was impregnable; but it seemed possible, under certain conditions, to penetrate the Intellectual Left.''

''Sounds dangerous,'' Bark said. ''What conditions?''

''Bark's mad for spy stories,'' Laney said.

''I studied the globe and then told everybody that I was a Russian from Tashkent, which is way over in Asia so who in Paris could possibly be from there to find me out?''

''Sonya learned Russian as a kid,'' Tape bragged. ''Her father was a White Russian named Count Osinoff.''

64

"Golly, I'd never have the nerve," Laney said. "How did it work out?"

"Beyond all expectation. Overnight I became the darling of the Marx–existentialist-syndrome set and the supreme judge of all things dialectical. Of course I had to study Communist ideology madly to keep from falling out of the Troika."

"That's beautiful," Laney said, putting an impulsive hand on Sonya's arm. "What kind of things did you have to judge?"

"Oh . . . like, in Tashkent—I never spoke for Moscow, just Tashkent—we considered Brahms only half-bourgeois because he half-understood that the cello–piano dialogue in the slow movement of the Second Piano Concerto was in fact a dialectic that sounded the death-knell of bourgeois pseudo-values. You see, the whole clue to Communist esthetics is whether or not the artist *knows* he is ringing down the curtain on capitalism. If, like Joyce or Proust, he doesn't know, then of course he is not an artist. At least that was our position in Tashkent. It did wonders for my French."

To the tune of the Brahms cello part, Tape sang lugubriously, "Workers of the world unite. You-hoo have nothing to-hoo loo-hoose but your chay-hay-hains."

"Oh, Dad," cried Laney. "Stop or you'll ruin that for me forever."

"Turnabout," he said. "You murdered Claude's *Clair de Lune* for me, remember? Do you still play, always excepting of course nine-eight time?"

"She's great," Bark bragged. "Man, she sure did impress my folks last night with Chopin."

"Oh, I just mess around," Laney said. "Dad, are you still a mad record fiend?"

"I've switched to prerecorded tapes. In fact, Tape is what Sonya calls . . ."

"Look," cried Sonya, standing and pointing. "Those seals."

"The one on the left looks exactly like Togo," Tape said, and he told the don't-you-like-flowers story.

"Remember, Dad, that schizophrenic gardener back home who attacked Mom with a—" too shocked at herself to continue the

65

unmentionable subject, but too young to change it with ease, Laney floundered; Sonya flew to her rescue.

"Hey, won't anybody let me finish my Tashkent story?"

"I'm dying with suspense," Bark said. "Did they ever expose the clean-cut American?"

Laney relaxed. Sonya continued, "By the end of the Easter term, I had infiltrated to the point where they were openly discussing their weapons caches in front of me. Then, one night late, I dropped in at a party down in—what else?—a cellar. Cellars are a vice with Communists; they love them. I interrupted a stranger who was telling a long droll story in broken French. Waving at him to continue, I sat down and a girl whispered, 'He's a Russian actor.' I listened. He was describing one of the regular playgoers in the People's Theater where he acted."

Tape interrupted again. "*People's* Theater? What other kinds are there? Goats maybe?"

"Oh, Dad, stop! You know very well that in Russia people like us aren't people. Go on, Sonya."

"This particular theatre-lover the actor was describing came to every play and he always managed to get the same front-row seat. He would lower the seat, and put on it the following items: a leg of lamb, a bottle of vodka, and assorted delicacies. He always carried a prayer rug, which he carefully spread on the floor in front of the seat. Then he'd remove his shoes, place them on the seat beside the leg of lamb, and now he was ready to sit down, which he did in cross-legged style on the prayer rug, where he remained throughout the entire performance, all the while eating, drinking, and using the seat as a sort of garbage can. The man telling the story was a very good mime and I laughed like everything as he sat on the floor, peering at the actors' feet, which was about all the little man had been able to see. I thought it all very droll until someone whispered, 'Sonya, you must know him; he's an actor from your home city.'"

"Caught," said Bark. "Wow!"

"The story finished, the stranger came at once to me and said,

'Of course you're the Sonya from Tashkent, Comrade, and no doubt you have seen this little man many times.'

" 'Of course I have,' I answered in my iciest Russian. 'You have been making sport of my father, Comrade.' Well, the poor Russian actor almost died of embarrassment and humbly did his best to apologize to me, but I refused to say one more word to him, and so I escaped. A week later I went to Spain on my holiday and that was the end of Tashkent."

"That wife of yours would make a great spy, Mister Alberg," Bark said earnestly. "Or if you get down to that, a great anything. She sure would."

"Bark secretly wants to be a spy," Laney said, "but he's taking up surgery instead."

"What do you mean instead?" Sonya said. "A surgeon is king of the snoopers. But you two children must get those yacht stores stored, so may I be excused to go fix my face for the long journey back to Tashkent?"

"That reminds me," Bark said hastily. "I've got to oil my air horn. It's developed this bad case of laryngitis."

Sonya gave Tape and Laney twenty minutes to be alone, and when she returned, all said their goodbyes, Laney with kisses for both of them, the dear thing, and the two cars drove out of the parking lot, the Corvette turning to the right for Newport, the Jaguar to the left for Pobrecito, all waving, and Bark playing a well-oiled klaxon that sounded like six dogs being run over.

Tape was in ecstasy.

"What a charmer you are. You had those two kids drooling. Laney is just crazy about you, sweetheart. And Bark, too, of course. Me too, incidentally. When they ran to look at the seals, and you said what you said, it was the best moment of my life."

The best, the best, the very best. The one you are having is always the best.

"The greatest. Not that I didn't *know* it would work out the way it did, sweetheart, I just *knew* it would, in my bones. But the proof of the pudding . . . Oh, I admit I was a bit tense at first, especially during the trip down. You were so exhausted and beat I worried about your strength, I mean, but sweetheart, when you said what you said, Wow! Was I ever happy? Oh, by the way, while you were in the ladies' room, Laney had a private talk with me. She's very serious about Bark. They want to get married next year some time. It'll be the senior year for both of them, and then he'll go on to med school, and . . . I think Bark will make her a nice husband, don't you?''

"Yes, I do. He's a first-class boy."

"Apparently the money problem doesn't seem to worry his parents. They're all in favor of it, Laney said. Of course, you can imagine how a girl like Laney must have impressed them. She says she'll get a job while he's in med school. Anyway, I told her I liked Bark very much and even if I didn't, still I'd trust her judgment on anything anytime anywhere, up to and including marriage.''

"You did fine. I ate too much. And wine at high noon. I can hardly keep my eyes open."

"And no wonder, after zero hours sleep last night. You're just unwinding, after all the tension. Try to take a nap, sweetheart. I'll stop yapping."

He seized her hand, kissed it, and said, "Thanks for breathing, sweetheart."

"Don't mention it."

She turned her face toward the window and closed her eyes.

That sweet gracious sensitive child. What an ordeal it must have been for her, too. Was Laney now closing her eyes and pretending fatigue to escape Bark's commentaries?

Headache, sort of.

Did her father have any slightest notion of what his daughter had endured, for the sake of . . .?

Probably not.

My God, can this be madness, Clare's nothingness of scorn and noise?

This swelling, this bursting, my senses have exploded. I want to scream, to tear out my hair, split open my skull and scoop out my brain in wet spongy handfuls. Throw it on the pavement to

68

be flattened, obliterated, squashed, annihilated by a million wheels.

And why not the rest of my body with it? Let the myriad tires soak up my existence. So easy. Just open this door and . . .

Do what Werner's wife did to Werner and me? Oh, no. Nobody's going to pay that kind of price over my dead body.

Was Laney tortured, too? Or is he right, and I am the only casualty. And if I am, is that cause for . . .?

He was driving and humming. Happy man, happy tune. Schumann's "Carnaval." Doesn't he remember he once told me Laney played that piece for her first recital?

Probably not.

If he did remember, would he still hum it?

Does he know he's humming it?

Probably not.

I . . . must . . . not . . . blame . . . him.

"Laney says her mother's got a serious gentleman caller, *too*," he said. "Let's pray it's true."

My body is in a thousand pieces, each divorced from the other, my feet are divorced from my legs, my . . .

"Pobrecito, here we are," he was saying cheerfully, so she must have slept, although it didn't seem possible.

He was driving into the garage.

"Home again," he was saying, "from what I would call a very successful and very happy and very pleasant little journey. Eh, sweetheart? It's a great day for me, the greatest, and I humbly thank one and all present for making it so."

She ran into the house. The bathroom. The bed.

Soon he would find her, and he would be sure to say: "Anything wrong, sweetheart?"

And she would be just as certain *not* to answer: "I cannot speak. The Force has struck me dumb."

There was the splash of swimmers next door and outside the window a birdsong; on the other side of the room a door opened softly.

"Oh. Is something wrong, sweetheart? Anything the matter?"

While Sonya was resting, Tape stole out and bought champagne, not one but two bottles of the stuff, to surprise her. However, it was not a good night for champagne, especially on Sonya's empty stomach, for she ate hardly any dinner, not even the smoked salmon; and sitting in the living room afterward, listening to the Diabelli Variations, she begged Tape not to open the second bottle but he did, and in the end they both got sourly drunk, Tape on the staggering side, probably because he had added Courvoisier to the Cordon Rouge, while Sonya, who was never much of a drinker, simply became sleep-struck.

Tape filled the two glasses with the last of the second bottle and carried them into the bedroom, saying, "Let's finish these while we're undressing, huh?"

Then, Tape made the mistake of getting into Sonya's bed with her, and—this night of all nights—fooling around.

All this kneading of the sleepy dough which was her body seemed to Sonya in very *mauvais goût* and she proceeded to discourage it in a manner she would never have dreamed of adopting while sober.

You picked a bad time for sex, Dad, was her thought, as she said, "My defeat today was your victory, it seems, which you have chosen to celebrate in champagne. Well, all night you've been drinking toasts to the worst beating I ever took—and I'll bet it was the worst beating Laney ever took, too—so now you want to crown it all with a garland of sex, which you no doubt confuse with love."

Tape withdrew his insulted hands. Sonya sat up in bed. He decided to play it realistically, on the drunk side.

"After two bottles of champagne," he said, "what else could you call love, but sex? Is there any other kind?"

"One would hope," she answered with Cordon Rouge *hauteur*, "that somewhere there exists a kind of love that rises above *self* things. A kind of love that doesn't force its will on another person's *person*, speaking metaphorically as well as physically. Especially metaphorically."

"That luncheon with Laney still galls you, and for that I'm sorry," he said. "But I did not *force* you to go. Remember?"

70

Sonya got up and went to the dresser for a pill. It really had been a dreadful, disastrous day for her, and her face in the mirror was as Tape had seen it that morning, a bronze death mask, but the hunted, anguished eyes had changed to drunken, remorseless ones.

She hoped Tape would, in her absence, leave her bed; instead, he started asking personal, rhetorical questions.

"Why is it," he asked, "at times like most of the time, like now, that I don't feel worthy of you? I try to take an innocent feel, and it becomes an *unworthy* feel. Is it something I do to myself all by myself, or do you help me?"

He finished his glass of champagne and tried to decide if he should finish hers, too, but feared it would be yet another proof of his unworthiness.

"Why," he asked, "should I feel unworthy of your love just because I had luncheon with my own daughter?"

"Love," she said, standing by her bed as if waiting for him to abandon it. This hurt his feelings of course, and he said, "Yes, love. Sex is pragmatic love, so don't knock it. You're always dreaming of some airy-fairy kind of love that never existed. Impossible love."

"I don't suppose *you* could conceive of a love that transcended the Self, the Ego," she countered. "Even so, it can happen."

"Semantics," he scoffed. "It's impossible to define love. Because love is *People,* and people are Mrs. and Mr. Ego in person."

She sat on the edge of her bed, well away from him. She picked up her glass and sipped the last of the champagne.

"Love," she said softly, mournfully, accusingly, "can be a rare event. In which nothing done or said by either lover is ever . . . disappointing. It *can* be."

The way she said *disappointing* sounded just too goddamned personal, and angrily Tape insisted, "Love is *always* disappointing precisely because it's always two people. If one wants to go North when the other wants to go South, then one of them is gonna be dis——"

Suddenly he became suspicious and changing his tack said,

71

"Wait. I think you are referring to yourself in person. I think you think you actually experienced this perfect love, what you just called the rare event."

Sonya deigned not to answer, so he felt he had scored.

"Sounds like one of those moonlight-on-the-water memories of high school," he scoffed. "How old were you when you and Mr. Rare transcended each other's egos?"

His sarcasm was just too . . . and she snapped, "I was old enough to know it can be that way."

"What way?"

"A way you'll never know."

Until this remark, it could have been the kind of comic champagne night that both could have laughed over the next morning. Tape had always admired Sonya's extreme delicacy in never, never mentioning previous things; but of course he had always assumed that with such beauty as hers she had had certain experiences of course.

Now, she was flatly telling him she had loved before in a way he could never be up to—she had used Love's ultimate weapon, which is the invidious comparison and not the Rival himself. More than ever, he was the unworthy mate, compared to the rare one, the fabulous fellow incapable either of forcing or disappointing her.

"And so we fornicate," he said bitterly, close to tears, "in your second-best bed. While you no doubt think sadly back on a perfect lover who once took you to the most expensive motels. Love-love, money-money."

Outraged that he could pair those two words in reference to her, Sonya snapped, "That Wichita motel was not *money*. Any more than the St. Louis swimsuit was money. I could have slept in the wheat fields with a man whose deepest concerns centered around me; but I could not shop for cheap cabins with one whose obsession was to scrimp and save for other reasons in other places, at the precise, intolerable moment of the honeymoon."

"Intolerable? Our *honeymoon?*" This was the first time in four years of marriage that she had mentioned those tense unhappy days and he became convinced that she was not just being

72

driven by drunkenness, but was using it as an excuse to say the things and do the things that would destroy the marriage, leaving him broken-hearted in the rubble.

Regretting the terrible and ugly word she had used, Sonya tried to soften it, saying, "I only meant we had the intolerable bad luck to try to honeymoon with Them surrounding us. Before They existed, in Italy, I thought we were going to have that . . . rare event. But we never had a chance. They existed. And *They* were intolerable to the idea called honeymoon."

This seemed even more desperate to Tape and he rose from her bed to present his side of the case, weaving frantically around the room as he did so.

"A goddamn swimsuit, a cheap motel. Don't you understand? I'm a Swede. A tight-assed Swede. All that money-fear has been pounded into me for centuries. And to make certain I knew the lesson, they tossed me bare-assed into that Depression when I was only ten. Plus those Great Plains dust storms. I ask you to consider that all my Dad's plants died, even the trees, because we couldn't pay our water bill and they shut us off. And Grandpa Alberg had to come up from the farm to live with us and learn the trade of shoe-repairing at the age of seventy. First consider that, please."

"Oh, Tape," she cried, sincerely moved. "Why won't you understand that I am not talking about money?"

"I understand you're talking about how lousy I am compared to some guy you used to know," he cried in anguish. "Where is he now? What's he do? Why didn't you stay with him, if he was so . . . ?"

Tape fell across his bed and started to cry in earnest. Sonya closed the window, on account of the Brewsters.

Then she said, putting on her robe, "Listen, Tape. We're both very very drunk and very very foolish. We say too much. Much too much."

"*In vino veritas,*" he sobbed.

"Perhaps—but we must stop this nonsense. And I know you won't stop, in your condition, so long as I'm in this room, so . . ."

73

"Oh, no," he blubbered. "Don't abandon me now. Please. I'll never force you again. Never. I'll . . ."

But while he was begging and pleading with her to stay, she turned out the light and went to the spare room, which had been polished and scrubbed and made cheerful with flowers for the expected guest whose change of plans had changed so many other things, too.

CHAPTER 7

The point of no return. This time, she's through with me.

She's never said so much or gone so far before. And she's just not the type to abandon bed as an empty threat.

She's through.

A car screeched into the Brewster driveway, spraying light across the Venetian blind. The dressing-table mirror flickered briefly with Madame Pompadour's jewel box.

Through. Especially metaphorically. Especially physically.

Stop it. The only finality is death. But doesn't everything die, including marriage? I'm living proof of that kind of death. I send alimony to a stranger. A stranger who once shared my intimate unmentionable intimacies. But now, just the stranger-mother of my . . .

"*Arrivederci,*" shouted the Brewster boy to his departing friends as their car scratched gravel and again sprayed light against the blind; and, for good measure, "*Ciaou.*"

Those Brewsters. Do they really enjoy life in their luxurious wasteland of swimming pool and fun room and Bar-B-Que complex, barren of all culture except that Stanfordized son, thinly varnished with a year in Rome to write his novel, but returning scriptless with an Alfa Romeo and five or six Italian phrases?

Now, exactly what is young Brewster's problem? His problem is he cannot wangle a grant to continue in graduate school, and if you're in graduate school without a grant you are merely and blatantly advertising Inferior Goods. But Messrs. Ford, Rand, Guggenheim, Fulbright, *et al.* have thumbed him down.

Poor lost boy, too good for his old man's realty office, not good enough for Fellowship, condemned to wander twixt two worlds, one beneath him, and t'other above him.

Shit on his problem. What's mine? Imagine, running that idiot's *dossier* through my computer system at a time like this.

My problem is *not* final. She'll soften. She just got carried away. The tension, the pressure. We all have our secret little crazy little worlds we live in. Mine is fear of losing her. Hers is guilt at getting me. Guilt worked against me in Laney's case. But it'll work for me in this case. Telling me about that One and Only, First Great Love of hers . . . will make her feel so sorry for me that she'll probably wake me up tomorrow with

"Forgive me, Tall Boy."

There was nausea in his stomach and sickness in his soul.

Especially physically.

His feet were slowly turning numb; sleep was moving in foot by foot, inch by inch up his legs. He turned on his stomach, adjusting the pillow to bolster his right shoulder.

The condemned man's last waking thought was:

She'll be here, warm and golden. Especially, especially physically. Wait and seeeeeeeeeeeeeeeeeeee . . .

The black nirvana was broken by a splash and a boy shrieking girlishly; a girl laughed boyishly. Sunlight sprayed the black hole of Calcutta.

Last waking thought turned into first waking thought:

She's not here!

Especially phy—

Panicked, Tape turned and stared at Sonya's bed. Empty. But maybe it was still early, the clock . . .

The hands prayed hopelessly at ten minutes past ten.

This was the ultimate Rejection.

Had she left the house, like the bed? The town, like the house . . .?

"*Buon giorno,*" shouted the Brewster boy to a new, squealing arrival. "Race you ten laps free-style, *cara mia.*"

An image suddenly flashed on mind's picture-tube, of the bulldozer next door rooting out that beautiful acacia hedge, Self at the window watching helplessly.

No bulldozing on this delicate plant, you stupid Swede. Wait. She'll soften. Her guilt will "Forgive me, Tall Boy."

And stop playing back that old tape.

Especially physically.

He was ruminating and urinating.

Mixing her in with my kids was bad policy. Never again. I must go to them, not they to me. Keep her out of it.

Think up a good Plan and stick to it. Order of the Day. Number One: Do nothing, say nothing, and *wait*. Bank on Time. Good old Time. I mean Guilt. Good old Guilt.

He was washing his teeth.

Number Two: Don't press or force. Force is a dirty word, and it's worse on the end of your . . .

Play it cool *SPLAT* Be gentle *SPUT* Be laconic *SPLIT*.

He was shaving with the world's greatest blade: Wilkinson's Sword.

This is the tenth—no, eleventh—shave and the blade is still great. Liar! A Big-Spender would have changed five shaves ago.

Above all, be generous. She can't stand tight-assism. No more St. Louis. Never again Wichita. Eschew all petty economies . . .

Although it wasn't necessary, he removed the old blade and grandly unsheathed a new one. He'd show her a Swede farm-boy from Nebraska could be just as grand as a French-Russian countess-type from Long Island.

He was under the shower rehearsing the breakfast scene:

"Good morning, sweetheart. Looks like the morning fogs have finally . . ."

Sonya's waking-up dream was noiseless, a landscape dream; she was bogged down in a dismal swampland cratered with scummy pools of slimy water.

A dead scene, *natur mort,* where no snake snaked and no vulture vultured. A lifeless swamp. But wait! Over there, in that puddle of green slime, some living thing twitched to show life, then began to struggle frenetically, sinking, rising, flailing, writhing, the anguished slimed mouth gasping Help, Help, Help!

Sonya the dream-watcher desperately tried to scream encouragement, but the words wouldn't pass through her mud-thick throat; still, she silently screamed: *I'M COMING; HOLD ON, MOTHER, I'M COMING!*

She struggled to break out of the thick bottomless mud but could not move.

And was forced to watch her own mother's contorted face going down for the last time in the green muck, as the mouth tried to smile and did succeed in wrenching out:

Au revoir, Sonya.

Consciousness, semibenign, transported her from the land of terror to the state of misery.

The roses on the dresser, put there for Laney, had had their two days. Sonya turned the other way.

I am not fit to live with. And yet, what I did to him last night inevitably had to follow what was done to me yesterday.

On the Brewster side, water splashed and youths screamed. On the estate side, an electric garden clipper buzzed and hummed, with now and then a startled whine as it bit into more than it could chew. Hedge-clipping day at the Big House.

Totting-up time in the guest room.

He will be down there fretting in bed and waiting no doubt for a sexy reconciliation.

But what up until now has been the only possible solution has changed overnight into the most impossible.

Is there any solution?

She closed her eyes and invented the breakfast dialogue:

"You deserve a better wife, Tape, but . . ."

"Ah, sweetheart. It was just the champagne."

78

"No wife at all is better than a bad wife, Tape."

"Ah, sweetheart."

"Go back to Them. Where you belong. Oh, I don't mean Her, Them. Taking care of Them will soon make you forget what I made you do."

But that tack was too unrealistic. Try again.

"You're a normal happy sort, Tape. I'm not. You live in the rosy future, I live in the gray past. It's not your fault. I know what normal second wives do in these broken-family cases. But I can't. I simply cannot cover the hideous ruins with pretty climbing roses and forget what's underneath, or who made them ruins."

"Ah, sweetheart, love is not ruins."

"Love, you say? Love. I'm afraid I'm not capable of that, Tape—or, forgive me, its passionate facsimile."

Cheap talk. Trashy talk. But perhaps cheap-trashy true talk.

She rose and went to the window to close the blind, but paused for a moment to look down on the Brewsters' swimming pool. Five Pobrecito youths, three girls and two boys, were at the outdoor bar drinking. At the far end of the pool an unwatched (except by her) portable television was showing the Man with the Terrible Headache who yearned for Faster Relief. Suddenly came a newscast, and a man tossed out words like grenades: Viet Cong, Cuba, Freeworld, Red Students.

I am a miniworld, whirling from petty crisis to petty crisis, scorched with brushfires of the brain. Before the Laney crisis, I had an Ives crisis. Impossible to recover from both. And next will come, reasonably and necessarily, the Stan crisis.

Between his family and my . . . that was a sharp arrow he let fly, about First Loves and moonlight on the water.

Were Dante and Beatrice faking off? Not from Dante's point of view.

Am I? Perhaps, but only perhaps. I do not know. I Love You is a point of view, not a Law of Life. Whom does Werner Grunwald love, now, right this minute?

And who am I to set myself up as an angel of sensitivity

79

entitled to my version of Paradise? Do I not plague Tape as he plagues me?

In her private Prado, two life-size paintings hung together on a wall, a couple, side by side, facing each other, loving each other. Dürer's Adam and Eve.

Then slowly, as she watched at the window above the Brewsters' swimming pool, the figures began to turn, until they were back to back, their shoulders gradually bowing under the joyless burden of having to be together, forever, on the same wall.

In the room below, the shower started running, so Sonya put on a quilted robe of palest blue and went down to fix his breakfast.

I've either got to change, completely, my point of view, my values, my sense of my own value and how it should be valued, or . . . what?

Not fit to live with.

The icebox offered smoked salmon galore, but no milk for coffee.

So she brewed him a pot of tea.

We lead doubly flawed lives, his by Them, and mine by . . .

"Morning, sweetheart. Beautiful day. Guess the foggy season must be over."

Today will be fuller than usual of Sweethearts, poor thing. Has he ever noticed, I wonder, that I never sprinkle him with casual endearments?

Did I ever rename any person with one of the words belonging to the sugar family? If so, I don't care to remember.

She said, "Good morning, Tape. Sorry, but we're out of milk. Will you settle for tea?"

"Love it, sweetheart. Well, today's the big day."

"For what?"

"My appointment with the Mayor. Remember?"

"Oh, yes." The proof that I am not a proper wife is this, for what true mate could be so indifferent to his gallant business schemes?

"I wish you luck," she added.

80

"Thanks, sweetheart. Appreciate it. Didja bring in the paper?"

"Not yet."

She was cooking bacon and eggs and he said, "Call me when everything's ready."

He went outside.

On good mornings we always eat corn flakes; on bad ones, she *cooks*.

He found the paper over by the brush cherries. He kicked it out of range and watered them with the hose.

She sets the mood, not me; if she's cheerful, I'm joyous; if she's glum, I'm glummer. As Sonya goes, so go the Albergs. Meaning her and me. Stan was that way back home, back there. He's one of the Powerful People, too.

Seems to me most wives call the shots, set the mood, name the game, pick the movie. Why?

Probably has something to do with tnuc spelled backward. Maybe the wife learns through self-protection how to control the husband's cockiness, like nature controls her tnuckiness, and so she learns the technique of controlling everything else as well.

Not just Sonya. Betty, too. Betty didn't like, or was ashamed of, my dad. So we never visited him again after the first time. While me, I despised her mother and spent damn near every holiday with the mean old bitch.

And wives, not husbands, flounce off to the spare room.

If Sonya took a liking to Dad—and she would, I just know those two would hit it off—then we'd start visiting Dad. Must take her to Lincoln sometime. And also down to Beaver Crossing to see my farm. My half-farm. Half a farm for half a Hamlet.

Some rich husbands name the game. Or is that why they're rich?

I really must take her to Lincoln, first chance, or would that be Forcing, too?

Christ and Calvin, what a mess.

"Hey, Mistle Albell."

It was Togo, on a ladder, clippers in hand, peering over the ledge.

"Hi Togo. When you get *that* juicy contract?"

Togo beckoned, just like a World-War-Two spy. Tape turned off the hose, picked up the paper, and crossed the driveway.

Togo, nodding toward the Big House, whispered, "How they up there? They pay okay?"

"They're too rich to pay every month, but they'll cough up once a year or so. Did you sign a contract?"

"Not yet. First I show 'em good job."

"Take my advice and don't give old Carl the Caretaker a cut. They fired the last clipping service for that. Why they boot out the innocent and keep the guilty is too much for me."

Togo giggled his appreciation.

"Thanks, Mistle Albell. Keep nose clean, huh? Hey, watsa matter with your blush cherries?"

"They won't take hold. Can't figure out why. I treat 'em better than I do my wife, still . . ."

Togo snickered. "You treat 'em too good, Mistle Albell. Too much damn waller, too much damn food. No damn good. Same as wives. Don't treat 'em too damn good."

"Maybe," Tape said, knowing the lazy bastard was right, at least on the brush-cherry proposition.

"Breakfast, Tape," Sonya called from the kitchen window, and Tape turned, as Togo said, "Hey. Them Natal plums for Miss Nelly's hedge. You want? I got five hundred beauts."

"Stop it, Togo. Like I said, it's going to be dwarf myrtle."

Tape removed the rubber band from the newspaper and put it on his wrist; then the small economy scared him and he threw it away.

The table was set for one; she was emptying the icebox.

"Oh," he said. "Did you eat already?"

"Ages ago. This thing is so filthy. Really disgusting."

He sat down. "I must write Dad. I'm terrible about answering his letters, poor old guy."

"I hope your eggs aren't too cold. Nelly called but I told her you were talking to Togo and she said it wasn't anything and refused to let me interrupt you."

"I'll drive up to see her after I finish with the Mayor."

82

Now she had her head inside the great empty refrigerator, scrubbing the white gleaming interior as busily as if it were really dirty.

When the going gets tough, she always cleans something that doesn't need cleaning. Or paints a chair that doesn't need painting. Keep to the policy. Play it cool.

He ate his eggs fast to get to the tea and First Cigarette. He unrolled his newspaper.

"Oh, my God," he said. "Another jet crash. Terrible. Christ, ninety-three dead. No survivors."

"Horrible," she said. "Where?"

"Kennedy Airport. It was taking off for London when something . . . it just exploded, about five hundred feet up, and nobody knows . . . Oh! Jesus, this is awful. One of my favorite musicians was aboard. Poor guy."

Sonya pulled out the vegetable bin and put it on the floor. She opened the ice compartment and said, "Who?"

"You've heard him. That piano player who in my opinion is the Schnabel of this generation. Werner Grunwald. The Austrian. He's an American citizen now, though, it says here. Was."

She heard, but she must hear it again. "Who?"

"You know, the guy who did that Concord Sonata I'm so crazy for. And the greatest Prokofief Third. And the dazzling Chromatic Fugue, remember? Grunwald. Werner Grunwald. Seems he was headed out of New York for a London concert date, poor guy. His home is in New York. Was. Too damn bad. A great artist. It's a terrible loss to the music world."

She seized a cube of ice and squeezed it in her hand until the coldness burned right through to the back; she squeezed harder with all her strength, feeling the sharp stabbing ache in all her knuckles. Slowly she slid to her knees and stared into the empty refrigerator, still squeezing the agonizing ice cube.

"Well," Tape said, "I gotta try and sell His Honor a beauty treatment. Wish me luck. If I succeed, this could be the turning point in my career. The financial security for our future."

He decided not to kiss her, but instead played it cool, giving her head an amiable pat in passing.

"Bye, sweetheart."

She held her breath.

And held it until the Jaguar sounded its way out of the garage.

Then she fainted.

CHAPTER 8

Mr. Mayor, my name is Alberg. I'm a blackmailer. It's common gossip that you've got a mistress as well as a wife, and I happen to know both. Your mistress is a fading beauty by the name of Santa Teresa . . .

Improvising Sales Approaches, Tape drove down Mission Road, shaded its full winding length by great trees, mainly eucalyptus, which in Greek means, simply, Good Shade.

The trees had been planted in the 1890s, after the Eastern millionaires, mainly from Boston, had discovered Santa Teresa's rugged hills and mild climate and had decided, because of its elevation above the fog belt, to build their estates in Pobrecito, which in Spanish means, simply, Poor Guy.

Now, the name was merely ironical, but once it had been an apt description of an area where long-gone Mexican fruit-pickers had squatted in mean leantos and splendid gypsy squalor.

A couple of yards behind the two rows of trees under and between which Tape drove were the high estate walls; it was like driving through a damp greenish tunnel with here and there a few drips and drops of sunlight.

Seriously, Mr. Mayor, Jack Hoover claims any guy who knows how to rejuvenate your girl friend has got you hooked, so . . .

He turned into the fast, too-damn-fast, growing city at Padre Muñoz, winding through hordes of new, small, worrisome houses gnawing like bright hungry mice at the walls of the old estates; and headed downhill toward the ocean, where the little houses yielded to clusters of high-level apartment buildings set on handkerchief lawns in which scooters scooted, toddlers toddled, and mothers gossiped.

She's a total enigma when she gets *that* polite. But cleaning the refrigerator was a very bad sign. Patience. Play it cool. Stick to the Plan. Maybe by sundown . . .

It was Dedication Day for the new Junipero Serra Shopping Center and he slowed down and gawked. All that imported architectural talent and local money had combined to produce an effect no better than a string of highway motels and no worse than an airport. The five-story central building, a barn concealed by concrete lace, had nothing to do with its wings of one-story glass boxes which packaged several chains of stores. The air-conditioned shopping mall, a huge bubble with a plastic dome, stuck out like a water blister on a sunburnt nose.

The more we spend the uglier we get, Your Honor.

Tape slowed down again for the intricate cloverleaf, locally nicknamed Hell's Gate, and entered the Freeway just below where it ceased being earthbound and translifted itself into a two-mile bridge, dripping with runoffs, spanning the seedy section of the city.

The signs called it the Expressway; the advertisements luring tourists said Skyway; and on a clear day, like today, it could plainly be seen that Santa Teresa was no uglier than most downtowns, and in fact the Old Mission section creeping up the mountain back of it was still very attractive, in the Spanish style liberally larded with Ranch House.

From Tape's viewpoint, on the highest part of the Skyway, the dominating aspect of the town was the automobile. The buildings along the streets were like riverbanks for their ceaseless Stop and Go.

The Skyway itself was as pragmatic as a Roman aqueduct, and, forgetting the charm of ancient ruins, probably no uglier;

like them, it hugely scorned any esthetic pretensions, making no attempt to adorn the area over which it stretched.

In a few words, Mr. Mayor, your girl friend has lost her Mission Bells charm and is no better or worse than, say, Jacksonville, Florida, or a hundred other cities.

KEEP IN RIGHT LANE FOR CITY HALL

Tape left the Skyway and immediately got stuck in a traffic jam composed mainly of orange-laden trucks inching toward the sorting station.

Traffic marmalade. She wished me luck. If I have luck, maybe she'll . . .

The line of trucks moved like a hot orange-topped glacier to the corner; the Jag turned right and escaped.

If I have luck, I'll buy her a big bunch of roses, and . . . don't be a cornball, buy her roses anyway. No, something more permanent, a nice cashmere sweater maybe. There's a sale on at Bullock's. Don't be a tight-ass. Go to I. Magnin and buy it full price.

Tape parked in the City Hall lot and put a dime in the one-legged bandit, Jack Hoover's advice twanging in his mind's ear:

"Howie's a native son of a bitch for one. And third-generation rich, to boot. That seems to help in politics, these days. Maybe the poor trust the rich, for a change. At least the *old* rich."

Tape, lugging his portfolio of drawings, walked across the patio, a bit of Old Spain with a fake well in the center, and climbed the steps to the Mayor's office.

He presented his credentials to the receptionist, an acned case of obvious nepotism, who spoke into the intercom. "Mister Alberg is here for his appointment, Mayor Howard. You know, the landscape architect from Pobrecito. Mister Jack Hoover's friend."

And Tape, after all these months and months of the hardest kind of work and study, was In.

The Mayor greeted him with a steely handshake and a politician's heartiness. He presented the image of a prosperous rancher in town for Saturday night. Beautiful embossed boots, drill

87

trousers reinforced for riding, wide belt with silver buckle, twin-pocket shirt and string tie.

"Nice to see you again," Tape said. "We met once or twice, sir, at the Rattlesnake Canyon Club, and . . ."

"How's that beautiful wife of yours?" the Mayor asked. "I swear she's the purtiest thing to hit Santa Teresa since Carole Lombard honored us with a long visit. Now, there was a square-shooter, Carole. On the level all the way. Have a seat."

Tape sat and put his portfolio on the floor. The Mayor put his boots on the desk.

"You know Jack Hoover well, Mister Alberg?"

"I guess Jack's the best friend I've got," Tape said. "We're both afflicted with stereophonicitis, you know, and we started trading tapes, then ideas, and . . ."

"Jack sounds mean as a sidewinder, but underneath he's all setter pup. A sweet guy. And a durn good editor. What's on your mind, Mister Alberg?"

"Black . . ." Tape swallowed the *mail,* and decided to cut all that cute crap about mistresses and fading beauty . . . "I'm a Landscape Architect, sir, with special training at UCLA after coming out here four years ago, and . . ."

"Oh, I know and admire your work, Mister Alberg. That McCormack place was so pitifully run down and you . . . I hate to see any part of Pobrecito go to seed; I was born there. Those estates give us something that's fast disappearing these days."

Tape wanted a cigarette, but the Mayor had not smoked and his ashtray was ashless; if he had just quit for health reasons he would be contemptuous of weaklings who still drove nails into their own coffins, so . . .

Better not. The Client is always perfect. Just like in the ad game.

"One thing we both have in common," Tape said. "We both love this city. And I don't have to tell *you,* sir, that she's suffering from a malignant growth, beginning six hundred yards before the southern approach to the Skyway, and continuing to the Gila Hills cloverleaf on the north side of town. Now in your position, you have to listen to all kinds of nuts, and I'm the kind of nut who wants to do something about that steel-and-concrete cancer. So much so that I have spent two years, all my spare time, in the consideration of therapeutic possibilities; the results of that study are contained in this portfolio. If you'd care to spare the time to look, sir."

"Why not?" the Mayor said, removing his boots from the desk.

Talking all the time, just like in the ad game, Tape untied his portfolio. "My reasons for going to all that trouble of course are completely selfish. First, I live here and have to look at the monster every day. And second, nearly every city in the country is building this type of thing and I want to make myself known as a specialist in beautifying them."

"I think that'd make a great career," the Mayor said.

"So naturally," Tape said, raising the first drawing but still not showing it, "I need a sample. To show my future clients. And this can be it."

He placed the watercolor painting in front of His Honor.

"Hey," said the Mayor, "did you draw this yourself? It's beautiful."

"Yes, of course. That is how the south approach would look. Here's the photo as it now is. Eyesore Number One. We'll have to widen the highway here to allow for these artificial hills; they'll be topped by Monterey cedars, because the sea winds'll twist them and make 'em even more beautiful. The mounds will be completely covered with thyme bushes."

He dropped another picture in front of the Mayor.

"Here, at Cathedral Cut, is a detail of the cliff."

"But it's solid rock," objected the Mayor. "How can you get anything to grow on that wall?"

"By concealed hanging pots. It's cheap, practical, and beautiful, Mister Mayor, sir."

"Oh, call me Howie. What are you, Andy?"

"My wife calls me Tape. And thanks, Howie. Now, here's the killer. The Skyway itself. If we make this, Howie, the hanging garden of Babylon will hang its head in shame."

Slow down, Tape. Your prose is getting too purple. This is not Madison Avenue.

"Well, for heaven's sake," the Mayor said solemnly. "That's . . . spectacular. More, inspiring."

And it was. A flowering boulevard, tree-lined, soared high above the earth.

"Each tree will be in its own concrete housing, Howie, all of them interconnected with troughs for these oleanders, and everything irrigated and even fertilized from a central control station. I've checked the engineering and the extra weight is negligible, by the way. As you see, it will be formal, elegant, I might even say noble. That's why I want to use cypress."

"Cypress seems a little graveyardy to me, Tape."

"Only in sound. In Europe the approach to the Palace is usually lined with them. Of course we could get much the same effect with Chinese juniper, but they present more of a shaping problem."

"I sure can understand how you worked two years on this, Tape."

Next, Tape showed him the ideas for the north exit, the fern-covered underpass, the blanket of climbing roses covering the small-road overpasses; and finally a proposed sketch for a city nursery where all plants would originate.

"You think big, all righty," the Mayor said. "But where would I find the money in Santa Teresa for a project that huge?"

"We guys who love beautiful ladies can usually find a way to dress 'em fit for a queen," Tape said, and he felt he had found exactly the right remark to score with the Mayor. "Besides," he added, "It's gonna cost a lot less than you think if you let a real tight-assed Swede superintend the job. Meaning me."

"I wouldn't turn this dream of yours over to anybody else even if it cost me the next election," the Mayor said.

"Thank you, Howie. Appreciate that. I also propose to make it a tourist-advertising lure by calling it The Garden in the Sky."

"Not bad, Tape. Not bad at all."

The intercom spoke: "Mister Nixon to see Mr. Howard."

The Mayor rose and shook hands heartily. "I'm very glad you came, Tape. I like young men who think big."

"Not so young," Tape said, trussing his drawings. "About five less than you, I'd say."

"Call your five and raise you six. Better hide those pictures until you hear from me, huh?"

"From now on"—Tape patted the portfolio—"this is *our* baby. But just what is the next step, Howie?"

"I'd say convincing the city fathers to give us an appropriation to make a scale model. But that's my department. How about you and that beautiful wife of yours spending a weekend at the ranch? Does she ride?"

They were at the door, which the Mayor opened to greet Mr. Nixon, and Tape was out.

At the phone booth in the patio, he joyously called Sonya, convinced that this was the turning point in both his career and her depression.

But the phone didn't answer. She was shopping, probably. That reminded him to run up the street to Magnin's, where he bought a very expensive peach-cashmere cardigan with pearls sewn all over it. No more niggling for him.

He went to his car. His time had run out and there was a ticket, but who cared on a day like this?

But he couldn't neglect Nelly Finch, even on a day like this, so he drove far up the mountain to Spanish Monastery, her house.

Nellie insisted that he invite Sonya up for lunch and a swim, but again he phoned and again she didn't answer.

He was dying to go home, to tell Sonya his great news and give her the present, but Nelly, now under the influence of her after-breakfast martinis, wheedled him into staying for lunch. Besides, Sonya wasn't home.

By two-thirty, Nelly was stewed and sleepy, and he left in relief, driving fast.

The front door was locked. As he stepped into the hall he began to feel uneasy. Very uneasy.

"Sonya?" he called with pseudo-cheeriness. "Anybody home, sweetheart?"

91

He went into the living room. Then the kitchen. Everything was just as it had been that morning; the breakfast remains were still on the table, the refrigerator still empty and de-iced, with gaping door.

He ran in panic to the bedroom. Beds not made, either.

On the dressing table, where Madame Pompadour's jewel box normally sat, was a note:

> *Tape—*
> *Am rushing to New York on something*
> *important, urgent, and personal.*
> *Please don't worry about me, and*
> *I'll be in touch with you later.*
> *Sorry,*
> *Sonya*

CHAPTER 9

~~~~~~~~~~
~~~~~~~~~~
~~~~~~~~~~

She could not bear the bellboy's fussiness, so she turned her back on him and looked out the window.

Why did I come *here,* where once we . . . ? Us. Here. Not once, but twice. But our first night was here, and that must be why I came here.

She saw the Park Lane hotel across the street, and at a window on her same eye level stood a man. He wore a bow tie. He stared, smiled.

She turned away, withered by his glance, shivered by his smile, and saw that the bellboy was gone.

She was opening her valise. She was lifting the jewel box from its protecting bed of cashmere and silk and nylon and wool.

Not Madame Pompadour's. His. His jewel box, the only real thing left of him available to me, to my touch. The sound of him exists in stacks of records and miles of tapes, but . . .

I must inform Pobrecito of my whereabouts. Not my why and wherefores, just my whereabouts. He'll be frantic, poor thing . . . but if I do tell him where I am, nothing will keep him from flying back here and . . .

Even thinking *Tape* betrays Werner.

Dead.

Firmly she seized Thought and forced it to turn back to the jewel box in her hands.

Now I know why I came here. Because this is where he gave me the jewel box.

Not the first time, but the second, the last. He was still living in the Towers here and had not yet moved to Central Park West.

Dead.

Stop it, Thought. Stay *here*.

What had he said about the box?

All else was clear, a perfect image: his two hands offering the gift, the light brown hair musicianly fluffed, the eyes with their blond eyebrows, all—but it was a soundless image. *What had he said?*

"My madness, my Sonya."

Yes, of course, *that*. Now I envy Tape's memory machine; I *see* everything, I hear nothing.

Thinking Tape betrays Werner.

"My nicest aunt."

Viennese English must be the world's best; especially his voice, a flawless bell cast in a baritone key. But what had he said about the box, this box? Which is the greater curse, remembering too much or forgetting too much?

Now, holding his precious gift in her hands, memory presented her a more precious one, the music of his voice:

"It belonged to my nicest aunt in Vienna, and she swore it had been made for Madame Pompadour. In that case, dear auntie, you must keep it, I said. It is much too rare. But she said . . ."

The man in the Park Lane was still peering at her, expectantly, so she closed the draperies, putting down the jewel box to do so.

She returned to the box and picked it up again, struggling to recapture *all* the details of the giving-of, the taking-of the one thing left of him for her alone and was rewarded with the image of Werner, smiling with affection for his beloved aunt as he said:

94

"But she said, if it were not so rare, dear nephew, I should never think of giving it to you. So take it, on one condition, that when your time comes to give it away, she must be beautiful, you understand. Not merely beautiful, dear boy, but beautiful in a way that becomes Madame Pompadour's jewel box."

He said his aunt said.

"And so I more than fulfill my promise to my dear dead aunt, Sonya my beauty, my love, my joy and my madness. Here, take it."

She was putting the jewel box on the writing desk.

Here, writing desk, take it.

Of all the things I did not inherit from my mother.

Your exquisite casket.

I love you.

You loved me.

Past-perfectly.

And now? Do what?

Have I come here to attend your funeral, my darling? Shall I join your wife and child in a trio of grief over your broken bits and pieces as the sad birds sing?

She flung herself on the bed which became the great white sofa by the flickering flames, the Bechstein a soft black shadow in the corner of her grief, and the hands that had held the jewel box were playing, only for her, "Oiseaux Triste."

Dead.

"Now listen carefully, Benny," Tape said into the telephone. "I'll repeat it, to make sure you understand."

"I understood, Swede," Benny said.

"Listen. First make a list of every first-class hotel in Manhattan and start calling. Ask for Mrs. Andrew or Sonya Alberg, and then Sonya Osinoff. Got it?"

"Sure thing, Swede," Benny said. "When would she have checked in, timewise?"

"Probably yesterday afternoon. No, later. Evening. And call me right back."

"You know I will, Swede."

"I'll wait right here by the phone till I get your call. And Benny, you understand, this is . . ."

"I know, Swede. I won't even tell Gloria. Depend on me."

"If I didn't, I wouldn't be asking this favor. I'll hang up now, Benny, so you can get dialing. And . . . seems I forgot something important, but I just can't re—"

"I've got all the dope, Swede, believe me, I have."

"It was . . . oh, yes. It was thanks I forgot to say. Benny, I sure do appreci—"

"Shut up and hang up, you square-headed bastard."

He reread Sonya's note: I'll be in touch with you later Sorry Sonya.

But later could mean a month later. If Benny fails, I'll fly back there.

Especially physically.

I'll need money.

Tape looked at his watch. Eleven-twenty. Togo's clippers hummed, then buzzed and stopped with an angry burr.

Better get to the bank.

He went to the desk and looked at his checkbook.

Our checkbook. Joint Account. Bank of America, Main Santa Teresa Branch, ANDREW ALBERG

SONYA OSINOFF ALBERG

The joint account was her gentle idea on account of her steady inheritance and my unsteady income.

$1847.54.

Plenty for . . . unless she . . . she must have taken a big chunk of it, for a New York trip.

Why not? Actually, it's her money. I owe the account . . . he looked at a separate paper in his top drawer . . . $345.00.

But would this be using her money to . . . track her down?

"Andrew, bring Mother's bag here. You must never touch anybody else's money, even in play, son."

Honest mothers run the best policy.

No, I won't cash a check. I'll borrow money on the house. But we just theoretically own this house, the lawyer said. Our equity is only thirteen dollars a month, and we've only been paying on it seventeen months. The rest is interest and carrying charges.

The Jag is clean.

But her money bought it.

Dully his mind contemplated his insurance, but his first wife had confiscated all the policies. And a mortgage on the farm his Grandpa Alberg had left him needed his first wife's signature, and . . .

Has Sonya really left me? For good? But she promised not to. Why? The Great Love, or Laney, or . . . what?

Why was not the point. He considered there was only one point left:

Go back to New York and find her as fast as possible.

The telephone rang. Tape grabbed it, hoping Sonya, expecting Benny, but getting . . .

"Hello. Mrs. Howard here. Is Mrs. Alberg in?"

The Mayor's wife.

"Oh, hello, Mrs. Howard. I'm Mister Alberg. Sorry, but Sonya had to make a rush trip back to New York. A family matter."

"Oh dear. Pity. Howie and I wanted to invite you two out for the weekend. When will she . . . ?"

Would she really abandon me?

"You know how these things are, Mrs. Howard. She'll just have to stay a week or two. You know relatives."

Abandon also this old cherrywood table? That Tang horse? All these priceless things her mother left her? Leaving me alone and empty, wandering among her bric-a-brac?

The Mayor's wife was issuing rainchecks. He thanked her and hung up.

Mixing her with Them did it. It was not Laney, it was the idea; that luncheon made the family a Presence to her. An unbearable Presence. Like New York in the beginning. Until Laney came here California had been far, far away from them, . . . and in Italy, before there was any idea of Them, she was entirely different. We were completely a couple. But over here she found strings attached to me, and . . . when the strings reached California she couldn't stand it so she . . . escaped.

97

"I thought we had a chance to be that way. In Europe."

In another country, on another continent, had made a lot of diff— How had she put it, night before last? "Before They existed . . . in Italy . . . I thought we had a chance to be that rare event."

Suddenly Tape was hit with a wild idea, a wild solution, that seemed solider than anything he had yet thought of.

Take her back to Italy. Far far away from . . . mixing. Where there would never be any Forcing or suspicion of Forcing because there would be nothing to Force. Over there.

Stay until she recovers from her . . . but the Mayor. Screw the Mayor. And Nelly. And Katie. Forget business, forget time, forget cost, forget everything and take her back to Italy.

Tape strode from room to room, so carried away by the simple greatness of his great idea that he deserted his post by the telephone.

Not Italy, some more remote place. Give her a month or two in some really remote place and . . .

He thought of remote places.

Spain? Not remote enough. Greece? Too touristy. Yugoslavia?

Yugoslavia gave him pause. It was foreign. Strange. Almost out of Europe. And even communism was good therapy in this case. There would be no associations with anything.

He became obsessed with Yugoslavia, the panacea. He phoned a travel agency and jotted down the costs they gave him. He went to the desk and built a traveler's budget for two.

Including air tickets, three thousand'll be enough to do it right for at least six weeks. And it's gotta be right this time. No penny-pinching. No Wichita. If she admires a swimsuit, or anything else, in a window, sneak back later and buy it for her. We'll fly to Trieste, rent a car there, cross the border and crisscross the country. She loves strange sights and sounds.

But the money? Where?

To quiet his nerves, he turned on the hi-fi and scanned the shelves of tapes.

"If you had one more hour to live and could listen to any piece you wanted, what would it be?"

98

He chose the Thirteenth Quartet of Beethoven.

He sat down by the telephone, resuming his vigil, hearing Beethoven over there, and other sounds far and near, a passing plane, Togo's clippers, a bird that sounded like a typewriter, and the noonday sun flowing into Beethoven and putting a bright mustard glint on the arched snakelike neck of the Tang horse—and far farther farthest away sounds, the *Medea* at Verona, Saint Anne two rows below him in the stadium, the buzzing clippers, the sun, the moonlit stadium, Callas, all one sound, one sight, one time, Beethoven flowing over and above and through all.

But when the Adagio came he burst into tears and ran to switch off the complex of beautiful machines that man hath wrought.

The empty house pressed heavily inward on him. He went into the bedroom and made her bed. Ex-bed. He picked up *The Oxford Book of English Verse* and put it back on the living-room shelf.

The phone rang and it was Benny.

"Of all the goddamn places, she's at the Waldorf," Benny said happily, for no runaway would go to such an obvious place, or register under her married name. "Mrs. Sonya Alberg."

And so on.

Next, Tape dialed Long Distance, intending to call the Waldorf, but suddenly changed his mind and phoned Nelly Finch.

"Could you see me right away on something urgent and personal?" he pleaded.

Nelly could.

He put Murine in his eyes, washed under his arms, and in a clean shirt drove up to Rattlesnake Canyon.

CHAPTER 10

She was calling International Concert Artists, Ltd.

"Could you please give me some information about the funeral of Werner Grunwald."

"One moment, Madame."

The next voice, grave and baritone, must have been on tape: "Funeral services for Mr. Werner Grunwald will be held at two-thirty P.M. on Tuesday, April twenty-first, at Carnegie Hall. Repeat, Carnegie Hall. Invited mourners are kindly requested to present their invitation cards to the ushers; others who wish to attend are kindly requested to go to the balcony. Interment services will be held at six P.M. in the Powhatan Falls cemetery, Putnam County. Thank you for your inquiry."

Sonya hung up, outraged, for Werner, had he had his say, would never have permitted such a public entertainment to be made over his . . . fragments.

Whose idea? The wife's, probably.

And do I presume to resent a wife I've never even seen?

Yes, I presume.

And I will not go to such a spectacle.

So now what? If I am really a wife, I must inform my by-now obviously maddened husband of my wherea—

100

Am I really a wife?
No. Not really. Nor have ever been one, really.
Dead.
I love you, Werner.
No-body no-wife, no-thing needs a bath.
She went to the bathroom and turned on the tap.

Tape drove into Nelly's cactus-lined driveway and parked by
the first of many connected small buildings, all of them in
Mission Style. This one looked like a chapel but was actually the
library, seldom if ever entered, at least by Nelly.

When the news first got out that Nelly was giving Spanish
Monastery (the estate's name) to a School for Girls, everyone
put the astonished question to her:

"And why on earth change this fabulous place for a new
one?"

And Nelly always answered, "Because I want to, do you
mind?"

Reminding Tape of another anecdote favorable to his mission:

At Cat Cay, another one of Nelly's places, she kept a hundred-
foot schooner with a fifteen-foot draft, which prevented her from
sailing to Nassau the direct way, across the Bahama flats;
instead she had to sail north to Hen and Chickens and around to
Tongue in the Ocean, over twice the distance and more than a
day longer, which often raised the question:

"Wouldn't it be more convenient to have a smaller yacht,
Nelly?"

"It's impossible. I'm too rich."

Tape rang the doorbell.

Now how could a woman like that refuse my piddling request?
Maybe four, or even five, would be more to her style, than three.

And Jack Hoover had once said, Tape, ringing again, remembered:

"Nelly's husband latched on to somebody's basic patents and
retired to irritate his liver with alcohol until death severed his
soul from Nelly's, who is doing her best to join him, wherever

he may be. She's close on sixty and looking for ways to spend money that don't interfere with her drinkin'."

And besides, Nelly liked Sonya and, strangely enough, Sonya liked Nelly, saying, "I enjoy vulgarity when it's *that* eccentric."

The purple bougainvillaea by the doorway was sick. Probably rootknot. Nematoditis.

Tape saw cunning bloodshot eyes in the spyhole, and Mack the Butler opened the door.

"They get drunk together in the wee hours. Nobody knows who puts whom to bed. He's got some hold on her. Robs her blind. She couldn't care less."

I'll ask for five. Definitely.

"Oh, hello, Mister Alberg," Mack the Butler said. "She's out by the children's wading pool, sir, and she instructed me to ask you to stop by the bar for a drink on the way to join her. What will it be this time, sir?"

"Nothing, Mack, thanks."

He walked down the Hearstian hall, armor-cluttered and larger than his entire house; then into the loggia which enclosed on three sides the monastery garden. At the open end he spied Nelly, a floppy pink straw hat over her blonde straw hair.

Wearing a turquoise beach robe with the skirt tucked into the waistband of her salmon sunsuit, she was wading in the knee-deep pool.

"Don't drink this water unless you're constipated," she warned. "It's full of Epsom salts. Supposed to be good for my swollen feet."

"Why don't you just soak them in a tub, like ordinary people?"

"Because I'm not ordinary people, thank God."

Nelly waddled out and flopped on a chair protected by an umbrella. She poured herself a martini from a large crystal pitcher on which was engraved a frosty warning:

PERSONAL PROPERTY OF NELLY FINCH

HANDS OFF

The pitcher was half-empty, indicating that Nelly was half-full, and Tape considered that a good omen, too.

"Sit down, darling, and tell your old pal what's eating on you."

And they were, in a sense, old pals, sharing the foulest stories and all that. At parties Tape pretended to be her drinking companion, although he usually just added water to the same old tired Scotch.

A pal in need is a pal indeed.

Nelly exposed her varicose veins to the sun's healing light.

Finally he said, "It's sort of—well—personal, Nelly."

He sat and looked down on Pobrecito, the Skyway, and beyond the blue water slightly grayed over with mist. Far out, a yacht race.

Epsom salt in the children's wading pool. Don't believe it.

"Oh, stop being coy, you gangling squarehead. If you can't tell your old pal Nelly, it must be at least syphilis. Or have you suddenly gone queer on us?"

"Could I sort of skip the detail bit and just let you have the net-net?" he pleaded.

Christ and Calvin, I'm talking like an Army officer. Crisp, man, crisp.

"You can do it any way you like, so long as it don't interfere with my drinking," she said, tilting the pitcher.

The water on her feet had dried and he could *see* the Epsom salt glistening between her puffy toes. Imagine, a swimming pool full of . . .

As fast as he could, he said, "I need three thousand dollars. I'd appreciate a loan. Payable in three months."

Nelly shook down her bracelets and scratched at the bruised flab beneath.

"Or as an advance on commissions," he added miserably. "Whichever you prefer."

If I'd known it was going to be *this* tough I'd have gone to some other . . .

Pal.

"Why, darling," Nelly said, seeming not in the least surprised, disturbed, or even impressed. "You need something worse than money. You need somebody to examine your head, boy. Don't you know, haven't you learned, that nobody as rich as

103

I am ever lends *anybody* personal money? It's a sort of—not sort of, it *is*—an Unbreakable Law, Buster."

That Buster was just too much and Tape said, "My name happens to be Tape. I'm sorry I asked."

"You should be more than sorry; you should be ashamed of yourself. It certainly wasn't considerate of you, spoiling our funtimes together this way."

As she drank, he could see her eyes brimming with tears. What next?

My God, *she* was crying. Who was doing what to whom?

"That's the way it goes," she sobbed. "Everybody disappoints me. I thought I had found a friend, a real pal, at last, but . . . it's no use. I haven't had a real friend since Buddy died. My poor old Buddy. A real pal."

Tape found himself standing, looking at his watch.

"I've really got to hurry or the bank'll be closed. So, if you'll excuse me, Nell . . . Mrs. Finch, I . . ."

"You see," Nelly blubbered. "The damage is starting already. The rot. Mrs. Finch. Now I'm *Mrs. Finch*. Goodbye, Nelly, it was nice knowing you. Oh, why do people do these things to me? It's not fair. Shit."

"The bank," he said. "Goodbye, uh, Nelly . . ."

"Oh, Buddy," she wailed. "Why did you have to die and leave me friendless and alone, at the mercy of every . . .?"

And he escaped, almost at the cost of his life, for as he made the turn out of Nelly's gate, the Jag very nearly skidded into Rattlesnake Canyon.

The humiliation. The shame. But who in hell was Buddy? Old Man Finch had been named Georgie-Porgie, at least in Nelly's book. Besides, Georgie-Porgie had died over three years ago, not last year, so . . .

Then it hit him. Buddy was her dachshund.

A miserable old dog who had died at the overripe age of fifteen. Smelly, snappy, an eater of cashmere jackets, a foul farter in company, even black-tie company.

Good riddance. Served her right.

The blubbering old bitch, turning herself into a martini-soaked martyr, when *I'm* the one who . . .

Shut up. I just asked to borrow three thousand dollars and it cost me a six-thousand-dollar commission. What an idiot I was, taking all those Old Pals seriously.

Shut up. Money's the problem. Money *now*. Sonya's at stake. Sonya's *the* stake.

But who'll loan me that kind of . . . ?

As if answering his question, the Jaguar passed the Pobrecito Palace Hotel, and there, in front of it, was Katie-from-Chicago's parked maroon Rolls, complete with Katie's chauffeur.

Excited, he slowed down, looking for a parking place, finding one, then getting stung by a horrible thought:

Katie is rich too. Unbreakable Law. Can't lose two clients in one day.

Darling. My ass.

The Jag U-turned and started away, headed for . . . ? By coincidence, Katie came out of the hotel. She waved, shouted, beckoned. He pretended he didn't see her.

Cutie-pie. My ass.

Unbreakable law.

But who? Where?

Jack Hoover.

No harm in trying.

The Jag turned downtown, but suddenly Tape became nauseated almost to the vomit-point. He opened both windows and sucked in fresh air.

Why?

My stomach is screaming Swede go home. I just cannot take another turndown right now.

The Jaguar headed for home. What once was home. Until day before yesterday.

Three thousand. The most important three thousand I'll ever . . .

He parked the car by the kitchen door and was fumbling for the house key.

105

"Hey, Mistle Albell."

Togo was sitting in the shade of the privet hedge, opening his lunchbox.

Tape walked across the lawn and squatted beside him.

"Listen, Togo," he said. "Listen . . ."

CHAPTER 11

〰〰〰〰〰〰〰〰〰

No need for a coat on a day like this. And besides I don't have a black coat.

No jewels, just the watch my mother . . .

The Eternal Peeper in the Park Lane window looked like another man, but he was only wearing a four-in-hand necktie.

Out with it: the watch my mother gave me when I left for Europe. Her final gift.

Ten past two, time to go.

She walked up Park Avenue to Fifty-seventh Street and crosstown to Carnegie Hall, a figure in a dream among dream-crowds.

What am I doing here?

She joined the queues in black and went inside.

A grave old usher was saying: "Present your invitations for the orchestra, please. Those without invitations, upstairs to the balcony, please."

On the way upstairs, a woman said to her, "Are you a friend or just a fan like me?" and another woman said, "What a tragedy. Such a talent. And only thirty-seven." The first woman, happy to find someone to talk to, said, "I never missed one of his concerts and I'm . . ."

Not going to miss his funeral.

Sonya escaped and found a seat in the quietly filling, dimly lighted hall. A good seat, first row on the aisle.

The stage curtains were closed. In the orchestra below were about three hundred invited guests.

A woman squeezed past her to take the next seat. She peered below, excitedly identifying celebrities. She leaned far over, saying, "Here comes the widow. And the child. I don't believe in taking such young children to funerals, do you? It marks them."

Sonya saw the veiled widow and beautiful child, a girl of three. Front seats, the choicest, Double A.

His child knows she is a star, but I do not think she knows what drama she stars in.

"Doesn't she remind you of Jackie?" the woman, deeply moved, whispered. "That same nobility."

And what am I doing here?

The curtains parted, and . . .

There he is, in that box. His charred bits and pieces. Or so they claim. Who knows for sure? Those crashes. Whose head, whose body, whose hands?

She wanted to run back to the Waldorf and get the jewel box and take it to the stage and put it in the casket just to be sure there was *something* of him in it.

Then, of course, she didn't want to do any such macabre thing.

There was a Bechstein concert grand behind the bier, draped in black; she supposed it was the one from Central Park West, his favorite.

The minister prayed an Episcopalian prayer.

The widow must be Episcopalian, for Werner and I shared, among so many other things, Couldn't-care-lessism.

Prolixly, the prayer dwelt on the world's loss, God's will and unknowable ways, all that.

We shall meet in the Hereafter—all four of us. The suicide will climb up from Hell, or at least Limbo; the present wife will fly in from Heaven's château country; and I, I shall come skulking out of the black, twisting alleys. His harem of angels.

108

"She's his second," the woman next to her whispered. "His first committed suicide."

The world's most famous composer read the eulogy; it was very like the one in *The New York Times*.

We had planned to live in London, not New York, and if we had been living in London, then he would not have had to catch that particular plane, and . . .

All this is therefore my fault, as the self-killer killed only *my* will-to-marry, not *his*. He begged, implored, phoned, followed— and I escaped, avoided, desisted, refused, ran . . .

Not from him, never from him, but from the monster who killed herself to pay him back for me. The monster and me. We're the collaborators. We co-produced this show.

"Werner Grunwald," the eulogist was saying, "although only an adopted child of America, loved his new country so passionately that he became one of the truly great interpreters of its music. So it is fitting and proper that on this tragic day those of us who mourn him should close his farewell concert, so to speak, with one of his most celebrated recordings."

Oh, no! Not again! I cannot bear it.

Sonya went rigid and pressed back into the seat, waiting in anguish, as several days ago she had cowered against the book-shelves in her living room.

The music commenced, and the woman next to her, thrilled, turned to Sonya and stage-whispered, "It's the Concord Sonata. By Charles Ives." And proudly, "We've got the record at home."

Sonya bore the first three movments with stony fortitude. But the fourth, the Thoreau, always her beloved, broke her.

She heard herself moan, and fought against a repetition, but she was unable to stop the tears, as the piano (Werner!) dreamed through the Indian Summer day at Walden, with the philosopher-poet sitting in front of his cabin on the pond's tranquil edge, listening to the attractions of the restless world outside, but sternly keeping aloof.

"Most people live lives of quiet desperation." Himself included. Myself, too.

Sunset, twilight, and creeping darkness over Walden. The poet raises his flute, for this sad, strange, lyric day must have its swan song.

The pond faintly echoes the dusky, woody notes.

And what had Ives himself written about this passage? Oh, yes, "A train passes . . . But Thoreau much prefers to hear the flute over Walden."

The flute, like the day, ended with a sigh; and the piano (Werner!) thoughtful and hesitant, whispered to the end that was not an ending, to a death that *was* a dying.

The audience did not know whether to applaud or not. A few nonconformists tried to clap the entertainer into his grave, arousing outraged sobs and indignant shushes.

It was like the big tragic moment in a play; all over the hall, members of the audience were wiping noses, dabbing eyes, cleaning glasses.

The widow, leading the child, climbed the steps to the stage and slowly approached the closed coffin. She paused, looking down at the cover. Her lips moved.

Was it really he in there?

Then the first four rows of mourners arose on a signal and moved—from Sonya's viewpoint above—in a human oval around the coffin and back down the steps.

Then the casket was lifted down and placed on a wheeled bier in the center aisle, and four men (were they stagehands?) pushed it up toward the exit, the pallbearers and invited mourners shuffling after.

As the Center Attraction of this performance passed beneath Sonya, she wished grief-strickenly that she had thought to bring a sprig of azalea; she wanted to drop it on his passing remains.

Here, coffin that slowly passes, I give you my sprig of azalea . . . please, please, *please* don't be Whitmanesque.

Lights up. The show was over. As Sonya reached the street, the hearse was just leaving, followed by a truck on which was mounted a newsreel camera.

Next stop Powhatan Falls. Last stop, for the old connecting line to heaven went out of business years ago.

Jostled by dream-figures, she walked down Fifty-seventh Street.

In the Waldorf lobby there was a well-bred squeal, "Sonya! Precious!" It was her stepmother stepping out of Peacock Alley. Her ex-stepmother, since her father's death.

"But aren't you in California, precious?"

"I'm just here momentarily."

"Oh, you must come see me. Same old place. Dinner tomorrow, precious?"

"I'm leaving tomorrow. Early."

"Tonight, then."

Lying, she escaped.

Must get out of here. New York is impossible when you don't want to see anybody you know. Impossible here. But where? Never mind where. Just check out of this hotel, get out of this city.

She went upstairs to pack.

On Tuesday morning, foggy and early, Togo brought the three thousand dollars as promised. In cash—tens, twenties, and fifties —which Tape grandly refused to count.

He had the promissory note signed and his luggage was already in the Jaguar.

"You're a real pal, Togo," he said. "Now, don't worry, in three months you'll have this all back."

"I don't worry, Mistle Albell. Why should I? Your wife is rich."

"But you're loaning this dough to me, not my wife. She's got nothing to do with it. And I definitely am not rich, you lazy bastard."

Togo's plump, boyish sixty-year-old face expressed understanding of a poor husband's pride, but his eyes gleamed with confidence in a rich wife's ability to pay.

Tape locked the door and got into the car.

"Thanks again," he said. "I won't forget this, Togo. And if anybody asks you when I'll be back, say in six weeks or so. Okay?"

111

"Okay. Keep nose clean, Mistle Albell. And don't worry about your blush cherries. I give 'em swift kick in the ass and make 'em grow."

The Debtor backed away from the Creditor and nosed out the gate. The Creditor shouted, "If you know somebody needs five hundred Natal plums, I got 'em. Maybe Miss Finch . . ."

Tape waved a cooperative hand, and on that understanding the transaction was completed.

He drove to Los Angeles too fast, ninety most of the way, until stopped by a highway patrolman, with whom he pleaded, "My wife is critically ill in New York and I'm rushing for the plane. Give a guy a break, officer."

He got the break and a warning.

In Santa Monica he parked the car in dead storage and took a taxi to the airport.

He had plenty of time, over an hour, and he spent most of it buying the complicated tickets: one round-trip LA to NY, two round-trip NY to Trieste, and one one-way, NY to LA.

While paying, he had thrifty second thoughts.

Am I crazy, spending all this borrowed money on a trip I don't even know she'll take with me? Maybe I should have phoned the Waldorf first. Maybe she won't even see me. Maybe she's checked out already and gone who-knows-where. Am I crazy?

And he answered the Swede within:

No. Definitely no. It's one thing to phone the Waldorf, another to show up in person. It's one thing to *suggest* a trip to Yugoslavia, another to spread out the tickets in front of her. No more Wichitas for me.

He checked again to make sure he had both their passports, still valid for one more year, thank God; and he scrawled a hasty note to Laney at the Brentwood address, apologizing for having to leave on a New York business trip, ending with:

> *Sonya sends all love to her newest*
> *favorite girl. Best to Bark,*
> *Your loving Dad*

112

He was at the newsstand buying a *Hi-Fidelity Review* when his plane was announced. He crossed the concrete field, the smell of jet fuel worse than smog, the sonic boom an outrage to his ears. He boarded his plane and strapped himself into his seat.

In times of crisis, I can't think. I hear and smell and see *more,* I feel *less,* and think *nothing.* Should I have phoned the Waldorf? Can't find any reasons for or against. At least I'm moving toward her. In space and time. It's twelve my time; but it's three her time. What time is *our* time? Or does time exist for *us?* We have had a Past, but we do not at least this moment have a Present. And we may not have a Future. True of anybody. All philosophers screw up Time by including the future, which is not real time, just potential time.

The stewardess brought luncheon.

This buzzing-semianesthetized Present which jets me East is like, is like . . . the Western flight I made, twelve years ago, to the bedside of my dying mother.

But the image of the old sick woman turned into that of a pretty, young one, seated at the Knabe upright; and he became a tow-haired boy of nine, bellied on the stained red-brown-yellow Axminster rug with his crayons, sketching green pines on a snowy slope thrusting into a purple sky; and listening to "Anitra's Dance" from the *Peer Gynt Suite.*

The carpet smelled musty, the piano was too beautiful, his love for the mother-artist and mother of the artist too ecstatic, the authority of the soft bright crayons too awesome——

So he could not eat the prefabricated luncheon on his lap.

"Take it away, please," he begged the stewardess.

"Coffee?"

"Nothing, thank you."

"So to make a long story short, sweetheart, I got this thing about Yugoslavia, and I hoped you might like to spend a month or so there and so—big spender that I am—I just flared up and bought us some tickets. Here they are. How about it, sweetheart?"

The Past happened, the Present is happening, but the Future may or may not happen.

"Play it again, Mom, please."

113

The tow-headed boy added an orange half-moon to the purple sky, the old-dust smell of Axminister heavy in his nostrils.

And Grieg dripped down like rain all over him.

At Kennedy Airport, Tape, a new man with money, splurged on a taxicab, urged haste on the driver, and then sat back to study his tickets, passports, and travel folders to avoid thinking about the next move.

But by the time the cab crossed into Manhattan, he had become an emergency case, to whom every second seemed a matter of life and death.

He ran into the Waldorf, instructed the porter to check his bag for an hour, and hastened to the house phones.

Room 915, Benny had said.

"Yes, please?" the operator said.

Haste became waste. Trembling and sweating, he hung up without answering. Suppose she . . . ? Suppose there was another . . . ?

Disgusted by his disgusting, unthinkable thought, he backed away from the frightening phone.

Anyway it's more discreet, more genteel, if I call from someplace outside the hotel, so . . .

"Swede Alberg, you old bastard."

"Oh, hi, George," he said shaking hands. George who? Oh yes, George the Account Executive on the Vexol account, whatever his last name was.

"Still landscaping out in California, Swede?"

"Sure am, George."

George pulled a younger man into the picture. George wore glasses and looked like Barry Goldwater; the younger man was bald and looked like a youthful Ike. George said,

"Eddie Lamb, Swede Alberg. Swede's the only guy I ever knew had the guts to quit this mouse-hassle and go back to nature. You lucky bastard. How's existence?"

"Pleasure," Tape said, shaking Eddie's hand. "Great, George. I can't complain."

114

"Wish I had your guts," Eddie said, and George repeated, "You lucky bastard. How about a . . . ?"

They were by a bank of elevators, and one of them opened, giving Tape his chance to escape.

"I'm late as hell," he said. "Sorry. Nice seeing you again."

"You lucky . . ."

The door closed.

"Floor, please?" the operator said.

"Nine," said the lucky bastard.

It took a lot of courage to knock on 915, discreetly; and to announce, loudly:

"Sonya? It's me. Tape."

Will it upset her that I didn't phone first? Will she think I suspect she may be in there with . . . ?

He felt his coat pocket, checking passports and tickets.

The door opened.

Sonya had on her coat and hat and gloves; her suitcase was packed and standing by the door.

"Oh," she said. "I should have . . . informed you."

"I was going to call from the lobby," he lied, "but all the house phones were busy so I just . . ."

"Come in. I was just leaving."

Does one kiss one's wife who has just run away from home for reasons or reason unknown?

Tape squeezed her around the shoulders and let it go at that.

"Leaving?" he said. "Then this is my lucky day. If that plane had been ten minutes later I'd have missed you."

"I should have phoned you, Tape. Forgive me."

"Skip it, sweetheart. So long as you're okay, it's . . . you *are* okay, aren't you?"

"Yes. Yes. Of course."

"You look a little pale. You're losing your gorgeous tan already."

"I was just making a last-second check, to see if I'd forgotten anything."

She retreated to the dresser and began opening drawers. He

115

came farther into the room but remained standing, a gentlemanly caller.

"Black is very becoming to you," he said. "In Pobrecito, you never wear it, and I'd forgotten you in black. You're real citified, all of a sudden."

"Uh, please sit down," she said, closing the bottom drawer.

He sat in the easy chair by the window.

She sat in the straight chair by the desk.

"On a clear day you can see the Park Lane," he said.

She looked out the window. The man in the bow tie was not there.

"Did you inform the desk you were checking out?"

"No."

"Good. We can order some Waldorf Room Service Hamburgers. The world's greatest. I'm starving. Missed my lunch in all the rush."

"Oh. You must eat."

He phoned for room service.

"Nothing for me, please."

"Then join me in a drink."

"All right."

"Hello. Two Scotches with soda, and one hamburger, medium rare," he ordered. "Room 915."

Now that they had something to wait for, they waited. Tape found himself staring at the blank face of television. Our household barometer.

Who said that?

Struggling, he found the answer: Nobody *said* it. I thought it, the other night when all this started. And it was *before* Laney's call, so don't blame her.

Room Service came and went. Tape served the drinks.

"Cheers."

He started in on his huge hamburger, saying, "The winner and still champion. Here, take half."

"No, please. I'm not hungry."

"Sure?"

"Please. No."

116

So he ate alone, wishing he'd ordered Coke instead of whisky.

He finished and went to the bathroom to wash his hands. Then he came out and stood at the window looking down on Park Avenue.

He craned and tried to catch a glimpse of the old building where he used to work, 247 Park, but could not.

You lucky bastard.

She said, "Of course we must talk about this, sooner or later."

How dead her voice was, how cold her hands looked. He had the feeling her skin would be icy if he touched it, which he had no intention of doing. She was too far away, too involved in something that had drained her spirit, destroyed her purpose.

Had he ever been part of her purpose? Now he doubted it.

He said, "I've been thinking things over, sweetheart, and I decided I talk too damn much for my own good as far as you are concerned, at least."

"Oh, Tape."

"So the fewer words I spout, the better off I am . . ." In the fading afternoon light, her face was toward him in three-quarter profile, the eyes, lids half-shuttered, were not looking at him, but at something down on the floor, giving her an oblique, enigmatic beauty that intensified his suffering.

Oh, if I could ever know the glory of being yours; why won't you let me belong to you? I found the flawless creature and tried to make it mine, tried even harder to make myself hers, always pretending success, always knowing I had failed, but always hoping, even in the bitter center of failure, even in the bitterest center of it, now.

"But, look, sweetheart, I came back here to, well, try to win you back, I guess. To make things like they once were in Italy, when we were bouncing happy as two pups in that rented Fiat. Anyway, this morning in Los Angeles I bought us some plane tickets. To Yugoslavia. I thought maybe a month or so of that would . . ."

He removed the evidence from his inside pocket and dropped it on the desk in front of her.

"They're dated for tomorrow, if you agree. To Trieste, where

117

I plan to rent another rented Fiat and sort of explore Titoland. There's a music festival at Dubrovnik. And Split, that's on the Dalmatian coast, too. And . . ."

Where did he find the money for all this, poor thing? Trying to make up for St. Louis. Wichita. As if that had any bearing on . . .

Dead.

"Another thing I'm excluding from my life," he said, "is Forcing. This decision is entirely up to you and what you want, sweetheart. Look, my bag's down in the lobby. What say I leave now, and get myself a room, and give you the night to think it over? In solitude, so to speak. Then, if you want to go, just call me, or I can phone you tomorrow morning. The plane leaves at three P.M. and . . . This one's your passport, by the way. It's still okay for another year."

She put her hand on the tickets, which lay on the exact spot where Madame Pompadour's jewel box had so recently been, and slowly said:

"Yes. I would like time to think it over. The trip, I mean. But you're . . . I mean, taking another room sounds . . . why don't you go down and arrange to come up here?"

Tears sprang into his eyes.

"That's awfully . . . if you've no . . . in that case . . ." he was moving toward the door, opening it, leaving.

"I'll be right back," he said.

Running-water sounds, river-of-car sounds. Where am I?

Sleepy vague flowing water-car sounds; babbling brooks of falling water and Mississippis of flowing honking autos.

Park Avenue. The Waldorf. And he's in the bathroom taking a shower.

Sonya awakened fully.

And today he will use all his Force to make me go to Yugoslavia with him.

No!

Why not?

To go any place with the living betrays the dead.

118

I must be alone.

Yugoslavia is unnecessary torture to both of us.

I must not yield.

The sound of the running water in the shower had long since stopped, and now Tape emerged from the bathroom completely dressed, even to his necktie.

Our modesty is pathetic. Poor thing.

But I *will* be alone.

No yielding.

"Morning, sweetheart. Sleep well?"

"I didn't even hear you get up."

"It's nine-fifteen. Let's order breakfast. Eggs? Cereal? Juice?"

"Just coffee."

"Sonya!"

"And a Danish roll, then."

While he was at the phone, she took her clothes and went to the bathroom and stayed there until breakfast was announced.

When she came out, also fully dressed, Tape was conspicuously studying the tickets. He conspicuously put them down by the breakfast tray and poured her some coffee.

The Park Avenue traffic sounds were at the flood.

Eating, even a Danish roll, seemed some kind of heresy that outraged mourning. Why?

Perhaps because it is an expression of life that the dead bits and pieces cannot share.

Silly, in that case I wouldn't take Doridene or smoke, either. Or sweat, or . . . suffer.

"Oh, that reminds me," he said, running to his bag.

She unwrapped with dismay the I. Magnin gift box, with its cashmere sweater which she did not know how *not* to accept.

"Lovely," she said. "But far too expensive. Thank you."

Mind's pencil jotted down the rough draft of a speech:

"Tape, I'm sorry, but I have to be alone. At least for now if not forever. Please don't ask me why. You must believe me when I tell you that my being alone is as necessary as . . ."

"I wonder if we ought to take any shots?" he asked. "My

119

smallpox is still valid, but I think I'm out of date on all the . . ."

"Oh," she said. "About Yugoslavia. I don't know, Tape, I'm so . . ."

Rejection turned his hopeful blue eyes into smoky gray clouds of misery; his lips twitched as if she had slapped him; and she discarded—postponed, rather—her speech for a kinder, vaguer one:

"In the first place, I couldn't possibly leave today. I really must go to Southampton. That trust-fund thing. And I don't know whether it's wise to go to Europe right now. But forgetting that for the moment, for today at least, *you* must run up to Connecticut to see your son. You can't just come all the way back here and not see him."

"I suppose I *had* better run up there today, while you're out on Long Island, hadn't I? That means I'll have to change the date on the tickets. To some other date. And I'd better do it now."

She moved away from the phone to let him get to it.

"What date shall I tell them to change it to, sweetheart?"

"Why not just leave them open?" she said. "And decide what to do when we meet here this evening."

It's better to tell him tonight. Now, it'd just spoil his day with his son, and . . . tonight, I'll just say that I'm totally unfit for any human society, that I must be alone, that I am a no-thing, no-person, no-wife.

Waiting for the airlines call, he said, "Anything you say, sweetheart. Tonight will be the night."

They left the Waldorf together and got into a cab.

"Take me around to the Forty-second-Street entrance of Grand Central," Tape ordered the driver, "and then continue with this lady to Penn Station."

This lady.

Who happens to be my wife.

In name only.

Especially physically.

120

CHAPTER 12

For nine years, twice a day, this was my habit. My morning duty to depart, my evening's pleasure to return.

Tape stood on the old, familiar, exceedingly strange station platform and faced the freshened guilts, the ever-renewing worries, the continuing fears and unburyable shames which were the price he had had to pay for Sonya.

He walked through the underpass and into the telephone booth, and put in a dime, *E pluribus unum.*

But he had forgotten his own telephone number. Ex-telephone number.

He swiveled the book and started looking under the *A*s for Alberg, but before he could find it, his finger suddenly remembered the number and started dialing.

Proving Finger is Mind. Or sumpin'.

"Hello."

"Betty? It's me. Tape. Uh, Andy."

"Oh. Hello again. Where are you?"

"Here. The Oldtown station. I had to come to New York on business, and . . . how's everything?"

"Like always. Except the cost of living. In case you haven't heard, it keeps going up."

Same old Betty. Everything she says embarrasses me. Or is it same new Betty?

His thought was even more embarrassing than her remark, and he said miserably, "I wanted to spend a few hours with Stan, maybe have lunch with him. That is, if you have no objections."

"Why should I?"

"He still at Beech Grove?"

"Who knows? At least that's where he started out for a couple of hours ago."

First worried, he then took it as meant, a Stan-type joke; the family name for Stan had always been, probably still was, Our Master's Voice.

"In that case," he said. And she said, "Look, why don't you drop by the house on your way over? There's something that should be discussed with you. If you don't mind. You can call the school from here and arrange the luncheon date with Stan."

"Love to, Betty. I'll be right over."

"Are you alone?"

"Sure."

"I'll pick you up."

"Oh, no thanks. I'll grab a taxi."

The taxi driver said, "Revere Lane, that's in New Oldtown, ain't it? Don't I know you?"

"I doubt it. I haven't been around here for, oh, almost five years."

"Your face is familiar. But all you durn commuters look alike to me anyhow."

The shrubs and trees were much larger but the house itself hadn't changed much. The filbert was starting the new season in great shape, the flowering quince would soon be in bloom, likewise the red crabapple. But the forsythia bushes were sick, and the mountain ash twins he'd cornered the lot with, dead.

Two young corpses.

The lawn needed fertilizer.

Any guy naïve enough to start looking for nature analogies is sure to find 'em.

122

And the house still looked like thirty thousand dollars. It was split-level, despite all the jokes a nice design when there are children.

If I can keep up the payments, it'll be all hers in seven more years.

His 1959 Rambler station wagon was still in the garage, but the old Buick convertible had been superseded by a red Ford Mustang.

The door opened before he rang the bell, and there he was, facing his ex-wife *and* the dilemma of how to greet her: kiss or handshake?

Betty solved his problem by saying, "Hurry, Stan's on the phone. I had him called out of class, so . . ."

Tape ran inside to the telephone, and with tears in his eyes cried happily, "Stan!"

"Who's talkin'?"

"Stan. It's Dad."

"Yeah. I know."

"It's wonderful hearing your voice again. It's much deeper now, by the way. Look, Stan, let's have lunch together?"

Betty said, "Tell him you'll meet him at the school cafeteria. The food's not *that* bad, despite what the kids say."

"At the school cafeteria," Tape said obediently.

"Lunch? Why?"

Christ and Calvin, he was maddening.

"Because it's my one and only chance to see you, Stan. When is lunchtime there?"

"Twelve-thirty, like always."

"Maybe I can get Mister What's-his-name, the Principal . . ."

"Now it's Bevin, a new one," Betty said.

"Mr. Bevin to give you the afternoon off."

"I got track," Stan said.

"Oh. We'll settle everything at lunch, then. I'll be waiting in the cafeteria for you at twelve-thirty, Son."

"Okay. Gotta go now."

"I know. Class. Goodbye, Stan."

Tape hung up, frustrated. Laney used to say "That's Stan's profession, frustrating people."

The hall was the same, except that the Duncan Phyfe table he'd got for a bargain in a New Haven junk shop had been replaced by an ugly blond one.

"It's only eleven-thirty," Betty said. "How about some coffee?"

"Love some."

"Come into the kitchen."

"Oh," he said, following, "new stove, huh? Fancy."

"The other one just disintegrated. Like . . ."

Like certain other things. I'm talking to a stranger. More, a total abstraction. Her letters are more real than she is.

And yet . . . there'd been little physical change. Pretty as ever. Damned attractive, in fact. Bright and sharp, cool blue eyes not missing a trick. Hair a little blonder, chin up a little higher, neck thinner, cordier, body a little stringier.

"You're looking great," he said.

Then, she'd been . . . thirty-five. So . . . forty next month. Still young enough, plenty pretty enough. Was there really a serious boy-friend?

He looked out the kitchen door. "Suburbia creeps closer and closer," he said. "Where's Pete?"

"Dead."

"Oh. Getting old, I guess."

"He was twelve. We had to put him to sleep. Hemorrhoids. Your coffee's ready."

He sat in the breakfast nook.

Nook like in nooky. I used to call her Nooky-girl. This abstraction. *My* Nooky-girl, with never a thought that it would ever change.

Sonya was right (he admitted for the first time to himself) when she said my marriage was fine, my wife fine, and everything else about my family, especially the kids, the greatest. And I have always been wrong to deny it with all that passion. Methinks.

So, what is the truth? It's time I faced it.

124

My main argument, that my solo flight to Europe proved how tired my marriage was, is not really true. Face it, I wanted to make the music-festival rounds, and Betty gets bored by that kind of thing. No, I left for Europe convinced I had a damn fine marriage, a lifetime set-up, never questioning anything about it, anything *big* at least, until . . .

"Still no sugar?" Betty said.

"That's right. No sugar."

Until Verona. Where I chanced to meet a masterpiece, a Mozart Piano Concerto, Number Twenty. As compared to a Gershwin rhapsody.

Bad analogy. Rather, the "Apassionata" compared to "Sweet Sue." Or Da Vinci is better. Saint Anne on those rocks compared to a . . . *Vogue* cover.

But that was too raspy, for Betty when he had met her had been a student at the Conover modeling school, and he did not wish to be unkind to her obvious good points.

"Great coffee," he said.

So . . . the only really honest explanation I can give myself is simply: I yielded to the superlative. Even if the superlative did not yield, or at least at present is not yielding, to me. Looking for excuses, I found 'em, but that came later. At that moment of decision, though not of truth, the masterpiece dimmed out the plenty okay nice gay pretty dutiful wife. And, as though she were helping me find excuses, this abstraction sitting across from me with her coffee and her Pall Mall and her smell of Apple Blossom put dozens of bitter ones into my eager hands. But Sonya is right, my life before meeting her was perfectly okay, at least plenty okay.

"Laney wrote me you met Bark," Betty said.

"Yeah. Sure did. Nice boy. Stable *and* bright. Mad for Laney, too. Did you give them your blessing?"

I walk on hummingbirds' eggs again; once she told me I had lost the right to advise her children and I guess I have.

Two young corpses. Flawed lives. Especially physically.

"Laney's got more sense than both of us put together," Betty said.

"Laney's a champion," he said, flooding with sickness from the blows, from the really cruel and wanton blows he had given this woman's pride and dignity, and her security, and her Present, and, yes, her Future.

The coffee tasted like quinine.

He lit a cigarette.

He wanted to do something to lessen the hurt, to restore her lost pride and dissolve her new bitterness, but still he knew that he would never do the one thing that could work those miracles; he knew that if crazy happenstance should put him back here, in this selfsame breakfast nook, he'd do again what he had already done once, for who can trade, retrade, throw away forever the "Appassionata" for "Sweet Sue," although in itself a plenty okay tune?

Betty, who had left the kitchen, returned with a folder.

"I think it's about time we discussed Stan's college problems," she said, sitting in the breakfast nook across from him.

"Does he know what he wants to make out of himself?"

Probably Ph.D. Doctor of Phrustration.

"That's for him to decide," she said. "I was referring to the financial side. Judging from that last income tax report you sent me, his college is going to take more money than you're making now."

"I keep building. Remember, it's a new business."

"Anyway, I got to thinking about that property in Nebraska."

"Grandpa Alberg's farm?"

"Yes. I find we can borrow eight thousand on it—a first mortgage—and if I invest that for Stan, it should at least take care of the first years, just in case your affairs don't . . . improve."

"But he's still got one more year after this one in high school," Tape said. "Why don't we wait and see how next year works out businesswise? Besides, the interest on a mortgage loan will eat up whatever income you make on the investment, won't it?"

"There is such a thing as a mother's peace of mind. I had this fixed up to send out to you, but since you're here . . ."

She handed him a document, prepared by the same lawyer who had four years ago charged Tape seven hundred dollars for writing five one-page letters dealing with the possibilities of sharing certain personal effects which never, in the end, got shared.

"It needs your co-signature, of course," she said.

"I sort of forgot that arrangement on Grandpa's farm," Tape said. "What exactly was it?"

"The deed was assigned by you to to the trust fund as guarantee of alimony. But it still remains common property, like the . . ."

Like the insurance and everything else. It's a trick. The one solid thing I thought I still owned, and now she . . .

"I never liked the idea of borrowing money," he said. "Why don't we let things ride, at least until Stan's ready for college? Then, if necessary, I'll . . ."

But all the while he was listening to himself saying this, Laney's voice was coming through on his private sound-track. They were in Malibu, standing at the rail, looking at the seals. Sonya was discreetly in the ladies' room, and Bark was discreetly tinkering with his Corvette. "Oh, Mom enjoys life, Dad. She's got this new boy friend. You know. And somehow I think it's serious this time. He's new to Oldtown. Wall Street, I think. And it's obvious he's crazy about Mom. You know. I mean . . ."

Betty said, very bluntly, "Do you really expect to double your income out there in one year? If you'll pardon me, that sounds a little dreamy. I'm only trying to be practical. When you made the decision to toss over a twenty-two-thousand-a-year job for a risky—very risky, if you'll pardon me—venture in California, it was—well—your decision. But it hardly took the children's college into consideration, to say nothing of . . ."

Excited now, but craftily concealing it, Tape said, "Do you happen to have that settlement paper handy? I'd like to refresh my mind, if it's no bother."

"It's in the desk. I'll get it."

Ex-Nooky-girl left the room; Tape juggled happily with hopes and possibilities.

"Here," she said. "This is the clause on the farm. Number three."

He scanned the long legal-length page. Number four: Andrew Alberg to maintain all present insurance, with Elizabeth Alberg as beneficiary; and if payments are not kept up, then the cash value of the policies will be taken and placed in abovementioned trust fund. Nope.

Number six: Andrew Alberg will guarantee full college costs for both children at any college of their choice, said amount to consist of tuition, room and board plus one hundred dollars monthly for each, plus four round trips by air between school and home each year.

Nope. He turned the page. Ah.

Number eleven: If Elizabeth Alberg should remarry, then the trust fund will be dissolved and she shall share half the then-remaining amount with Andrew Alberg.

The then-remaining.

BUT—mind's grammarian capitalized the tricky little conjunction—whatever she can turn into cash *before* she remarries shall remain hers with no ifs, ands, or *BUTs*.

And I'd be stuck with a farm mortgage to pay on my then-remaining half.

It sounded bad, *BUT* . . . Grandpa Alberg's preacher-voice came on, saying gravely:

"No bad without some good, my boy."

Axiom: Cashing-in the trust fund is an incentive to remarry.

Corollary: The worse my business gets, the more she'll feel like marrying.

If I were still earning that twenty-two-five, she'd never marry; it'd mean giving up seven thousand a year tax-free, plus all the extras. But my present income scares her. A new marriage would be a safer investment.

No bad without some good. Even losing Nelly Finch had its advantages.

"To tell you the truth," he said, "business this year is running under last. Mainly because a few days ago I lost my biggest client."

128

"That's why I'm trying to protect Stan."

Madame, you may have your dowry with my blessing. Eight thousand should more than take care of the trousseau.

"I see your point," he said, and signed the paper.

"My gosh," he said, "it's time to meet Stan."

They walked through the living room. The Maize Goddess was still on the mantelpiece, but the Dufy over the sofa had been replaced by a mystic Op maze, whether painted by a pro or Betty herself, he could not tell.

The missing Dufy gave him even more hope. And the Duncan Phyfe table—liquidation seemed to be setting in. Dowry, I love you.

A mess of 45-rpm records was on the Garrard; there was no sign of his old magnificent collection.

Okay, Madame. Go to, Madame. Good luck, Madame. Let whoever will that wishes wander amongst my bric-a-brac, fish with my flyrods, and watch birds through my binoculars. My blessing on thee, Madame.

Betty said, "And please tell Stan to come home right after his track practice."

It was only five past twelve, so he walked to the Beech Grove Day and Boarding School for Boys.

In my financial condition, Stan should be going to the public high school, but tuition is in the settlement and that's that.

Even so, he felt he had never done a better day's business in his whole life. Betty's marriage would erase years of double-struggle; on the psychological side, Sonya would breathe freely.

He was in a street of large well-gardened homes. Spring was hemming and hawing, backing and filling, trying to decide: To be or not to be.

God tempers the wind to the shorn husband.

He passed a magnificent stand of Persian lilacs, sepia-budded; soon they'd be blooming like pink snowdrifts. The lawns around were new-sprouted and pale jade-green. The air was chill, the sun warm. There was, oh yes, the old Gunniman place. Bridge fiends. Bores. Next, the drunken Fitzhughs. He wondered if poor Billy was still having his troubles with the delivery boys and his wife's ways with them.

It was astonishing to know a town so well and still be such an utter stranger in it.

At this very moment, Sonya must be walking through her old home town. I wonder if it feels *this* strange to her? I didn't really like her looks. So drained, no vitality.

Could sickness be her reason? Bad sickness that she preferred I didn't know about? Maybe that's why she's so cold on Yugoslavia.

Like what her mother died of. Some say it's inherited; others, psycho—

Cancer.

Oh, shut up. Of all the idiotic . . .

He passed through the school gates and admired the campus, magnificently adorned with beeches and maples, with here and there an open lawn, and the one old building sedately mimicking the Ivy League, while the other newer ones looked like motels.

Twelve twenty-five. He walked up the gravel road and found the cafeteria. A bell rang and youths poured out of all the buildings, making incredible noises.

He found a table by the cafeteria door and waited. About two hundred boys stormed the place, but Stan was not among them. God, the noise. An atonal chorus ranging from shrieking soprano to rumbling bass in full bay. Teachers are martyrs.

And the conversation: "I've decided to take up medicine."

"So this guy calls on the lady, see, and he sits in her living room, and right before her eyes unzips and starts beating it."

"Yeah. Our doctor, who's really *stupid,* makes a hundred thousand a year."

"Dreamer. By the time you're out, Medicare'll be all over the place."

"Gahhhh. How gross! Don't you know anything but jack-off jokes?"

"Lay off, man, let him finish."

"Finally, the guy lets fly, and all this time this very elegant lady is speechless, and then he fixes himself and speaks for the first time, real polite: 'Madame, do you mind if I smoke?' ''

"Man, he sure grossed me out on that one. Yahhh."

"Have an oyster."

"Kackkkk. You're the grossest."

"Hey, Frankenstein applied to twelve colleges, all tenth-raters, and they all turned him down."

"It's the Army for him. Poing! Keroooow!"

At ten minutes to one, Tape got worried and went to the Principal's office next door, but it was locked. He returned to the cafeteria and asked random kids if they'd seen Stanley Alberg.

"Stan? No sir. Didja try the gym? Sometimes he does karate during the lunch hour."

He tried the gym. Then back to the cafeteria. The waitresses were shooing the kids out.

A bell rang. He went back to the Principal's office. An old man was there.

"Could you please tell me what classroom Stanley Alberg would be in now?"

A study hall. Room ten. Main building.

Tape went there. A huge room, filled, but no Stan.

He went to the teacher, a young man with soft flesh and a permanent frown.

"I'm trying to locate Stanley Alberg. I'm his father."

The teacher checked his list. "I'm afraid he's cutting study hall today, Mr. Alberg."

The teacher walked to the door with him and opened it. He stood eyeing his charges. Tape said, "Any idea where I might find him?"

"Since he's not here, no. You should have phoned first. Too bad."

I did phone, Tape thought but did not say.

A scuffle started in the back of the room. The teacher said "Sorry" and started menacingly toward it.

Tape left the building and wandered about the walled grounds. When he realized there was only one entrance, the main gate, he went to it and sat in the warm sunshine on a very cold stone bench.

No passing youth escaped his eye.

Two-thirty. Boys in track suits began to prance out of the gym.

He decided to wait until school was completely out, then phone Betty.

Could she have . . . ? Bitter waters run deep. No. He knew her better than that. Besides, she had never been able to exercise any more control over Stan than any of the rest of them.

He wondered if he hadn't been too hasty, signing that paper.

Three motorbikes roared by, out on the road going past the gate, and he turned. He heard them stop. The cyclists were parking them alongside the outer wall, but still he couldn't see them.

Three boys came through the gate and the tallest one was Stan.

Tape rose. "Stan."

"Oh. Hi," Stan said, and to the other boys, "tell coach I'll be there in a minute."

The boys left. Tape said, "Stan! We made a luncheon date. I waited in that damn cafeteria until . . . you shouldn't do things like that, Bunny boy."

"Don't call me Bunny," Stan said.

Our Master's Voice. He doesn't have pimples, thank . . . and his hair is getting dark, like mine did at his . . .

"You're a big man, Stan. How tall? Six-one?"

"Yeah."

"That Honda out there. Yours?"

"Yeah. I gotta get into my track suit."

He started to go past Tape, but his father grasped his arm, the first touch, as they hadn't even shaken hands.

"Can't you skip track today, son? Like you skipped study hall?"

"Skip track? We got a meet Saturday. Are you kiddin'?"

"I can't say your manners have changed much, but you're a

fine-looking kid and I for one am sure as hell glad to see you, Bun . . . boy. You look great."

"I'm late. Gotta go."

"Okay." Tape released him. "I'll wait here until you're through practice and then we can spend an hour or two together, huh?"

"Can't make it. After track, I gotta date."

"But . . . I'm leaving New York tomorrow. This is my one and only chance to spend some time with you."

"I can't help it if I already got a date."

"Stan! Don't be that way. We've a lot of things to talk about. Your college plans. And maybe we can wangle you a trip out to the Coast to see us this summer sometime, and . . ."

"You tryin' to get me in trouble with the coach?"

Again Tape took his arm and prevented him from leaving.

"Why are you this way, Stan? Why?"

The boy looked his father in the eye, his own eyes smoky blue with hate and said, "Because I don't like you."

He jerked out of Tape's grasp and walked away.

Out of control now, Tape said, "Where do you get off, boy, biting the hand that's feeding you? How do you expect me to pay for this, pay for your college later, when you . . . ?"

The boy stopped and turned slowly, all Power and poison.

"You're not feeding me. Mom is feeding me. Get it? And you're not educating me. The law is. Get it? So stop bothering me. Get lost."

He turned, and, now loping, a tall handsome blond long-legged boy loping, disappeared into the gymnasium.

Tape walked back to the station and got there just in time to catch the four-ten to New York.

CHAPTER 13

I love you, she said or maybe just thought; and then, as
if to leave no doubt that she meant to say it aloud, she
spoke up firmly:

"I love you, Werner."

Love among the funeral wreaths, pyramids, and circles and
sprays of them, dozens of hugest size, still fresh but not so fresh
as the dirt on the fresh grave they adorned.

Yellow, moist, spade-marked clay, drying fast; flowers dying
fast.

The peonies were first to give up the ghost; the roses had one
more day, the calla lilies several.

And here I stand among death's flowers, staring at the ugly
yellow spade-marked clay which only yesterday was a neat
mound on one side of a neat hole, the neat mound no doubt
covered by an undertaker's carpet of bright green artificial
grass.

And I stand here with no proper thoughts, no suitable feelings,
to fit this moment.

I stand in apathy. Lethargy. Deathargy. And yet I came for
some purpose, but what? Just to say I love you? Ah yes,
that—but more. I came to say . . .

134

The smell of calla lilies sickens me.

This is only the third grave I have after-visited. The first was my father's, out of love and duty; the second, my mother's, with love and guilt; and now I have just learned that the death of a parent is as nothing to the death of a . . .

Mate.

Now that I have lost my mate, I know that when a parent dies there is at the heart of grief the sure sense of going on with life, but without the mate, go where?

And for what? And why?

I must be alone. Out of life. There is no other solution.

But why did I come here? I wanted to say, to say . . .

Out of the corner of her grief's eye she saw a massive black sedan stop at the cemetery gate. A solemn chauffeur got out and opened the rear door; a veiled woman in black emerged, bearing flowers.

She was chic and there were no other beflowered graves in the small country graveyard and she was carrying an enormous branch of azalea in fullest flower.

Therefore I must go. I trespass on another's property.

But must I retreat without saying what I came to say? It was more than I love you. Ah yes, and you loved me and I came here to say that I am sorry I was not strong enough to carry her dead body on my conscience and I am also sorry that I ran away from you because because because . . .

And then she whispered, "Goodbye, Werner. Forgive me, mate. *Adieu.*"

The woman was coming toward the grave, so Sonya walked the other way, among the old, tipsy stones which bore the vital statistics of the Powhatan Falls dead, idling to read one here and there. Love among the epitaphs.

JEBEDIAH BURR
Born 1790   Died 1827

Werner's age, poor thing. In other centuries they died young, too.

But not from airplane crashes.

As she reached her waiting taxi, a Volkswagen slid in behind
the black Lincoln Continental with the chauffeur. Two men got
out with cameras and, checking their instruments, moved solemnly yet in a businesslike way toward the widow, now standing
with bowed head at the graveside.

There but for the grace of guilt stand I.

Sonya felt a spasm of sympathy, a stab of authentic pain, for
the woman. Poor mateless creature. Even after she recovered to
the point of wanting another man, who could follow Werner?
And if she did re-marry would not the memory of Werner's fine-
ness turn to dross the . . . other? Poor thing? Poor, poor thing!

But sympathy turned into the suspicion that the woman had
made a date with those cameras, a rendezvous with News.

Even at his grave, I am an ugly person with ugly thoughts.

The woman was fussing with her huge azalea branch, trying to
get it to stand on the grave. It was blood-orange, his favorite of
all the azalea colors.

"It is April, sweet Sonya, so let us drive south. And how far
south? Why, about a hundred miles on the other side of spring.
Until we reach, that is, the azaleas. Ah, the azaleas—I love them
even more than I loathe the tulips of Holland."

From Norfolk on, all the way to Charleston, azaleas were the
Appearance and the Reality.

Mind's album turned to a great pine forest full of them, each
bush six feet high and eight feet in diameter, solid with blooms,
not one green leaf or bare twig visible.

Flipping images like pages, mind gasped at each onrushing
garden, the next one always more beautiful than the last.

And the public gardens—shattering, dazzling in sixteen
shades of optical intoxication.

Now, sitting in the taxi at the graveyard gate, she remembered
how she'd closed her eyes and hidden her face from him so that
he could not see how the azaleas had begun to make her nerves
scream, crying Too much, too much.

But he too had finally said in despair, "I must stop looking, or
I will be sick."

Turning the car toward Charleston and the soft sensuous . . .
Bed.

GRAVE!

They had passed a cemetery, she now remembered, where each grave had its great blooming bush; and he had stopped, pointing and saying solemnly:

"When my time comes to leave you, dear Sonya, do me a favor and bury me here."

She said to the taxi driver, "The railroad station, please."

"That's the widow," the taxi driver said. "His second wife." He lowered his voice. "His first committed suicide. Don't she look just like Jackie, standin' over that grave?"

When the mate dies, there is no sense of going on, for where is there to go? And with whom? And for what?

She caught a glimpse of her inflamed eyes in the rear-view mirror and put on her dark glasses.

At Poughkeepsie she changed trains; once aboard and seated, the coming ordeal, the necessity of saying what she must say to Tape, began to fill her with dread.

And as her train neared Grand Central Station, she became obsessed with wild ideas of escaping, of leaving this train and boarding the first one headed in the opposite direction, and thus avoid all the horrors of a face-to-face argument by sending a telegram to the Waldorf, and . . .

The train stopped and she rose, trembling, her mind almost made up to go through with her wild idea; but the train was not yet in the station, it was waiting in the tunnel for its clearance signal.

She sat again and stared out the window, across a pair of tracks at the opposite wall of the tunnel, composing the telegram:

THINK IT BEST TO INFORM YOU THIS WAY THAT I MUST . . .

On the other track, a train moved between her and the dirty wall. Rolling slowly into the station ahead of her train, car after

137

car passed her; and there, neatly framed in a slowly passing window, was her husband, looking out of his window.

Their astonished eyes met, his flicked away in terror and *gentillesse* as if not capable of believing he had seen what he had just seen; and then, he was gone.

Southampton, she said. On business about the trust fund, she said.

Penn Station, I told the driver, and she didn't disagree.

And here she is on a New York Central train, pulling into Grand Central.

So she didn't go to Long Island after all; instead, she went to upstate New York, or some other place north.

But why didn't she say so?

Did she see me? Couldn't tell, with those dark glasses. Maybe, maybe not. Who knows?

She knows.

She must have told that cab driver to bring her back to Grand Central, probably as soon as I was safely away.

Stop saying *safely*.

But what legitimate reason could she have for doing a thing like that?

Stop saying *legitimate*.

Although the reason-why as yet escaped him, Tape turned into a fugitive. He leapt from the train before it stopped moving and sprinted up the long dim platform, into the station, headed for Vanderbilt Avenue. Suddenly he remembered the exit (made after his time) through the Pan-Am building, so up that escalator he ran.

If she didn't see me—I couldn't tell on account of those dark glasses—then I don't want her to know I saw her.

He crossed Forty-sixth Street and went into the New York Central building, necessarily slowing down to a walk in its baroque splendor, as he had to buck the current of businessmen headed toward Grand Central, Westchester, Connecticut, and the first martini.

Their hats impressed him.

138

I first hit New York in the Age of the Sincere Necktie, and left it just at the close of the Gray Flannel Suit Period—now, it's the Epoch of the Narrow-Brimmed Hat.

Was I once one of these foreigners?

Yes, getting to the Waldorf before her is . . . better. *If* she didn't see me in that train. *If*.

Why? I don't know the reason, but . . . Reason-why, the First Commandment of Advertising—and here I am, in the exact center of Reason-why Country, but still I don't know the reason why.

He plunged into the whirling door and there he was, on Park Avenue.

Shock! There was a huge hole in it: 247 had disappeared. *His* building, where he'd worked for a dozen years, was gone without a trace.

The hole it left was merely temporary, of course; the sign on the wooden fence around it said:

245 PARK
47 stories will be erected here
Available for renting in 1967

All are gone, the old familiar façades. But it was not funny; the hole in the avenue had left him with a feeling of loss, the sense that there was nothing to go back to anywhere. And changing the number from 247 to 245 somehow made it *final*.

He paused, looking around at all the strange new buildings. Park Avenue had become a monument to the glazier's art; and the great glittering People-Cases reflected so much light that the eye was forced in self-defense to rest itself on the pleasant gray of the Waldorf, the black brick-red of the Park Lane, the lemon-tan of St. Bartholomew's, all three of them now relics of the Past as surely as Chartres or the Parthenon.

And now he knew the reason-why; like most reasons-why it was rooted in self-interest.

If we get into a hassle over Grand Central, she'll say No to Yugoslavia; and I want her to say Yes.

The sidewalk under his feet trembled, Park Avenue rumbled, a man snarled at a woman: "Take it easy, won'cha?" The afternoon sun threw golden shafts across the valleys, blue-tinged with gasoline fumes, and the furious woman cried, "Who you telling to take what easy?" but the dominating image was the image of Sonya sitting on the bed with her champagne glass, and the overriding sound on the mind's track was her voice saying:

"I was old enough to know it can be that way . . . A way you'll never know."

Of course, there could be some simple explanation, some change of plans, some friend she'd visited up north somewhere . . .

Friend.

Who is he? And where does he live? Not on Long Island, that is the only thing I know for sure.

You know nothing for sure, you stupid Swede, except that she is . . .

"My soul," he said aloud, like a sob breaking, or an unconscious groan. "She is my soul."

He was waiting for the light to change at Forty-eighth Street, and of course the crowd with him in that sunlit gorge heard him, but such cries of anguish are a common-enough sound in that city and no one so much as bothered to glance up into the face of the extremely tall thin man hurrying uptown.

And the body does not lure back its soul by accusing her of betrayal.

I saw her in Prades, in Bayreuth, in Salzburg, and she was the only one for me, the only one for any man, and I spoke to her in Verona and the mystery of why she even answered me was . . . is . . . the mystery of why she chose me in all my ordinariness is a . . . was a . . . will always be a . . . and now I must admit I never felt her love. Her sometime bespoke passion, yes, but not her love. No, never. I just wanted to feel it, and spent these years hungering, scrabbling, begging for it, trying to force it out of her and into me; but always she retreated, held me at bay, always, and I never understood why until that night—My God, it was last Friday, and this is only Wednesday, and . . .

She refused to tell me *when* she'd had this rare love. I called it

140

first love, but she didn't; she said *only* love. And it could still be around, live and kicking, ready for another try.

Oh, the goddamned sentimental world is running over with goddamned sentimental books and movies and mushy tales of first and only loves, but what about us poor bastards who come after? What about us? The real romantics. And so I join that endless queue of fairly okay guys who stand around with egg on our faces as we hopelessly try to erase our women's old undying memories of only loves.

But she took the train *today*. It is not a memory, old or young. *She took that train today.*

Tape went into the Waldorf lobby, dim and cool and gorgeous as an Early Renaissance baptistery, and bought a *World-Telegram.*

Positioning himself safely behind the bronze clock tower, he watched the desk until she came for her key.

She was still wearing those black glasses.

She moved toward the elevators, noticing nothing.

Like a dislocated person, a refugee from the Present Tense—who said that?

He raised his paper and glanced at his watch, planning to give her fifteen minutes to get settled before he went to their room.

Nobody said it. I thought it, that afternoon in Salzburg. On the Festival Hall steps.

Dislocated Person.

She hasn't changed.

These dark glasses, those dirty train windows, that gloomy tunnel . . . perhaps he didn't see me. Oh, he saw someone, but did he recognize me?

If he did, then what? Explain with some airy nothing, a casual change of plans involving the New York Central and not the Long Island Railroad?

Any explanation would be just another lie, no better or worse than the one I told last night and put into action this morning when I pretended to go to Penn Station.

Serving no purpose that is good for him or me.

141

The truth? For a change?

Worse. Besides, I will not advertise my grief. It is not for sale, trade, or barter. Neither is it mentionable.

So if he saw me, recognized me, I have hurt him worse than I intended, for I *will* be alone.

She showered the day's grime from her body and was dressing when he came into the room.

"Oh," he said, "back so soon?"

"How is your son?"

"Oh, he's okay. Big, tall, healthy, even handsome. And full of beans. How was . . ." He stopped, feeling he would lose Yugoslavia, his last chance, if he forced her to lie, and besides, he did not want to hear *anything*, true or false. . . . "Hey, sweetheart, I just saw in the paper that Richter is playing at Carnegie Hall tonight. Maybe we can still get tickets. If you're not too . . ."

"Oh, dear, I really am much too tired."

Of all places to choose. Poor thing. Carnegie Hall. And that sudden stop after *How was* . . . proves, or almost proves, that he did see me.

"You do look a little beat at that," he said. "Maybe we ought to put you on some vitamins or iron or something."

He opened his bag for a clean shirt, and to get at it, removed his flyrod and reel and box of flies.

It struck her as odd, his bringing them to New York, and she said, "Fishing?"

"Well, according to the folders, there are trout in Yugoslavia."

"Oh." She hadn't thought of that, but once mentioned, it was now or never.

"Tape," she said, "I'm sorry I'm the way I am, but about Yugoslavia . . ."

Swiftly, desperately, he interrupted her.

"Sonya, before you say anything else, tell me, Sonya—and please don't try to spare me. Is there somebody else? Is there, sweetheart?"

So he did see me and of course he thinks I got rid of him for the day by forcing him to go to Connecticut so that I could go to wherever he thinks that train came from to have a rendezvous with my . . .

"No one else," she said gently. "Believe me, Tape. No one."

No one living.

"Forgive me, sweetheart. Of course I believe you. I just . . ."

"You know," he added, "I get sorta discouraged sometimes. But hearing what you just said, I take heart."

But suppose I do recant and advertise my grief by saying: I spent this day at the graveside of my mate and now I am alone and lost in his loss and therefore it is impossible for me to continue as your . . .

Can I do that?

"We all get discouraged sometimes," she said. "Now, about Yugoslavia . . ."

"Yes?" He froze for her answer.

So it comes to this: I must hurt one of us more, and the other of us less.

"Let's go tomorrow," she said.

And so I must hide my grief, my matelessness, put it away like some trinket in the darkest corner of the jewel box my mother never gave me.

"And stop mumbling nonsense about someone else," she commanded, mock-roughly, mock-roguishly. "Who do you think you are, Othello?"

"No, just half a Hamlet," he said, grabbing the telephone to make the reservation.

PART 2

CHAPTER 14

Dear Pal Jack,
How R U, Jack? Well Jack, here's your old pen pal, Old
Nick, on a letter-writing spree again. Old Nick hired hisself
one of them capitalistic little Fiats in Trieste—that's in
Italy this season, in case you ain't up on your history, Jack—
it's got a two-horsepower engine and a ten-hogpower horn,
the Fiat I mean. And guess what, Jack. I latched on to a
gorgeous Russian chick who hired me to gigolo her around
the country. Yugoslavia, that is. It's a beautiful country,
Jack, offering everything a tourist could want except maybe
service. We drove to Belgrade to see the Danube, and to
Sarajevo, where they have built a bridge to honor the
humanitarian who started World War One. Then we headed
for the Dalmatian Coast, where we are now. The Russian
chick is okay, Jack, she complains of asphyxiation but claims
the experience is worth it. Anyway, it sure is a grate coun-
try, Jack. Nervewise, that is. And Old Nick is having himself
a ball. Number Eight, to be exact. But Old Nick's business
is real good, Jack. In Belgrade, I sold blue sunglasses to
tourists to look at the Danube through. Down here, I changed
them to rose-colored ones for looking at the world with. The
natives is friendly as gila pups, Jack. Sure do wish you was

*here. And vice versa. Did you get my three postcards I sent,
Jack? You'd split if you knew where I was scribbling this—
we're sitting in the atrium of the old palace of that Roman
Emperor Diocletian (he was one of the local boys who made
it, Jack) having ourselves a slivovitz (it's a Worker's Café
now, Jack) and waiting for the Folk Music Festival to start
in the outdoor Roman Theater next wall. In the city of
Split, get it? I knew you'd Split. Ha-ha. More later.*

> *Your friendly guide,*
> *Old Nick*

Tape handed the letter to Sonya, and while she was reading it,
he filled up a post card addressed to Bark Scott, Swarthmore
College, Swarthmore, Pa.

Dear Bark,
*Old Nick the misguided guide is Fiating around Yugoslavia
with the Princess of Tashkent. YS is composed of six People's Republics, most with different languages but loosely
tied together by photographs of BB. That is all the space
I have so better let orwell enough alone. Love to L.*

> *Nick the Swede*

Sonya said, "I don't know whether it's such a good idea putting
stuff like this in the mail."

"I'm just testing the censorship," Tape said. "Besides, how
they gonna trace Old Nick to me? Unless you squeal."

"Well, don't drop any more of them into hotel boxes where
we're staying, then."

"Hey, you'd make a good spy. Who said that? Oh, Bark."

He sealed his letter, addressed it to Jack Hoover, Editor,
Santa Teresa *Herald,* Santa Teresa, California, USA; he took
the card and the letter to the box by the Roman theater. When he
returned to the table, Sonya said:

"That word you used, *asphyxiation,* happens to be true."

"You said it last week in Dubrovnik, remember?"

"Did I?"

"It impressed me."

"But why do we get this feeling? Is it something we bring to

148

Communist countries, or does it exist here without us? Independent of us? The feeling of not being able to breathe. The drabness, the grayness, all that is *visible*, of course, but . . ."

"One thing sure, you'll never find out from a Yugoslav. They just won't talk. They won't even *look* at a foreigner."

"With one exception. That nice old man, the desk clerk at our hotel. He's human."

"Still, he won't talk. But at least he *looks* at me when I ask for the key; that statement cannot be made about any other Yugoslav desk clerk."

"He does too talk," Sonya said. "He says Good morning."

"That's business talk. As a matter of fact, he promised to put me in touch with an English-speaking fisherman who hires self and boat by the day. The guy's coming tomorrow. Interested?"

He held breath; Sonya inspected watch.

"The concert begins in twenty minutes; we'd better start trying to pay our bill."

"Yeah, it'll take at least that long to catch the waiter's eye. If this fishing guy turns up, why don't you go fishing with me tomorrow?"

"Let's wait and see *if* he turns up, first."

Their hotel was at Kastela, seven or eight miles from Split. It had once been a Grand Hotel, and it was set in a large tree-filled park on the Adriatic shore. The main building was five stories, with immense public rooms and a princely marble staircase spiraling from top to bottom. There was an annex which once had been used to house the servants of the guests.

Sonya and Tape had been assigned (through no effort of their own; the key had simply been thrust at them by a clerk adding figures) a top-floor room with a large terrace facing the sea.

Now, of course, the elevators weren't functioning, which made the marble staircase a beautiful but athletic event; the furniture was plywood jobwork, the floors uncarpeted, the water cold.

There were no porters to carry luggage, but a sullen maid invaded their room once daily for a five-minute whisk.

Of necessity, they were on full *pension,* as there was no *à la*

149

carte menu in the dining room, which was run Army-style, with meals of an endless sameness.

Even so, it was the nicest place, in the loveliest surroundings, they had encountered since Sveti Stefan; swimming was fine, the sun bright, and the water perfect; the music festival at Split took care of their evenings, and so they stayed on, now, through their fifth day.

At least those were the reasons each gave the other for staying on.

The hotel was always full, of Germans and Austrians mainly, who didn't seem to mind the general do-it-yourself attitude the hotel staff took toward the guests.

Ordinarily both Sonya and Tape would have minded; they were too accustomed to the amenities to enjoy paying for anything less, especially in a rather ordinary country which seemed so devoted to the principle of antipleasure.

But something made them stay on; at times, despite all their complaints, it was almost true that they welcomed the inconveniences.

Perhaps because—Sonya, waking up on the eighth morning, thought—it gives us something to fasten to outside ourselves. Something in common. Last night he said that misery loves company. In his case. In my case, does masochism accompany grief?

At leisure is the soul.

There was a bird on the balcony rail, and Tape was still asleep in the other bed.

Whatever made me think of Emily Dickinson? I cannot drive those lines of hers out of my head.

The bird heard German voices on the next balcony and flew away.

At leisure is the Soul that gets a staggering blow; the width of Life before it spreads, without a thing to do. It begs you give it work, but just the placing pins, or humblest patchwork children do, to help its vacant hands.

It's no use, Emily; I already tried knitting. Fly away, fly

150

away, poem. Three days of you is too much. *At leisure is the soul*—please fly away—*that gets a staggering* . . .

Tape turned in his bed, looked at her, then looked away from her and said,

"Another day, another sardine. I dreamed I was back home listening to Bartok. The Miraculous Mandarin. Sexy, huh? And the Mayor rode his horse right into our living room to present me with the key to the city. Maybe I'm going to get that Skyway job after all. Good morning."

He got out of bed and couldn't find his slippers.

"Christ and Calvin, in another week there'll be more sand on this floor than there is down on the beach."

"Good morning," she said.

He was in the bathroom. She went out on the balcony to get her swimsuit. It was still damp. He came to the doorway.

"If I ever again stay at a hotel where they won't serve breakfast in the rooms, do me a favor and have my head examined. Imagine walking five flights down for mudcafé, and then climbing right back up to get rid of it."

Yes, the misery of our life here matches our inner misery. That and not lethargy is the secret of why we stay on.

Lethargy, deathargy.

They dressed and went down to breakfast.

"We're late as usual," Tape said. "Look at the hate on our waiter's face."

The waiter assumed an official stance and announced, "The serving of breakfast discontinues at nine o'clock."

"Think I'll try the tea this morning," Tape said, for they had discovered that the waiter had no weapon left but grumpiness if they ignored him.

He took their order.

"Fishing again?" Sonya said.

"Old Nick," said Tape, "is gittin' kinda tired of chasin' them sardines all by hisself. You used to like sailing and fishing. Why not join me, for either or both?"

"Oh, I . . .," she said.

"Besides, you just got to meet Petar. His English is unbeliev-

151

able. Almost Shakespearean. How he ever wound up being a fisherman is more than I . . .''

"His story should be interesting," she said. "But of course you'll never get to know it."

"Don't be too sure of that. I'm making headway. Yesterday, for a starter, I pried one shard of information out of him. I was complimenting him on the way he juggles our language, and he said 'My father taught me!' Then I asked him what his father did, and he said, 'He *used* to be Professor of English Literature at Belgrade University.' Yep, old Petar is thawing fast. Maybe if you came along today, your charm would elicit a full confession. How about it?"

"Oh really, Tape. You know me. I just like to do nothing. Lie on the beach, pretending to read, but actually vegetating. Fishing tires me to think of. All that activity."

"Old Nick'll bait your hook."

"It's not that. I . . ."

"Well, if you won't join me, I could join you, and . . ."

Sonya stiffened and said, "And send your man back after you'd hired him for the day? That's not very . . . practical."

Old Nick didn't care to analyze that one, so Tape said, "I know. We'll catch two birds on one hook. Petar and I will sail you out to his island, Drvenik. It's only about three miles out, and it's got a superb little beach, all white pebbles and crystal water. And I've never seen more than three people on it, so it'll get you away from all these Germans. We'll drop you there, go fishing, and on our way back pick you up. How about that?"

Poor thing, back in the Waldorf he vowed never again to use Force on me.

"That does sound attractive," she said, deciding to yield, just this once.

Petar was waiting in the boat basin with his little fishing dinghy rigged with a lateen sail. He was a youthful forty-five, or even fifty, and very romantic, also distinguished, in appearance. No one around had poorer clothes, or wore them with such an air. Tape had already discovered that he lived on Drvenik Island with his wife and three children and made his living as a commercial fisherman at night, with occasional daywork like this of hiring self and craft to tourists.

Tape introduced Petar to Sonya. He bowed gallantly and helped her into the boat. Indeed, he did have an air.

The day was glorious. Back on land, the sun had been burning hot, but out here, a fresh steady breeze kept it in check. The little boat scampered through the waves. Sonya Copper-toned her body, and donned sunglasses to cut down the sea's glitter.

They were enormous glasses with curved lenses, and Tape's hurt expression reminded her that she had been wearing them that day in Grand Central Station.

So when he was engrossed in fixing his fishline, she removed them. Out of sight, though never out of . . .

Tape looked up to say, "Now your skin is darker than your hair. In California, they were . . ."

"The lovely thing about sailing," she said, "is you just fly along thinking about nothing."

"That's even truer of fishing," Tape said. "Right, Petar?"

"If one thinks one doesn't think," he replied, "then thinking so will make it so."

Tape caught Sonya's glance, pleased to have his Shakespearean remark about Petar confirmed so brilliantly, and said, "I don't really come out here to catch sardines; my secret mission is trying to find out what Petar's ambition in life is."

Petar smiled tolerantly at Sonya. "Really, Madame, your husband asks me the most personal questions. Sometimes I am almost tempted to shock him by answering them."

"Oh, oh, I'm stuck here for the summer," groaned Tape. "I bet that's how he keeps his clients. The Tease method."

"Please permit me to be present when you do, Petar," Sonya said.

"I'm only trying to find out his point of view so I can change it for him," Tape said. "A man of Petar's obvious breeding shouldn't fritter away his life catching sardines. You could be a success, man, in anything you wanted to."

"Any suggestions, sir?" asked Petar, still joking.

"Well, with your languages, how about hotel management? Ours, for instance."

"Nobody could be worse than the bureaucrat we've got," Sonya said.

"When the Kastela was the finest hotel along this coast," Petar said, "they had a wonderful manager. But now he's just one of the desk clerks."

"Really? Which one?"

"The old man who told you about me."

"Oh, he's our favorite. A wonderful old guy," Tape said. "Do you mean to tell me he used to be the *manager*?"

"He was the owner."

"Oh."

"There is Drvenik," said Petar.

"Where is your house?"

"On the other side of the island, Madame."

Tape said, "Just wait till you hear Petar sing, Sonya. He specializes in Dalmatian folk songs and English madrigals. You should hear him ask the pretty maid if she'd care to break a little barley. He's got the authentic lilt."

"Please, Petar, now," Sonya begged.

"I have not my guitar. Otherwise I'd be most happy to oblige."

Tape said, "We've been thinking about driving up to the Plitvice lakes, Petar. Are they worth it?"

"They are natural marvels, sir. Sixteen of them, all at different levels, connected with each other by fantastic waterfalls."

"Any trout?"

"Two kinds, sir. Marxist graylings and capitalistic rainbows imported from your California."

"Sounds lovely," Sonya said. "Tape loves to liberate trout of any ideology."

They were sailing into a little cove. Petar dropped his grapnel and let the boat slide to within a few yards of the deserted pebble beach.

"Sweetheart," begged Tape, for the day had been so nice and amiable thus far, "sure you don't want to go with us?"

154

Sweetheart. It's the first time I've called her that in days. Why did I stop? It didn't seem seemly. So why now? Because there's a third person present which seems to make it seemly.

"Fish? With that lonely beach beckoning me?" laughed Sonya.

"Well," he said, convincing himself that trying wasn't exactly forcing, "Maybe we should give Petar the morning off to fix his nets and stuff, and I'll skip the sardine chase, and . . . beach a bit with you."

"Oh, I wouldn't be cruel enough to deprive you of your sport for anything, Tape. Go out and have fun. Pick me up whenever you're through."

Because I must, I must, I must be alone. At least part of the day.

And she took her towel and bag and waded ashore, saying:

"Thanks for the ride, Petar."

"It was a pleasure to be of service, Madame," he said.

The day was made remarkable by Tape's snagging a two-foot eel, his first catch to date measuring more than six inches.

"They're really exquisite eating, too," Petar said, mashing the ugly creature's head.

"Ugh. I wouldn't eat that thing for all the . . . if you want it, take it home to your family."

"I shall be most grateful, sir. When we return to Drvenik, I shall drop it off at my house, with your permission."

"Let's go now, before my poor wife gets charred. This is one hot day. I shoulda brought my sunglasses."

"What means *shoulda,* sir?" "Oh, excuse me—should have."
"Excuse *me,* sir."

Petar tied the boat to a rock and went up to his house with the eel. A poor little house in a poor little village, isolated from the other houses, as Petar must have been isolated from the other villagers.

A girl of twelve or so was in the dooryard. She looked down at Tape, and waggled her fingers at him, in the same foreign way all the Yugoslav children waved at tourist cars.

155

"Hey, Petar," Tape shouted. "Don't forget your guitar."

Petar returned with the guitar.

"That your daughter?"

"Yes sir, my youngest."

"She's very friendly, like all Yugoslav kids. The grown-ups won't even raise their eyes to us, but the kids waggle their fingers like crazy. All of them."

Petar smiled. Tape said, "It's an odd-type salute. I suppose it's centuries old, the traditional greeting."

"No, sir. It's part of the campaign to attract tourists from the West. The schools have Friendship Drills. That's the Official Youth Salute, but it's only required for bona-fide tourists."

Tape, feeling gulled, went ashore and bought wine, salami, bread, and fresh goat cheese; then they sailed around the island and picked up Sonya, still alone, and shades browner from the long morning in the scorching sunshine.

They set a course for the mainland and Tape served luncheon. Petar accepted his share with easy grace. He ate, drank, and chatted as a gentleman should. Tape plied him with wine.

Tape winked at Sonya and said, "My turn at the tiller."

She shoved the guitar toward Petar. "You promised."

Petar smiled and uncased his guitar. He looked around; it was just past one o'clock and all the other boats had gone in for lunch. Drvenik was a mile behind them, the mainland two miles ahead.

"When I am all alone on the water like this," he said, "I often amuse myself with my hobby. Perhaps it will amuse you also."

He was tuning the instrument.

"I make new words, in English, to old Dalmatian, Serbian, and Montenegran folk songs. The melody you shall hear"—he plucked a few chords—"is called 'The Dying Soldier's Message to His Mother.' It is a sad little seventeenth-century tune, and the words of the original are even sadder: A soldier, dying in battle, tells his friends to take a message back to his mother, that he has found a beautiful bride and has married her and is living

156

in a palatial home. The bride, of course, is death, and the home is the earth."

"Oooh," said Tape. "Cheerful, ain't it?"

"I have made funny new words in English, and the new title is . . ."

He plucked three minor chords and went, "Shhhh."

And with none of the apologetic fumbling usual with amateurs, he began his song:

> You ask me my ambition, sir;
> It's just to be a . . . shhhh!
> If I dared breathe ambition's name,
> I'd die of . . . shhhhame.
>
> Oh, the Land belongs to the Workers,
> But the Workers belong to . . . shhh.
> You know his face, it's everyplace.
> His million eyes, his million ears,
> Are greeted by ten million cheers,
> And tears . . . shhh . . . and fears . . . shhh.
>
> Oh, the Land belongs to the Workers,
> But the Workers belong to . . . shhhh.

Petar paused, leaned toward Tape, and his mock-melancholy voice became low and confidential:

> Your face so kind has changed my mind.
> I'll whisper my ambition, sir.
> It's just to be a foreigner,
> A patriotic foreigner,
> Shhhhhhhhhhh.

Sonya, trying her best not to, was crying. Petar cased his guitar and said, "It was meant to be funny, Madame. I'm sorry."

"*I'm* sorry," she said; and Tape added, "So am I, Petar. Sorry as hell. Sure do wish I could grant you *your* wish."

"It was just a joke," Petar repeated, taking the tiller.

And wordlessly they sailed for a few minutes; then Sonya

said, "What sort of work did you do, Petar, before you became a . . . ?"

"It could hardly be called work, Madame."

Tape broke the next silence. "Some fine day, Petar, why don't you just head this little boat of yours toward Italy, and . . . ?"

"My children," murmured Petar, "are very well-adjusted to the present conditions. Remarkably well, sir."

Tape remembered that the little girl waggling the Official Youth Salute hadn't even spoken to her father.

They were at the hotel dock.

"About tomorrow, sir?" Petar asked, pocketing his fee and refusing a tip.

"Well," Tape hedged. "If Mrs. Barkis is willin', I sure am."

He looked hopefully at Sonya, even expectantly, for today had been . . . better.

"Oh. I really don't know. I mean, making advance plans on a holiday is so . . ."

Failure. Again. Rejection. Again.

Petar said, "That other island. Hvar. It has a beautiful Romanesque church. Exactly, I should think, to Madame's taste."

"Really, I . . ." Sonya began. Then she paused and said, "Why not? What time tomorrow?"

It was the big breakthrough Tape had been waiting for, a notable First, but victory had come from the wrong quarter, and he muttered gloomily, "Okay. Anything you say. How's eight, Petar?"

CHAPTER 15

"You'd think that even the Communist Party would put curtains on a Western exposure," Tape griped, and in truth the afternoon sun flooding through the glassed terrace doors of their room was maddening. The breeze had died and he was sweating. The glare of the sea stayed on his eyeballs even when he closed the lids over them.

"I'm burned beneath my tan," he complained.

"We overdid it," Sonya said. "The sun's over Cancer."

"Over Split," he corrected. "And furthermore I don't feel up to eating the so-called dinner here. What say let's go into Split now, have ourselves a decent restaurant meal, and sit in the square until concert time?"

"What's at the Festival tonight?"

"Don't remember." He found the schedule and squinted through it, for it too glared at him, glossily.

"It's that tra-la-la folksy group again, hop-skip-and-jumping all over the place. If Diocletian was still around, betcha he'd never let those cornballs perform in his palace."

"Petar's song today sort of spoiled native music for me, too," she said. "Let's just go in, eat, and window-shop or something."

Tape showered and dressed first; he waited at the desk

looking at her jewel box. Odd, she'd never before lugged that cumbersome old heirloom around with her on their travels.

"Bet Madame Pompadour'll be glad to get back home," he said, outlining the portrait with his forefinger.

She swept the sacred object from under his touch. "It's folly leaving it there," she said. "Tempting the maid."

She wrapped it in sweaters and put it in her bag. She locked the bag and put the key in her purse.

"What's to keep the maid from stealing the bag?" he asked. "First time I ever saw you so security-minded about anything. Remember all that money you left lying on that dresser in Spoleto?"

She went into the bathroom to do her eyes.

Out of sight, out of conversation.

As they drove down the noble avenue of cypresses leading to the main road, Tape said, "If per lucky chance Katie-from-Chicago has remained faithful to me during my absence, I'll reward her with a driveway just like this one."

But it was another incompleted conversational pass, and he added, "We've got to butter up the Mayor, first thing we get back to Pobrecito. He's already toasted."

If we get back to Pobrecito. She's never been interested in my business, but never so little as now.

"Isn't that the old desk clerk?" Sonya said.

He was waiting at the bus stop, the shabby, defeated old man, dispiritedly slumped on the bench in front of the majestic hotel which once had belonged to him.

Tape said, "It's so hot, let's offer the poor old guy a lift to town."

Picking up strangers is absolutely against my policy, but now . . . *two's* a crowd.

"Oh, let's, poor thing," she said.

It is better with a stranger along; the conversation is not so false or desperate, and a third person lets me slide to the rim of things.

Tape stopped by the old man, who discreetly pretended not to notice.

160

"Going to Split?" Tape said. "Hop in."

The old man seemed not able to make up his mind, so Sonya got out of the front seat, scuttled into the refuge of the back seat, and held the door open, saying brightly, "Men in front."

"This is most gracious indeed," the flustered old man said, having no choice but to get into the car.

Along the road they passed some children. Who waggled. Tape felt like thumbing his nose at them. Same as Jag drivers.

"By the way," he said to the old man, "thanks for finding us Petar. He's wonderful. Have you known him long?"

"Since he was a boy," the old man said, now relaxed and comfortable. "His father was one of my dearest friends."

"Excuse me for being so nosy, sir, but why is a man of Petar's obvious—you know—a fisherman?"

The old man shrugged. Tape persisted. "I bet he was a professional singer."

No comment.

"Look, sir," Tape said. "Petar told us you used to own the hotel."

"He shouldn't have," the old man demurred.

"So, turn about's fair play. I know how *political* things are around here, but we're all alone in the world's noisiest Fiat. And my wife and I are dying with curiosity about Petar. Come on, please, tell us. What was he?"

"*Please* tell us," Sonya begged, leaning forward to encourage the old man and joining in the conversation for the first time.

Ah, now she's interested. Well, well, and well.

The old man looked around as if to make sure Sonya was alone in the back seat, and said, "In the old days, he was our greatest actor."

"It figures," Tape said.

The old man loosened up and said with pride, "His Hamlet, his Liliom, his Uncle Vanya . . . the best in memory. And as to singing, his *Student Prince* ran for a whole year."

"I knew he was Somebody," Sonya said.

Tape kept probing. "I suppose he lost out because he was Right when it was wrong."

"No, sir. Petar never took sides."

"Then why . . . ?"

"The Actor's Union canceled his work permit."

"But why . . . ?"

"In the old days, all the bad actors were Communists, and it may have been a device used by them to get rid of the talent that was keeping them off the stage. It is true that most of our finest stars were accused of fascism at the time. But Petar's position was so high, the public so idolizing, that he would have stayed except for . . . love. Yes, he was destroyed by love."

"Aren't we all?" Tape said.

"Whom did he love?" Sonya asked.

"Some princess probably," Tape said.

"Oh no, just his wife," the old man explained. "But another woman, a young and very terrible actress, loved him. She pursued him, flung herself at him. And he rejected her."

"The ultimate insult," said Tape wisely, trying but failing to catch Sonya's eyes in his rear-view mirror.

She said, "But how could that make them revoke his work permit?"

"This bad actress—she is now the star of our National Theater, by the way—was then the head of the Actor's Union. And when the Union voted to renew his permit, she in her hatred brought new charges, of treason, and then personally led the Voting Committee to Petar's door, with her gun ready to kill him when he opened it. But he left by the back door instead."

"Hell hath no fury like a lady Commie spurned," Tape said, and Sonya said, "But he did nothing. Won't they give him back his work permit?"

"No, Madame. He has been officially branded."

"He should go to some other country," she said.

"He has considered that, Madame. But his family, his old father, too, is still alive, and . . ."

They were approaching a long viaduct entering the city, and the old man interrupted himself to say, "Please stop this side of the bridge, sir. I . . . am getting out here."

162

They let him out and drove on. Sonya said, "How nervous we made him. He seemed glad to talk, but afraid, too. Poor thing."

"These Titoites don't seem to bother with any of that crude concentration-camp stuff here," Tape said. "Just work permits."

He looked into the mirror. The old man was walking across the long bridge, so Split had been his destination, after all. But he'd been too scared to be seen in town with the visiting Enemy.

Their dinner at the city's chief restaurant was no better or worse than it should have been, and afterward they wandered through the shopping section.

The stores were still open and the merchandise in the windows provided them with food for comment.

Tape studied a window displaying sleazy rayon underwear in rainbow colors. "The Sell is neither hard, soft, nor seductive," he criticized. "Just Marx-awful."

At the adjoining window Sonya surveyed a chaos of cheap handbags, gaudy swimsuits, and coarse yard goods. "Yugoslav fashion," she declared, "has yet to rear its pretty head."

The swimsuits reminded Tape of St. Louis.

"Nothing worth buying in this town," he declared. "Let's go back to the hotel."

But on the way to the car they came to a store with windows that would not have been out of place on Rome's Via Condotti or even New York's Fifth Avenue.

"Oasis," exclaimed Tape. "Let your eyes drink."

"Unbelievable," Sonya said.

A sign in English announced that it was the State Shop for Tourists, and that all purchases would be discounted twenty per cent if paid for in any foreign currency.

"Well, that should include the natives out," Tape said. "But you see, they do know how to sell, for the right kind of currency. Dinars just don't interest them."

"Look at that leather coat," Sonya said. "Beautiful."

Strange and beautiful. The coat, of finest antelope, had been dyed shining satiny black and was designed for evening wear, with a Givenchy stand-up collar.

163

"It's a killer!" For weeks Tape had kept his eyes peeled for something smashing enough to . . . cancel out the St. Louis swimsuit. And this was fabulously it.

"I never saw a lovelier leather coat," she said, obviously as impressed as he was.

"The store's still open," he said. "Come on."

He strode to the door and opened it for her, but she just stood there, not moving.

"Come on," he urged. "Maybe we'll be lucky and find it in your size."

With something like nervousness, Sonya smiled. "Oh, Tape. I don't want to *buy* it. I was just . . . remarking, that's all."

"Oh, come on. At least let's see how you look in it."

With something like panic, she pleaded, "No. It's lovely but . . ."

He closed the door and went to her. He tugged persuasively at her arm—feeling manhandled, she pulled back.

"Tape! Let's sleep on it. Decide later."

But he had worked her close to the door, which he opened. Defeated, she gave up and entered with him, not knowing what her next move would be, but determined not to let him buy her that coat.

There were no customers in the store, just two women preparing to scrub the floor, and back of the counter a male clerk, taking inventory.

"Do you speak English?" Tape called to him. "We'd like to try on that black leather coat in the window."

"No," Sonya begged. "Please."

The manager put down his paper and pencil. He pointed at the clock, then at a sign on the door. "We close at eight," he pronounced severely.

"But the clock says exactly eight," Tape argued. "We only need a minute. If it fits her, I'll buy it."

He advanced farther into the store, but was halted by a woman splashing and sloshing water in front of him.

The manager came from behind the counter. His face was peevish. He made a shooing motion and spoke harshly.

164

"Closed. Can't you even read your own language? It says *closed* there. In English. Out. We scrub. Out."

This was too much for Tape. He moved toward the manager menacingly, stopped not three feet from him, and pulled himself up to a stiff military attention.

Then he made the fascist salute and barked, "Heil, Tito."

The manager was outraged and enraged beyond speech. He pointed at the door, and Tape slumped, waved languidly, and ambled out, where Sonya was waiting; she had run outside when it happened, hating herself for doing so and loathing the scene, which had terrified her.

The manager slammed the door and locked it.

"Come on. Let's go back to that crummy hotel," Tape said, and Sonya followed him obediently to the car, resenting the insufferable manager, but on the other hand relieved at not having to try on the coat.

As they were getting into the Fiat, she looked at Tape. He was still trembling with rage. His chin quivered, his lips twitched.

His disposition gets worse and worse. And no wonder. Oh, why did I come? Why didn't I stop him, stop *this*, back in New York?

They were on the long viaduct.

"Screw them all," Tape said.

And all over a coat she didn't want, as she didn't want the I. Magnin sweater—she has not worn it once on this whole trip.

He added, "And I for one am forgetting that shitty little incident as of this second."

"Please don't drive so fast," she begged.

He slowed down and in a few minutes calmed down.

"Hey, Old Nick forgot to send his daily Wish-I-was-there."

The Fiat was on the main road. Ahead of them, laboring up a long hill, was a column of Army trucks, fifteen or more. Tape, unable to pass safely, fell in behind the last one.

They were World-War-Two ten-wheelers, U.S.-made, and he grumbled, "Stuck behind our own tax bite. I helped pay for those goddamned things. That's the ticket; give free military

165

supplies to all our enemies so they won't be short of anything to clobber us with, when the time comes.''

They finally got to the top of the hill and he accelerated to pass. But just as he was abreast of the truck, headlights approached, coming fast, so he was forced to brake hard in order to fall in line again.

The Fiat veered sharply to the left—not to the right and into the side of the truck, thank God, this was no time for ideologies —the two left wheels ran off the pavement, and frantically tussling he managed to straighten out, and get back of the truck just in time to avoid a head-on collision.

"Christ and Calvin," he said, sweating and weak and sick from the near-disaster. "We need a brake job bad."

Sonya opened her eyes and said faintly, "Please don't try to pass again."

"Don't worry, we're gonna play snail until I get these brakes fixed."

They drove in silence for a few more miles.

Then Tape said, "Ejection."

"What?"

"Nothing. Just thinking what that clerk did to me. I guess I'm the ejection type."

He is trying to sting me. But it is not rejection in his sense of the word. Nor is it caused by whatever he thinks causes it. The name of my hermitage is sadness. I am as unredeemably sad as . . . the Concord Sonata. Things around me are like shadows. Sounds are not real. Memories are like touches. Yes, now I understand my love for, my kinship with that flute across the pond. It is like me, *more* than lonesome, *strangely* lonesome.

And Tape has nothing to do with it. I was always this way. Even with Werner. Yes, even with him.

"Please let me share your loneliness, Sonya my madness, for loneliness such as yours is a kind of ecstasy."

He said. Past-perfectly. Dead-rightly.

Tape said, "What say let's take a picnic lunch to Hvar tomorrow?"

166

"Poor Petar. Forever trapped," she said.

"Yeah." Petar brings out all her . . . sensitivity. I hate that goddamn word. Me, I bring out . . . zero. If she is my soul, then I have ceased to be. Old not-to-be Alberg. To be half a husband, or to be no husband, that is the question.

And they were gliding into the parking lot.

As they climbed the marble staircase, Tape said, "They get steeper by the hour. Old Nick's calves are trembling like aspirin trees."

He paused for rest on the fourth-floor landing and grimly added, "Old Nick's humor is failing step by step."

In the room, Sonya just sat. Tape put Murine into his eyes. "That sun really third-degreed me today. Don't let me forget my sunglasses tomorrow."

But her mind was still on Petar. "I don't suppose there is anything he *could* do, is there?"

"At least nothing the poor guy *would* do."

He walked out onto the balcony and looked at the sea.

Old Nick said, "Not a leaf stirred, not a horse stirred."

Far out, a constellation of fishing lights glowed. Closer in, like an etching, a man standing in a small boat rowed steadily toward Drvenik, the drip from his oars gleaming in the quarter moonlight.

Could be Petar. If so, it's a long way home in this flat calm.

A German on the next balcony huskily said *"Schön."*

Tape returned to the room.

"Such a waste of human value," Sonya said. "Poor thing."

Her compassionate remark, not twenty seconds before completely shared by him, hit a nerve.

He said, "Tomorrow maybe you can charm him into liberating himself. Or sumpin'."

"No. He's trapped. The old man's remark about his family, his father, proves it."

"Oh, we're all trapped, thisaway or thataway. I bet old Petar's happy as a lark, right this minute. Doing . . . guess what?"

She didn't answer. Perversely he continued, "Yes, ma'am, I bet old Petar is busy as a bee composing a new song to buzz you with tomorrow. A romantic song for a change."

He's jealous. He thinks I'm interested in Petar.

To prove she wasn't, she said, "But *we're* not trapped here. Tape, let's stop this nonsense and go."

"When?"

"First thing tomorrow morning. Early."

"Why not? We should be able to make Plitvice by afternoon; see the lakes, maybe catch a trout or two, spend the night there, and the day after hightail it for Trieste."

"I vote to skip Plitvice and go straight to Trieste; that way we can be out of this country by sundown."

Tape was washing his teeth.

"Okay, if that's the way you want it. But Plitvice is to Yugoslavia like the Pyramids are to Egypt; they're something you're supposed to see, especially if they're only one day away."

"I just cannot bear to stay in this suffocating country one hour longer than absolutely necessary."

"Would you miss the chance to see Niagara Falls, if you were this close to it?"

"What's Niagara Falls got to do with it?"

"Anyway," Tape said, "we can't leave Split until I get those brakes fixed. So I'd better get up early and go in. These Commie garages close for the day at lunchtime, you know."

"I'll pack while you're doing that, then," she said. "But let's plan on going direct to Trieste."

Suddenly Tape felt pushed too far.

"Oh, sure," he said. "Anything Madame wishes. Who cares what Old Nick wants to see? I yield. I yield. Of course it gets me nowhere, still I yield."

"Nobody's yielding. You'll be just as glad to cross that frontier as I will. We've both gotten as irritated by this country as . . ."

"As by each other," he said, and she looked at him in anger and surprise, for never before had he taken *that* tone with her, or used words *that* cutting, *that* bitter.

168

"Yeah," he said, "this country and our marriage have a hell of a lot in common. They sure do at that. Well, it's easy to criticize *them* . . . but I for one can't see much difference between us personally and them collectively."

He walked into the bathroom and flipped his toothbrush into the glass; he rinsed his mouth with water and took a leak and washed his hands.

Then he went back into the room to say, "I got a sneaking suspicion that what you really want to get out of is both."

"Oh, let's stop it and go to Plitvice," she said, loathing herself for stooping to such a petty quarrel.

For days I've been trying to stop my self-pity, and now I am indulging myself in the only thing worse, self-loathing.

"Up Plitvice's ass," he said. "Old Nick'll drive you nonstop to Trieste. Old Nick is square as hell, but he does serve a certain purpose, after all. When all forms of communication, and I do mean *all,* stop between a twosome, then three's company and not a crowd. So, whatever else he is, square or rectangular, Old Nick sure as hell serves a therapeutic social function."

Since he was speaking the truth, she remained silent and let him rave on.

Which he did with bitter pleasure.

"Today, of course, we didn't need Old Nick; we had our Third Man in the flesh. I noticed," he said nastily, breaking off the first thought and substituting a more violent one, "that unlike me, Petar didn't not amuse you. I noticed you talked *and* listened to *him* with fascination, not to mention sympathy, compassion, and a few other things that in your relations with your husband are conspicuous by their absence. *I've* been singing sad songs for weeks, but I've yet to raise a single tear."

All this infuriated Sonya, perhaps because there still was a certain truth in his attack, and she snapped, "I've never before heard such ridiculous nonsense from you. Not very pretty nonsense, either. You sound like a stranger."

We're two strangers quarreling.

"You made me one," he said. "Maybe I'm just sore because

169

Petar succeeded where I failed. In bringing you out of the Past. For two whole hours, he managed to put you into the Present Tense. You've always been a Dislocated Person, at least where I'm concerned. Dislocated from the Present Tense."

She was cleaning off eye makeup. And thinking:

How perfectly he puts it. I *am* dislocated from the present tense. This quarrel is as meaningless to me, as far outside and away from me, as . . .

She said, "I really think we both should stop this pointless bickering and get some rest so the trip to Plitvice tomorrow will be as tranquil as possible under the circumstances."

"Oh, no," he said. "We're barreling nonstop to Trieste. You don't sandbag me into going to Plitvice the way you did with that Laney luncheon. And as to the bickering, it's the only way I got of making contact with you. All the other ways are blocked."

She was slipping her nightgown over her head, brassiere and panties still on, for Christ's sake. The worst insult yet.

"It was a mistake coming here," she said, "for, oh, lots of reasons. But now that it's done, please let's concentrate on getting out, and let all the other things yield to that. Please, Tape. Oh, I know I'm not fit to live with, but first things first, please."

He was removing his shoes and socks; she turned her back to him and slipped the bra and panties off. Challenged, he furiously removed all his clothes, and nude, walked to the dresser to get his pajamas. He'd show her.

"I've got a glare headache," he complained. "Can't stand light. These goddamned naked bulbs, why can't that two-bit commissar who runs this joint put a two-cent paper shade on them?"

The sand on the floor irritated his bare feet and he said, "Goddamn this goddamned sand. Where's my slippers?"

He put on his pajamas, took aspirin, brushed the sand from his feet, and went to bed, pulling the covers over his head until she turned off the light.

In the darkness, the placating darkness, she said, "I'll pack while you're at the garage." But he did not answer.

170

"I'm sorry, Tape," she said. "And believe me, I do understand your . . . irritation."

Still he did not answer.

Poor thing. I came here just to spare him; I could not bear sending him back to California thinking there was . . . someone else. But this is crueler. Oh, why do I always do the wrong thing, the ugly thing, the cruel thing? There is only one right thing to do and I have known what it is ever since . . . The Concord Sonata.

If his train had not passed mine in Grand Central.

I keep saying it to myself, promising it to myself and to him, the right thing—but I do not do it.

I must no longer try to escape from the unpleasant cruel moment—that's all it would take, just a moment—and think of the prolonged cruelty of weeks, these weeks, of months . . . yes, yes, yes, I must stop the way we are—I must tell him.

Tell him what? Anything, the words do not matter. They are mere preludes to the deed that must follow.

But tell him when? And where?

Anytime. Anywhere. It doesn't matter. Trieste, or—

Lights went on in the black tunnel, and there they were again: Adam and Eve. This time, not Dürer's painted couple, but white marble statues by an unknown sculptor in Young Bernini's style. They were standing back to back, as last she had seen them in the painted transformations; but no longer were they sorrowfully slumped—they were erect and taut with bitter anger and separateness. They were tense and uncoupled, two lone inhabitants of a miniworld called marriage. Two antagonists who had just fought a war without victory.

Stalemates.

And they were moving in mind's gloomy tunnel, the two statues, farther and farther apart, never once looking back at the one once paired with, later warred with, now through with.

I want to be a foreigner. Shhh.

Dislocated Persons.

Leather coat.

Azaleas bloomed in the cemetery near Charleston.

In the *triste* darkness, she tried again.
"How do you feel now?"
This time he answered her.
"Headache."

CHAPTER 16

At seven she rose and began to pack, very quietly. Even at that chill hour, the sea churned with Nordics who liked whatever it was that icy water did to them.

The day brightened the room. Tape covered his head.

She put on a Madras blouse and canvas skirt for the journey. At eight she awakened him. He sat up, then lay back and closed his eyes.

"Still got this damned headache," he said.

She brought aspirin. "You need coffee. Some food."

"Not if I have to walk five flights to get it. I'll starve first."

"I'll go down for my breakfast," she said. "And get them to bring up yours. It's just nerves. And no wonder. All this tension. You'll be all right after coffee."

She went down to the desk. The old man was on duty, luckily. But despite, or perhaps because of, their previous night's camaraderie, he did not smile or even say Good Morning.

He's afraid he said too much to us; they all carry their own little portable Iron Curtains with them, and so he's closed his, at least between him and me.

She explained her husband was sick, and asked if breakfast could be **sent** up to him.

He looked sympathetic but dubious.

"That's too bad, Mrs. Alberg. Let's discuss it with the Director and see what we can arrange."

He escorted her to a private office and explained the problem of the sick husband to the frowning man behind the desk. Sonya's presence was not acknowledged.

Mrs. Alberg. I've never once thought of myself as Mrs. Alberg. It's just a forgery I put on documents now and then. The Herr Direktor looks like a Jesuit during the Inqui— no, one of those cunning Lorenzo Lotto priests. He needs a shave, too, just like them.

The old man turned to her and said, "The Director fears it is impossible to fulfill your request, Madame. He asks me to explain that the present plan of operation does not grant him the authority to permit the serving of meals in the rooms of the clients. Sorry."

Sonya, matching as best she could the Director's cold, scholastic manner, said, "Will His Honor the Comrade Director be so gracious as to permit me to go to the kitchen and get a tray for my husband? I'll take it up."

The Director did not seem to care for this departure from the system, but finally he granted her request, scrawling an order to that effect.

"Give this, please, to the head chef," the relieved desk clerk said.

Sonya glanced at it. On the bottom of the memo form was printed in English, German, and French: *Thank You, Come Again*.

"The Director's generosity overwhelms me," she said. "Would you tell him I am almost reminded of the Good Samaritan?"

"This way, Madame," the distressed old man said.

He hustled her out of the office. She said, "Can you send Petar a message saying we won't be going to Hvar today?"

"Oh, I forgot. Petar was here earlier. He said to tell you he couldn't make it either."

Another portable Iron Curtain had clanged shut.

174

She went to the kitchen and presented her note, upsetting the chef enormously, which pleased her immensely.

Tape refused everything but the coffee. She touched his forehead.

I touch a stranger.

"No fever," she said. "Look, I'll take the car to Split and get those brakes fixed. So sleep off that headache. I'll put you in the back seat and you can sleep all the way to Trieste, too."

"Oh, I'll be okay. We'll split the driving."

The first time she's touched me since . . . especially physically. The driving's the only thing we'll have split in Split.

"It's just too much sun. Last night everything glittered, even in the dark."

"You should have worn dark glasses."

"Yeah. Tell the mechanic the car pulls left, like him."

She was looking at herself in the mirror. "I am certainly not dressed for the city. Maybe I should get a doctor."

"Not from here, please," Old Nick muttered. "My headache's on the right side."

She disappeared into the bathroom. He dozed.

When she came out of the bathroom, he noticed that she had changed from her Madras blouse and gray skirt into her orange linen dress. Even the dress hurt his eyes.

She went to the terrace and opened wide the double doors. The sun blazed on the bougainvillaea vine which framed the doorway. It was in full flower and it burned his eyes like purple fire; the hot orange dress in the center of all that purple, too, glowing fiercely, scorched his eyes.

But there was on her face a look of something that frightened him and he watched her face warily, squinting in the glare, trying to figure out what she was up to.

For a long moment she just stood there looking at him, indecisively; then, suddenly, as if under the terrible necessity and force and pressure of getting it over with, all these three long deadly weeks of strangeness and hell since those two trains passed in Grand Central Station, she said, clearly and deliberately in a strange way in a strange voice that pronounced every syllable with metallic distinctness:

"Tape, you were right last night. It's not only this country I want to leave. I want to leave you. I'm sorry, Tape, but I must leave you."

He flinched and closed his eyes against the purple-orange assault and said stupidly, "Why?"

"You have a right to ask that, Tape. Do you remember that afternoon in the Waldorf, when you asked me if there was someone else?" He nodded.

"And that same day, earlier, when you saw me on the train entering Grand Central Station?"

Again he nodded, numbed and speechless, waiting for the next blow, and after that the next, until finally the final.

"Well, I lied to you. I did not go to Southampton, of course. You knew that. Instead"—her voice began to lose its forward drive, and began to fade, slow down—"I . . . went . . . somewhere else . . . to see . . . someone else. Now . . . I've said it. Now you know!"

He could not bear to look at her face any longer, and shifted his gaze to the purple bougainvillaea, glaring in the bright morning sunlight.

"Now . . . I know," he repeated stupidly. "Yeah. What . . . what's next?"

The answer came as if long-thought-out, firmly and decisively, ultimate, with depersonalized clarity:

"I suggest we drive to Trieste together. And part there."

The orange dress moved out of its dazzling purple frame and crossed the room to the door. He closed his eyes.

Now her voice came softly, there was even a hint of kindness in it. "I'm sorry to hurt you, Tape, but it . . . just popped out. I had intended waiting until we got to Trieste or at least until your headache was better, but it just . . . popped out."

A pause, then, "I'll go fix the brakes now. Try to sleep."

He opened his eyes and she was gone.

She drove to Putnik, the State travel agency in Split, and

176

found out where the State garage was. She drove there, and found an English-speaking foreman. He understood the brake problem and told her to come back for the car at twelve-thirty.

"Can't you please make it earlier?" she pleaded. "I simply must get to Trieste today. As a favor?"

"Twelve-thirty," he said sourly, and as with everything else in Yugoslavia, that was officially that.

She sat in the prettiest square, which was sort of Northern Italian Late Renaissance in its architecture, drinking coffee, reading a week-old London *Observer,* and killing time.

Two tables away, an American woman was complaining about everything to an English couple, one table away.

"But you came here from the wrong direction," the Englishman explained. "To appreciate Yugoslavia, one must first visit Poland, Romania . . ."

"And especially Bulgaria," said his wife. "Now there's a garden spot. We must have been daft, Robert, to . . ."

"After them, you see," the husband continued, "this is rather better than Paradise."

When Sonya returned to the garage at twelve-thirty, the Fiat had not even been touched yet.

"But you promised it for twelve-thirty," she protested.

The foreman shrugged and found something more important to do. She kept doggedly on his tail.

"But when will it be ready?"

Still not looking at her, he said, "Not today, of course. We close at thirteen o'clock. There's no time now."

"Over three hours ago, I told you I must get to Trieste tonight. And you promised it at twelve-thirty. You simply cannot do this."

"It's closing time," he said. "Bring it back tomorrow."

"How long will it take tomorrow?"

"An hour. Less. It's nothing. Just the brake lining."

You bastard, she thought, I'll Tashkent you. And she exploded with rage, in Russian.

"You breaker of promises. What kind of Socialist example are you setting, Comrade? Shame on you. A Worker, and . . ."

This was her lucky day, after all. He not only reacted with understanding, he answered her back in Russian.

"Are you Russian?" he asked in astonishment. "My mother came from the Ukraine and . . ."

"My name," she announced regally, "happens to be Sonya Osinoff."

"Then why"—he checked his worksheet—"did you say it was Alberg?"

"None of your business, Comrade."

"Excuse me, Comrade," he apologized. "But I thought you were American. Or at least English. And you must admit the car is Italian. So how could I know?"

"In Russia," she said, "the Workers help one another. Kropotkinism still lives, thank G— . . . the Politbureau."

"Please be patient, Comrade. Please."

He shouted for mechanics; they swarmed over the Fiat; in thirty-five minutes the car was ready to go.

Sonya drove back full-speed to Kastela, thankful that it was on the same road they would take to Trieste, not one kilometer would she have to go out of her way.

But no bad without some good, as Tape was so fond of quoting his grandfather, for the extra hours of rest would be good for him. She hoped he would be up and dressed and ready to go.

Dislocated from the Present Tense. Not today. This day I must force myself to exist entirely in the present; the goal was Trieste, and nothing from the Past must intrude. Until Trieste happens, I must live in the Now. Now-this-second.

At the hotel desk she stopped to tell the old clerk that they would be checking out in ten minutes and to have the bill ready.

"Ten minutes," she repeated through the portable Iron Curtain.

He nodded and bent lower over the register; his face was not visible, but he was saying something. What?

She leaned over the desk to catch his mumbled words.

"Please tell your husband not to write any more Old Nick messages," he was mumbling. "They're checking him."

178

He turned, coughed, and grumpily put the ledger on the shelf back of him, never once glancing at her.

She climbed the great marble staircase feeling like a criminal for some silly reason, and frightened for some other silly reason.

By the time she reached the third-floor landing, her logic calmed her. After all, they would be safely across the border sometime tonight, and all it could possibly mean was that the government would be as relieved to get rid of Old Nick as Old Nick would be to return that favor.

Poor Tape didn't have much to laugh at these days, but his so-richly unearned James Bondish adventure should amuse him, add a little spice to the journey ahead.

Now relieved, she ran lightly up the fifth-floor steps—one more trip down them and *that* was finished forever. She hurried along the hall to their room.

As she was opening the door, Tape groaned.

He was lying on the bed, one hand holding a wet towel pressed hard into his forehead; he had kicked off the sheet and his large bony feet dangled over the edge of the bed.

Although it was nearly two o'clock, he had not touched the toast and marmalade left over from breakfast. An even worse sign, there were no cigarette butts in the ashtray. It was the first time in their four years of marriage that he had been sick enough, excluding occasional hangovers, to not smoke.

"Tape," she said, alarmed, "what's the matter?"

He groaned again. "I'm sick. My head's killing me."

She felt him; his flesh was burning.

"I think you're a bit feverish," she said, looking for the thermometer. "Any other symptoms?"

"Stomach cramps. Sort of. Not too bad, though."

"Perhaps you've picked up dysentery. All this bad food." She found the thermometer at last, in her jewel box, of all places. "How is it in that department?"

"Zero."

While the thermometer was in his mouth, she felt his pulse. A little fast, but not . . .

"How much?" he asked, as she held up the thermometer.

179

"Oh, you've a little fever. Almost a hundred and one."

Actually, it was a frightening hundred and four.

"Must have bumped into one of the local viruses," he said. "The car fixed?"

"Yes. Finally." She started to tell the foreman anecdote, then stopped herself with a firm: No Past Tense today, please. Not even *that* past.

He tried to get up. "Then let's hit the road to Nowhere."

Nowhere? Oh! Firmly she pushed him back.

"Not yet. Not until we find out what's the matter with you. You probably need an antibiotic."

What a time and place for this, whatever it was, to happen. One hundred and four. Old Nick. Big Brother is watching Old Nick.

Fears and tears beneath the cheers. Shhhh.

She made him eat a little of the toast, gave him aspirin, and then went out to find a doctor.

An English-speaking doctor. Or French-speaking, it didn't matter. Although Russian would be the likeliest to find, probably.

One hundred and four. On top of everything else.

As she pseudo-cheerily left the room, he muttered, "Headache."

CHAPTER 17

"Grippe," the doctor diagnosed, pronouncing it *grippy*.

He counted out twelve capsules of terramycin. "By tomorrow, with the aspirin, this should reduce the fever."

"But grippy," argued Sonya, using his pronunciation to save time, "shouldn't run his fever up *that* high. One hundred and four."

"He has no immunity to our local virus," the doctor explained. "There is no sore throat yet, but doubtless there will be."

He gave Tape two aspirin. "For your headache, sir."

"Aspirin for this headache is like trying to go to the moon on a Roman candle," Tape joked. "But seriously, doctor, I have to get to Trieste. It's urgent. When can I leave?"

"Not until your fever drops, of course."

Sonya accompanied the doctor downstairs and arranged to keep the room until further notice. The doctor sternly ordered the desk clerk to order the chef to provide Madame with whatever invalid diet she chose to order.

She went to the kitchen and got some soup, custard, and tea.

Cheerfully she carried the food up to the patient, who cheerlessly swallowed a little of the soup, nothing else.

An hour later his fever had dropped to 101. He slept.

Two hours later he started shivering and his fever was 104. Even so, she trusted the terramycin so much that she slept quite well between dosage times.

But next morning, the fever remained high and she phoned the doctor, who advised patience.

That evening, Tape rushed to the toilet with a severe attack of stomach cramps, which started a violent dysentery that kept him running, as he complained, "Every hour on the half-hour."

Sonya considered the humor, such as it was, a good sign, for she had long held the theory that really sick people don't make jokes.

The new development worried her more than it did him; his one, only, and great complaint was the headache. At midnight, she phoned the doctor, but the nurse at the clinic just kept saying, "*Demain, demain. Domani. Domani.*"

By sunup Sonya was frightened. The fever, which would yield for an hour or so to aspirin, kept generally around 104, after three days of terramycin; the dysentery would not yield to entero-vioform, the usually trustworthy Traveler's Best Friend. And Tape refused all food.

After terramycin-time, the only real time that now existed, she drove into Split and waited for the doctor to come to work.

She noticed his name on the desk-sign: Mestrovic, like the sculptor. He was a small, colorless man, somewhat resembling the Prince of Monaco. His English was like his personality, painstaking, correct, and frustratingly slow.

She described the new developments, and Dr. Mestrovic said, "I do not like this dysentery. Now in Split are several serious cases of—I do not know the English term—in Serbo-Croat we simply call it the Unknown Intestinal Virus."

"Oh, intestinal flu," she said.

"No. It is more—"

"Serious?"

"So far, the virus has not responded to any antibiotic. I should like to see your husband again, Madame."

Sonya bought some ice cream for Tape, and they left for

182

Kastela, she in the Fiat, the doctor following on his motorcycle.

Tape as usual complained of nothing but his headache. The doctor gave him some nerve-reaction tests and told him not to worry about that.

Then he took a blood sample.

"Although I still believe that it is simply grippy," he said reassuringly.

The ice cream had melted and besides the patient didn't want anything to eat.

The day passed; when afternoon came, she hung her blanket over the terrace doors to keep out the sun. Although the doctor hadn't told her to, she started a record of the fever and the pulse.

At his 6 A.M. terramycin-time, she made a chart of her figures. The fever was very nearly a straight line, slightly above 104; the pulse ranged from 88 to 97.

At eight she drove to town for alcohol, talc, money exchange, and gasoline.

Then she hurried back to give him an alcohol rub, which he greatly appreciated.

"You're one hell of a fine nurse," he complimented. "But it's too bad you have to stay here bothering with Old Nick."

"No comments," she answered, nurse-breezily, "and not even any thoughts, please. Just concentrate on getting well, Buddy."

"Old Nick's tour of duty is about over," he said.

"Shhh."

Now, when he wasn't cramped over the toilet, hunching in agony, he just lay in the bed passively, clutching his head with one hand.

It was his characteristic position, the manifestation of whatever it was that was wrong with him.

Many times she tried to go into the toilet with him, but he wouldn't hear of it, and always closed the door.

But more and more, as time went on, she felt, strongly and powerfully, that she must insist and be firm and see for herself what she could see in there.

He was very touchy and grumpy, but finally he yielded and let

183

her come in, as he sat on the toilet, clutching his head, bent over, cramping and groaning; when he finished, he cunningly tried to flush the toilet, but she was too quick for him.

"Go to bed," she ordered.

And she examined his stool, not knowing what to look for, except blood maybe, but there was no sign of blood.

It was shockingly *green*. Green as spattered moss. Frightening.

A laboratory test was indicated. She made her arrangements, then told Tape what to do next time.

He did not answer.

She turned out the light and got into bed; although it was almost morning, she had not yet slept, but she did not lie down. With knees up, arms around them, she sat thinking.

Grippe? I never heard of a case this violent.

The Great Unknown Virus?

Did the other patients have moss-green stools?

Doctor Mestrovic's ability? She heard her father's voice saying:

"The cult of Doctor-worship is wery silly, Sonya. The world has many doctors, but wery few smart men."

She got up, washed a teaspoon.

"Open your mouth," she said. "I want to see your throat."

Another shock. His tongue was like whitest cotton speckled with angry red spots. The throat far back was, seemed, looked fairly normal, but the palate and gums were masses of loose shredded skin.

It was twenty minutes past five. Still dark. Outside, in the sea, there was a healthy German splash, a breathless female voice screamed *"Ach, wunderbar. Kommen sie—"* Then another great splash. Tooth-chattering laughter.

The old man is night clerk this week. Good.

She dressed and went down to the desk. Ever since his mumbled Old Nick warning, the old man had not once looked at her. She leaned far over the desk and gripped his arm, forcing his glance.

"My husband is sick. Very sick. You understand?"

"Yes, I know. Grippy can be very bad. Especially in a strange country."

"It is not grippy. Look at me, please. I beg you to look at me and listen."

"Yes, Madame."

"You must try to understand me. I am desperate. You must understand that I am desperate, because you must help me."

The old man looked cautiously around the lobby, then removed her hand from his arm and patted it gently. "Now, now, Mrs. Alberg. You must control yourself. Of course I will help you. But how?"

"I want you to find two more doctors for me. The best. Language does not matter. I want them to meet here with Doctor Mestrovic as soon as possible. I am desperate, you understand?"

The old man reached for the telephone book.

All three doctors came together, at seven o'clock. Dr. Mestrovic introduced his two colleagues. For the old one she caught the name Nijaz, but missed several syllables; and she completely lost the younger doctor's name as he was making a gallant remark in Russian at the time. He told her proudly that he had studied in Moscow and seemed more interested in her than in the patient.

They examined Tape. She examined them, with something of her father's skepticism. For Dr. Mestrovic, respect, though not exactly trust. Doctor Nijaz, who spoke good French, was a middle-aged mixture of professor and bureaucrat: Forms first, People last.

Dr. No-Name was stethoscoping Tape and smiling at her.

Finally, they beckoned Sonya to follow them to the terrace.

Dr. Mestrovic said, "I still think it is only grippy, Madame."

"But the mouth?"

"A localization of the grippy. A most fortunate development."

"But—" she closed the door and whispered, "Diphtheria?"

Dr. Nijaz understood that much English, and he said, in French, "Impossible, Madame." She turned to him.

"The blood test made yesterday shows a very low white-cell count," he explained. "Most unusual with such a high fever, but

185

a characteristic of the cases we already have of the Unknown Intestinal Virus."

She turned to Doctor No-Name, who looked into her eyes and said in Russian, "I am withholding my diagnosis until further tests are made."

"What tests?"

"Oh, the blood, the feces, the spinal fluid"—he was very nonchalant about the whole thing—"we must rule out the possibility of—forgive me, my dear, but we must—meningitis, encephalitis, et cetera."

Alarming Sonya, irritating Dr. Mestrovic, and startling Dr. Nijaz.

They returned to the sickroom. Tape opened his eyes and said, "Oh, Captain, my Captain. Poor Togo, gambling all his cash on my rich wife. Well, you can't win 'em all, Togo, my boy."

Sonya decided that she had gambled and lost on all three doctors. There was nobody in command.

He is afraid of death in a strange land and—

I am all he has. Such as I am. All he has.

"Come here," she ordered. "Into the bathroom."

Although it had already been shown to them, she unscrewed the Nescafé jar which held the fecal sample.

She felt cold on the outside and hysterical on the inside, but with a wild flaming sense of complete self-possession.

"Look," she cried, thrusting the open jar at them. "This stuff runs out of him in gallons. Like green rotten swamp water. But completely odorless. Look at it. I tell you my husband is seriously ill. And I do not in my heart believe that any of you knows what it is. He's been burnt up with five long days and nights of that fever. And the mouth. And this. And we do nothing. Nothing." She opened the bathroom door and pointed at Tape. "Look at him. Deranged. Delirious. And we do nothing."

She had said this in English and she waited, trembling and panting, while Doctor Mestrovic translated what she had said.

"Please, Madame," protested Doctor Nijaz, in French. "I pray you not to lose control of yourself. Your husband is not in the slightest deranged."

186

She broke. She sat on the edge of the bathtub, defeated by the professionals who would not listen to her.

"He is deranged," she sobbed. "How can you say he is not when you do not know him? I tell you that when he is normal his mind is clear, clever, and above all, sunny. Now, he is arrogant, a way he has never been. He speaks grandiose nonsense, unfinished . . ."

"Please to stop your tears," Doctor No-Name soothed in Russian, gallantly caressing her shoulder.

He is more interested in stopping my tears than in saving the patient's life.

She shuddered.

Doctor Mestrovic said, "First, to quiet your mind, Madame, we shall settle the question of the derangement. Let me question him."

They all went to the bedside and he conducted the test, translating at times for the other two.

"Would you mind answering a few questions for our records, sir?"

"Why not? Records are what makes the world go round."

"Fine. How old are you, sir?"

"Forty-four."

"And where were you born?"

"Lincoln, Nebraska."

"And have you ever had any serious illness, just for our record, sir?"

"Just this headache, sir."

"Can you remember what schools you . . . ?"

Tape was on a ship. Although he had forgotten where he had boarded it and where it was bound for, still it was a ship, rolling slightly in a swelling sea.

But what kind of ship? Freighter, probably, because a passenger ship would have a doctor aboard, and there was none here, which was a pity, for a doctor would at least know how to kill the headache. When you are dying with cancer of the brain you don't expect any medical miracles, but at least a doctor around would give you something to knock the headache.

So the captain of the ship had brought the First and Second Mates into his cabin, as if they could do anything except smile and look sympathetic.

Cancer of the brain.

Nice guys, all three, who had thoughtfully not worn their uniforms, the innocents, probably trying to convince him they were medics.

But they were polite and he was not going to be outpolited in doneness.

The ship rolled again and he had a moment's fear that he would disgrace himself with seasickness in front of these brass-guts officers, but the feeling passed. Good.

"Since you, sir," he said to the captain, "are polite enough to inquire as to the extent of my education, if any, then let me . . . hmmmmm. I spent three years in the pursuit of philosophy, another kind of voyage into unknown seas, sir. And even to this day I still agree with Professor Carnap, who agrees with G. E. Moore that all metaphysical statements are nonsense. Since no proof can be forthcoming on either the True or the False side, they are simply without any meaning whatsoever. Indeed, sir, the great Wittgenstein should have included metaphysics as one of his games; I might say it is the titular head of the whole family of games.

"But on the other hand, sir, I also agree with Plato that one of the lower Forms, or perhaps I should say Steps, leading to the highest form of the Good, is fiction or myth. And therefore, metaphysically speaking, sir, a good myth is better than a mile.

"But alas, sir, my philosphical education came to an abrupt end on that chapter, and I started learning how to doodle from the noodle, which is how I happened to become The Man in the Red Flannel Tongue."

The captain, smiling his total agreement, explained the point to the two mates and they smilingly withdrew, probably back to the old sextant as the sea was getting rougher.

Cancer of the brain.

On the terrace, Doctor Mestrovic argued, "Any man who can relate Wittgenstein to Plato, Madame, is not deranged."

188

"I give up," said Sonya. "Deranged or not, what next?"

They decided to send a microbiologist out for further specimens of this and that, and to continue with antibiotics.

As they left, Sonya said to Doctor Mestrovic in crisp English, "Please do me the favor of keeping that Russian-speaking Don Juan off this case."

"Your wishes shall be respected, Madame," Dr. Mestrovic answered with deepest understanding, not to say relief.

While Sonya was trying to force a few swallows of rice gruel into Tape, he became nasty, increasingly arrogant.

"Why don't you go on to Trieste, like you planned?" he said. "I got the message."

"Shhh," she said. "One more spoon now."

"It took me four years to learn *this* philosophy lesson."

Oh why did I have to say those things? That stupid quarrel, everything, now trapped in his fever. And when he complained how everything glittered, that night, I should have known he was sick.

"Shhh," she said. "You mustn't talk like that."

"Just popped out of me," he sneered, sarcastically.

He slept finally, and she lay down, though not to sleep. This was her third night of no-sleep, still she didn't feel sleepy, just numb in body, her mind a buzzing instrument.

In the morning the microbiologist came, a lady scientist. They could not communicate with each other, but Sonya could see she was terribly disturbed by the green stool.

After Tape's midnight antibiotic, Sonya finally slept.

She was awakened by a . . .

In trying to get up from the toilet seat, he had fallen.

She turned on the light and helped him to bed. He muttered, "Missed the goddamned doorknob, thassall. I'm okay, just missed the . . ."

He had soiled his sheets with the green spattery stuff and when he saw what he had done, he cracked.

"Look what I did," he sobbed. "Look. Me. What I . . ."

"Shhhh. It's nothing."

But she wasn't strong enough to hold him up; he slid to the

189

sandy terrazzo floor sobbing, "I'm done for. My God, I'm done for."

"You're not. Courage, Tape. Courage. It's just an acci—"

"Done for," he screamed, keening and unable to bear the thought of . . . the meaning of . . . whatever it meant for a grown man to do *that* in his bed.

She managed to get him into her bed, where she washed him tenderly.

"Like a goddamned baby," he grumbled, ashamed but also relieved to be clean again.

She removed the sheet from his bed and put it to soak in the tub; she remade his bed with one sheet and got into it.

"See," she said cheerfully. "Everything's fixed. No trouble. No harm done."

"Done for," he moaned, his voice trembling, quavering, breaking her heart and almost her nerve.

I'm going to pieces and this man is sick and I'm all he has in this country. *All he has.* My God how sick he is, and the doctors do nothing. I must do something, but what? Find a plane. Fly him to Rome, Vienna, Zürich . . . now. Yes, a plane.

But fly? In his condition. Impossible. I must not waste his time. I must not waste my emotions. What can I do now? More doctors? More diagnoses?

She lay there and thought, her mind running through every disease she had ever heard of.

Finally, she went to his bed. "Feeling better?"

"Headache."

She tried to count the days that hand had pressed into that head, but could not remember them all.

"Euphemism," he said.

"What?"

"Headache euphem for cancer," he explained obligingly.

"Don't say that. It's not true. The doctors . . . you mustn't think such things."

"Just popped out," he said cunningly. "Like things pop out of your mouth. Get it?"

She dressed and waited for dawn. She drove to the Clinic.

190

Finally Doctor Mestrovic received her. Doctor Nijaz was with him.

"Speak French," Doctor Mestrovic said. "I understand."

"His fever has climbed up to one hundred and five," Sonya said. "The terramycin has had no effect whatever. I want the truth, now, about this Unknown Virus. Does it kill?"

"We have had three deaths so far," Dr. Mestrovic admitted.

"He is sick enough to die," she said. "He thinks he is dying. Of brain cancer."

Of the cancerous memories I have put into his brain.

"With that fever? Impossible, Madame."

"But Unknown Virus is no diagnosis at all," she said. "Tell me, does it cause such headaches?"

"Headaches are merely a symptom, Madame. Many patients are prone to them."

"My husband never has headaches. And his stool. Do the others have such bright-green stools?"

"Hmmm. They suffer dysentery. But . . . however, he complains of no great enteric pains."

"You could cut off his leg and he'd still say headache. Beside it, all other pains are trifles," she cried with passion, struggling against their professional lethargy deathargy. "Oh, please, please try to think of other things besides grippy and vague Unknown Viruses. Forget the coincidence that there happens to be nine cases and three deaths of a certain intestinal ailment in Split. Think of everything that produces such a headache, such a fever. Even cholera, even the black plague. The killing fevers: Yellow fever, swamp fever . . ."

She paused and then added, "Typhoid fever."

Dr. Mestrovic's mouth dropped slightly open, giving him a foolish, baffled look. His eyes . . .

I know that look. It's guilt. Is this the Recognition Scene?

Dr. Nijaz said, "But . . . impossible. Because, of course, he has been injected against typhoid?"

"Not for five years," Sonya said. "Or I'd have known about it."

"But that is impossible," Doctor Nijaz protested. "All Americans are injected against everything."

Doctor Mestrovic was taking some medicines from the stores and putting them into his bag. "If it is typhoid," he said reassuringly, "then of course we can cure it."

"How?" she asked.

"Chloromycin and more chloromycin. Fifty grams in all. It is the only antibiotic that kills the typhoid germ."

Doctor Nijaz made some telephone calls. The lady microbiologist came.

Sonya drove all of them back to Kastela.

"But that low white-cell count, Doctor, would that fit typhoid, too?"

"Yes, Madame. It is another one of the rare cases."

"Do you have much typhoid here?"

"I have never seen a case," Doctor Mestrovic confessed, and again that certain look entered his eyes.

On the long climb up to the fifth floor, Doctor Nijaz said, "And how do you like Yugoslavia, Madame?"

She gave him a completely honest answer.

"Yugoslavia," she said, "has disappeared."

They were outside the door, Sonya hunting for her key. When she put the key into the lock, from inside the room came a great, agonizing groan as if the doorkey had been thrust into his brain.

She ran to him, crying, "Tape! What's happened?"

"Been listenin' for you," he said. "So I could groan."

"Silly."

" 'M a tight-assed Swede. Won't waste groans. Hi, Captain, Mate. Glad to have you aboard."

There was a knock.

"I took the liberty of calling the Chief of the Army hospital," Doctor Nijaz explained. "It is very near here."

A short fat man entered. And instantly took command, by virtue of that something which certain doctors possess and other doctors, no matter what their knowledge, never possess.

Even Tape felt it.

192

"Didn't know this was a flagship," he said. "Who piped the Admiral aboard?"

"Your husband," smiled the new doctor, speaking English easily and lightly, "has humor."

"Sick humor," Tape said.

The admiral looked into Tape's mouth. "Stomatitis. Antibiotic reaction. Unimportant."

He flashed his light into Tape's eyes.

"Where do you hurt?"

"Headache. Can't stand light."

"Sorry. And where else, sir?"

"Nowhere else that matters, sir."

The admiral uncovered the stomach. Sonya flinched. And accused herself for not discovering it first, wondering with shame how long it had been that way, huge, swollen, distended. The admiral tapped it. Thud, thud. The hollow tympanic boom was almost like an echo.

"Ouch," Tape said, for the admiral was fingering his spleen.

Then the stethoscope on the chest.

"It's in the lungs, too; and of course the lining of the brain is affected, producing your headache."

"Euphemism," Tape said, winking at Sonya.

The admiral instructed the microbiologist to take blood, and verified that she had a specimen of the stool.

Then he said, "I think you are in luck, my friend. We shall look for the microbe, but I am almost sure it is typhoid."

"There are all kinds of luck, Admiral," Tape said, looking hard at Sonya. "Even death is relative. Get it?"

Then he closed his eyes and lost all interest in anything except clutching the head with the hand.

Sonya asked, "How long will the tests take to make sure?"

"Four days."

"But of course you'll start the treatment immediately. The chloromycin."

Doctor Nijaz was against that. "Until it is known for certain, we are not wise to pour more antibiotics into a body already poisoned by them. Let us wait for the tests."

193

Then he spoke in Serbo-Croat to the admiral, who said stiffly to Sonya, "It is only fair, Madame, to tell you that Doctor Nijaz is reminding me that it is against regulations for the Army hospital to accept civilian laboratory work. And that giving chloromycin now may affect our results."

Dr. Mestrovic said, consolingly, "Fortunately the heart goes well. It is a very excellent heart, Madame."

Sonya felt trapped in the world's stickiest bureaucracy, the scholastic one of Medicine.

Tape muttered, "Typhoid, huh? That's why it's unfinished."

The admiral bent over him. "What, sir, is unfinished?"

"The symphony. Typhoid finished Schubert before he finished the symphony. Great loss to the world. Pity . . ." Again he lapsed into somnolence.

Sonya said, "It is not his fault that it is so very late. Eight long days of this fever. Who knows how much longer he can fight?"

She had started her appeal to Mestrovic, to that certain look of guilt in his eyes, but she felt his weakness, and turned toward strength.

To the admiral she said, "Sir, I implore you to start the chloromycin now."

Nijaz said, "And if it is not typhoid?"

The admiral said, "Madame, my colleagues and I have agreed to start the treatment at once."

While Mestrovic was giving the first injection, the admiral took Sonya to the terrace.

"Your husband is dehydrated," he explained. "In shock. His body fluids are seriously low. We must get him to a hospital immediately. I suggest the Army hospital. It is closest, and more important, as Chief of Medicine there, I can get him admitted without delay."

"Would you be in charge of the case?"

"If you wish."

"With all my heart," she said.

"I shall call the ambulance."

194

Dr. Nijaz re-entered the case on another basis. Very officially, he said, ''Exactly how long has he been in Yugoslavia?''

''Three weeks.'' But she had forgotten to include the eight days of illness. They were real days, too; sick time was just as real as healthy time.

''Four weeks and one day.''

''The law requires an accurate report of what he has eaten and where. It is a serious matter of public health.''

''Of course. Tomorrow, I'll . . .''

''Immediately,'' snapped the doctor, drawing his pen.

The admiral was at the telephone. ''Not now,'' he said. ''Madame may write her report after we get to the hospital.''

Dr. Nijaz ungraciously yielded. It was not his day to win.

CHAPTER 18

~~~~~~~~~~~~~~~~~~~~~~~
~~~~~~~~~~~~~~~~~~~~~~~
~~~~~~~~~~~~~~~~~~~~~~~

This was the roughest sea yet, and the ship was pitching and tossing, yawing and rolling wildly. Maybe because it was going into harbor, crossing the bar. Sunset and evening star and all that crap.

Then everything got quiet and they were gliding along nice and smooth, nice and slow, which made Tape feel triumphantly correct in his analysis of the situation.

Movement came to a stop. They were docking, of course.

Will they let me walk ashore?

No, they carried him down the gangplank and he became terrified with the fear that they would drop his stretcher into the water with him in it.

He was in an elevator and Sonya was holding the hand that wasn't holding the head.

"Bougainvillaea," he said.

"What?"

"I didn't mean to say it until we got to Trieste, but it just popped out of me. Get it?"

It was night and he was in a bed with rubber under the sheet. Hot hard slippery rubber.

They were gouging his wrist. And jabbering in Japanese.

196

He said, "My name is Alberg. My serial number is eight eight nine five three and under the terms of the Geneva Agreement concerning prisoners of war that is all I am required to tell you."

Just like the war movies he said it. The admiral said, "He is reliving his war experiences, poor fellow."

Okay, let him think it. Who cared? Only a movie.

Sonya was holding the hand they were not gouging. He tried to pull it loose to put it on his head but did not have the pull to do so.

Sonya was bending over him, whispering.

"The doctors say I must leave the room for a few minutes," she whispered.

"Don't leave me," he whined, and she felt like thanking God for his wanting her to stay with him; all this hostility he had for her was so bad for his morale, and this was the first sign of . . .

But he spoiled it all by adding grumpily, "Alone with this goddamn language. It bugs me. Jesus, tell them to stop yapping."

"The foreign language upsets him," she said to the admiral. "May I stay?"

She was staying. His hand went back to his head. They were taping the needle buried in his other wrist.

He drank a bitter draught.

"This laudanum will stop his dysentery," the admiral was explaining.

The rubber tube ran from his wrist to a jar of liquid hanging on an iron rack.

No, two tubes and two jars. Twin carburetion, just like the Jag.

"Thought is brain and brain is cancer," he said.

"No, no," Sonya said. "Don't you remember? It's typhoid. The doctor just explained it to me. We didn't start the right treatment soon enough and . . . he says it's really in your intestines, but that two secondary areas are affected. Your lungs and your head. That's why your poor head aches so awfully but the real trouble, the center, is down here, in your abdomen."

197

Your drumlike belly, the skin at burst point. How well I understand the look in the other doctor's eyes. We speak the same language, the great common Esperanto of guilt. Oh, why did I quarrel, and in my egocentricity not see the sickness starting?

"Sleepy?" she asked.

"Cold." He started to shiver; his teeth took up the rhythm and then his entire body jerked and vibrated like an old jalopy out of time.

The doctors were leaving. The admiral told Sonya that the youngest one, the resident, would be in every two hours, to take pulse and temperature and check the heart.

He introduced her to the nurse, a leathery hunchback of middle age, almost a dwarf. Her name was Behka.

Behka pried Tape's chattering teeth apart and poured a thick pink soothing medicine over his tongue, which had changed from splotchy white to shocking red. There was no outer skin left.

Sonya saw the raw tongue and, frightened anew, ran down the corridor and caught the admiral.

"But what if he's allergic to the chloromycin, too?" she asked in terror.

"That would be most unusual, Madame."

"But if he is, what then?"

"There is no other antibiotic for typhoid. You must calm yourself and write the report I promised for you. List everything he has eaten the past four weeks. And the places, both towns and restaurants. It is most essential."

She returned to the room. It had an armchair, not very soft, and a footstool. The nurse made her sit down, feet on stool. She kicked off her shoes.

The nurse sat in a straight chair. She was so short, her feet dangled a full ten inches from the floor.

Sonya neither liked nor disliked her. She was just an object in the room.

Sonya watched the liquid bubble slowly in the jar as it ran into his veins.

The room was cold. Damp. Smell damp, like . . . new

198

plaster. She got up and felt the walls. They had given him a brand-new room and the plaster was not yet dry.

On account of the plaster smell she opened the window, but the night air was fresh and chilly, so she closed it.

Tape started to cough. A loose, gargly cough, from the very bottom of his lungs.

She ran to him.

"What's wrong?"

"Headache," he said, again coughing the frightening cough.

Oh, that hand. If that hand ever leaves that head . . . I'll do anything to make that hand leave that head. Anything.

She bent and kissed the hand on his head—his other hand lay flat, palm up, the tube running into the needle buried in the vein in his wrist.

"Darling," she said. "You're going to be all right very soon. You're getting the right medicine now. Very soon. Your suffering will soon be over, darling."

She kissed the hand again, and it twitched with irritation, dislike, distaste. She withdrew her defeated lips.

"Fair play," he said, and she shivered for all the times that she had . . .

He coughed again, a racking paroxysm this time, and Sonya became possessed with a new terror.

Pneumonia. This wet cold room has given him pneumonia.

She ran out into the corridor and found at its far end the head nurse.

But she could not make her understand anything.

"Me want doctor," she cried, in her desperation falling into pidgin English. "He sick. Need doctor quick. Where?"

Men's faces appeared in opened doorways—sick soldiers in striped flannel pajamas, old flannel robes; unshaven faces, haggard faces, primitives with ogling eyes, curious eyes, sick eyes. Someone laughed.

That enraged the head nurse, and she took it out on Sonya, imperiously ordering her back to the room.

And Sonya the Timid, who had run like a coward from the

incident of the leather coat, suddenly metamorphosed into Sonya the Bold.

"Shut up," she screamed at the nurse. "And let me by." She forced her way past the indignant woman. Ignoring the elevator, she ran down the four flights of stairs to the main floor and found the Chief's office.

The attendant there also refused to call the doctor for her, so she just stood and screamed until the young resident came running. She bullied him into taking her to the admiral, who was in the washroom preparing to go home.

"You've given him pneumonia, chills, a horrible cough," she cried accusingly. "That cold wet room. I did not give you my consent to put him in a room that would kill him. All that wet plaster. He must be moved immediately. Now."

"Please, Madame, calm yourself," the admiral said. "It is the only room available. The hospital is full. It is that room or nothing."

"Medicine should be above ideology," she argued, as if *that* were the issue. "Communist and capitalist must be treated alike, you hear. He will die of pneumonia. I demand that you move him to a warm dry room. Now."

"He has no pneumonia. It is a condition of typhoid. But I shall order an electric heater sent up."

"Bring it here and let *me* take it up," she said, trusting nobody any more.

It was a big old but efficient electric heater with three huge coils, and soon the room was warm.

His shivering stopped and he went to sleep.

To spare his eyes, Sonya turned out the night light, for the glare of the heater was adequate for any emergency.

She settled herself in the chair, feet on stool. The nurse was dozing in the corner.

Sonya did not try to sleep, or even relax, for she was reciting her new Creed:

I must stop screaming at the doctor.

I must trust him, and above all, the Chloromycin.

I must not expose Tape to one word of this language that

upsets him so; I must always be here and awake and let them relay all communications through me.

I solemnly swear never to leave this room until that hand of its own free will leaves that head.

I am all he has.

His antagonism to me is bad for his morale, his will-to . . . I must find ways to win back his . . . at least, his toleration of me. His bitterness must be dissolved, the anguish must be cleared out of his mind, leaving it free to fight for its . . .

Leaning back in the chair, growing drowsy in the now-warm room, she saw the matter clearly:

He does not love me any more and who can blame him for that?

I have lost his love—just what I wished would happen. No, not really. I merely wanted to gain his indifference, not his antipathy. If it were only indifference, there would be no real problem; he would fight the disease without the added poison of his feeling for me.

And yet I must stay by his side, no matter what he does or says. Even if he reaches a point where he orders me away, still I must stay.

For I am all he has. Such as I am. The worst is also the best.

The red coils of the heater at the foot of his bed cast a fiery glow against the ugly yellow wall. The liquid in the jar above his wrist gleamed, and the bubbles, rising delicately and slowly in the jar with each drip-drip-drip, moments apart, were like rubies.

He was in the Muir Woods near San Francisco. God's second oldest temple.

He said as much to Sonya, breaking the metaphysical silence in which they sat, on a fallen Great-Tree trunk. Adding, as he looked up in awe, "If Plato had seen these, he would have changed his theory that the Ideal Tree does not exist except in Mind; here, in the living bark, is his Highest Form of the Good."

"Somewhere up there, the sun is shining"—it was Sonya's voice, cathedralized into a whisper by all the grandeur of the soaring redwood columns around them—"but down here you'd never know it."

He remembered an old joke that had served many generations of fourth-grade boys: "It was quiet in the forest," he declaimed, like a Shakespearean actor of the old school, "not a leaf stirred, not a horse stirred."

"But it's too dark," Sonya said. "Much too dark for high noon."

She spoke in an odd, pseudo-cheerful, breathless way that started worries trickling through his body like cold water, setting up little patches of shivers, like tone-clusters, on his tremulant skin.

The worries seemed to be entering his body in a series of never-ending drips, at his wrist, his left wrist.

Drip-worry. Drip-worry. Drip-shiver.

The idea startled him and he groaned in fright.

"Don't worry," she whispered consolingly. "It's just low clouds."

He coughed, and that gave him the clue. "Not clouds, smoke," he gasped. "Let's get out of here. Fast."

Frantically, he looked around for the closest way out; then he realized it was a stupidity, for every schoolboy knows that when you are in the center of any forest, even the Muir Woods, you are halfway in and halfway out, so all the ways out are the same distance. Get it?

Then he saw, at what the fighter-pilots used to call three o'clock, a great red glow in the smudgy grayness. Worry escalated into terror.

"Run. Forest fire. Forest fire. Run."

Who's screaming? I'm screaming. But I shouldn't. Scream. Nobody has the right to scream *Fire* in a crowded forest.

He had seized Sonya's hand and they were running for their lives, coughing-choking-sweating-shivering-stumbling through the asphyxiating smoke, away from the flickering red glow.

"The Jag," he gasped. "We must get to the Jag." But where was it? Where had they parked it? Where?

Terror jetted into panic.

202

"It's over here," Sonya cried, dropping his hand and running to the left.

He had no choice but to follow her, for now he had completely lost his bearings. Only she knew the way to the Jag. Or did she know? Or was she just pretending to know?

Still, he had no choice but to follow her, and she did know, after all; and they were standing on the lovely little road winding like a forest path through the immense graceful trees that may be only second in size or age, but are certainly first in beauty.

Sonya was pointing, and then he saw the good old Jag, parked far down the road, waiting to rescue them.

"Follow me," he screamed, and he sprinted into the lead, running faster-than-he-had-ever-run-before.

But when he was no more than fifty yards from the car, a flaming redwood fell across it, and the poor Jag was squashed like a stink beetle. Then it too burst into flame. Great car. Great loss to the world. Pity.

Now that the road ahead was blocked by fire, there was nowhere else to go but back. He turned.

And Sonya had disappeared. Gone. Lost.

Back and forth across the road he ran, in and out of the forest, desperately searching for a glimpse of her orange dress, her glistening brown hair that exactly matched the skin of her face and shoulders, Saint Anne in the forest fire.

He tried to scream "Sonya, Sonya." He could hear the name rattling inside him, ripping and tearing at his lungs, but it would not emerge through his throat.

Darting this way and that, far from the road now, deep in the forest, soundlessly screaming "Sonya," he hunted for her madly, until he realized that he had lost not only her but also himself, for now he was completely surrounded by the redness, the entire forest was aflame.

Had she escaped? He hoped so, but it was too late for him.

Giving up, he muttered, "Done for, done for."

Then he saw that the flames around him did not form a complete circle; over there was one small dark patch of nonfire.

His only hope was to get through that square of blackness; he must give up the Sonya-search. He must believe that somehow she had escaped, gone to call on someone else perhaps, and now his only hope was *There* . . .

His panicked-animal scream woke Sonya, just as he was leaping across the foot of the bed.

The jar of liquid in its iron rack clattered to the floor and broke.

In the moment of paralysis before she reacted, he was at the window, throwing it open.

She lunged for his hips; he shook the tackler loose, and she slipped despairingly down his body, but she managed to get a firm clasp around his knees, and despite his frantic kicks was able to hold him until the nurse got there.

Like a monkey, the dwarfish, tenacious little creature stepped on Sonya's back, using it as a stair, and scurried up Tape. She seized his hair and pulled back his head and got one arm around his Adam's apple and throttled him mercilessly, until all three were in one tangle on the floor, all three screaming, two of them for help, the third to let him go.

Another nurse entered the hell, then the night doctor, then another nurse, and the five of them managed to carry him back to the bed.

He screamed, he raved, he sobbed and slavered. "Done for," he raged. "Done for. Goddamn all of you. I could have made it. Shit 'n died, shit 'n died." His voice moaned on, softer now, and more heartbreaking, "Shit 'n died. Done for. Shit 'n died. Done for."

When the overhead light was turned on, Sonya saw that the floor was covered with blood and broken glass and his wrist was pumping blood from the great gash where the needle had been torn from it.

Now the room was full of doctors and nurses. One doctor was burying the needle, this time in his right arm; another doctor was bandaging the torn left wrist; a nurse stood by with blood for a tranfusion. Other nurses were mopping up.

204

A doctor was saying in French to Sonya, "In the old days before Public Health Control, when typhoid was common, I have read that the rule in all hospitals was never to put them on an upper floor, because of the jumping from the windows. I learn much from this case, Madame, the first I have seen in my eleven years of practice."

He started the liquid in the jar on its slow, dripping journey. Into the other arm the blood transfusion was started. Now there was no hand left to press the head, so Sonya put a wet cloth there. The doctor ordered two nurses to stand on either side of him, to hold down his arms and shoulders throughout the night.

She stood at the foot of the bed and spoke brightly, to give him the assurance of hearing his own language.

"That was quite an adventure, darling," she said brightly. "But now it's over and all's well that ends well."

"Fire," he explained calmly. "Muir Woods. Campers probably. Too bad. It'll take over a thousand years to regrow that forest. A great loss to the world. Pity."

"You see? He is lucid already," the resident bragged. "So now we leave you, Madame."

"Those redwoods don't grow on trees you know," Tape said.

"Anything you want, darling?" she said briskly and cheerfully.

"Lights," he grunted, for light was the Fury which plagued his headache.

But the instant she turned them out, he panicked again, screaming *Fire* and fighting to get his arms back from the nurses, and only then did she understand everything had been caused by the glow of the electric heater.

I am all he has and I do all the wrong things.

Quickly she turned off the heater and switched on the night light.

Slowly his panic subsided and his arms stopped jerking, but the nurses, taking no chances, kept him pinned down.

Sonya stood at the foot of the bed and tried to say tranquilizing words.

"I love you," she said, adding truthfully, "and I am going to stay right here in this room, never once leaving you, and you must not be afraid. Does your wrist hurt awfully, darling?"

"Old Pal Nelly Finch is wrong," he answered.

"Nelly? Wrong how, darling?"

"Old Pal Nelly thinks money is power."

"What is, darling?"

"Rejection," he said. "Rejection is power"—and she understood there was a note of victory as well as discovery in that thin muttering voice.

He added sarcastically, "Blessed be the rejectors for they shall inherit the earth. And the rejected ain't gonna find their reward in heaven, either, 'cause there ain't no heaven. Hah!"

"Do you feel much pain in your stomach, darling?" she asked tenderly.

"Headache," he said.

CHAPTER 19

The night of the forest fire was Sunday night, and all through Monday the fever stayed high; the doctors who came to measure it every two hours kept trying to give her hope by pretending it was all in the day's work, to be expected.

The admiral himself was in and out of the room all day and his theological position was as pontifical, and unbelievable, as any Pope's: "It will drop because it must, Madame. Be patient. Have faith."

But she noticed that in the other sickrooms along the corridor the nurses, not the doctors, wielded the thermometers.

Between Tuesday's 6 A.M. and 8 A.M. reading the fever did drop, to 103—two frail degrees of hope—and at 10 A.M. it was a joyous 102, where it stayed till 4 P.M., when it rocketed back up to a sizzling 105 and stayed there, three full degrees of blackest despair.

Sonya began to doubt that it was typhoid. Three days of massive chloromycin injection and he was right back where he started from.

She left the floor for the first time since the incident of the electric heater, and descended to the admiral's office.

"Do you really believe it's typhoid?" she implored.

"No one can be positive until we find the microbe in his blood or in the stool. Until the tests have been completed, we can only continue with what we are doing."

She was studying his face, weighing his points. It was not a kindly face—are really good doctors ever *kind?*—but it was strong, it had authority *and* intelligence. An ugly face, loose and flapping, with a double chin. Small wise eyes.

She had heard him cursing at his staff, and had witnessed his contempt for other patients and their worried loved ones—to them he was maddeningly brief, uninformative, rude.

But not to her. And his attention to Tape was beyond criticism. Of course, the very rarity of typhoid these days was an attraction, still . . .

The admiral took her hand and patted it.

"You are forgetting his heart," he said. "I put all my confidence in his magnificent heart. What a machine! It remains so . . . professionally indifferent to the most severe demands. It is a hero in every crisis. Trust that heart, dear lady."

Wednesday came and no change. But the heart kept her courage strong, her spirit up; whenever she got scared, she would steal over and feel Tape's pulse, steady, strong, and unbelievably slow considering the fever, the wasting, burnt-out body it was trying to save.

Oh, if his mind could be as indifferent as his heart. But it was obsessed with the old rejections, and new bitter ways to even the score for them. Now, in his delirium, there was no trace of the love and adoration he'd once had for her.

By Wednesday night the heart's message could no longer console her, and she just sat there, staring at the hand. Tonight it was the right hand; they had switched the needle back to his left wrist.

There was a row of empty bottles along the wall. She counted them. Sixteen.

Would the hand ever leave the head? Of its own free will? Alive and no longer interested in the head, just wanting to be a free hand again?

Can hands, like minds, develop obsessions?

If I *knew* it was typhoid, I'd depend on the chloromycin, trust the heart, believe the doctor.

But if it is not typhoid? For why doesn't the fever drop, the headache disappear, the hand leave the head?

As hand with head, her mind became obsessed with the hand, and throughout that entire night, from its dusk to its dawn, she sat and watched it.

Now it did not even leave the head when the nurse came and with Sonya's help turned him over for his injection. This time, the left buttock, next time, the right one. Sonya kept a written record, so that he would not undergo the extra pain of having the injections two times running in the same spot.

It was a little thing, to save a little pain, but there were no big things left to do, just keep track of left and right; and watch the hand.

The drapes at the window were misbehaving.

It's just a design, knocked out by some half-assed artist like me, and printed by the mile on cheap white cloth, still . . .

Whoever heard of grapevines sprouting black roses, maiden-hair ferns, and flowering peach twigs? Also a Passion-for-Christ's-sake flower and a black sparrow with a lark's bill!

Vine by vine, leaf by leaf, Tape checked the left drape with the right—*they were the same*. Proving it's just the designer's arty license and not my . . . just patterns printed on cloth. I may be stupid but I'm not crazy, still. . . .

That black rose was *moving*. Paralyzed, he watched the ominous phenomenon. Slowly the petals became *ears,* then eyes and teeth, head and body of a saber-tooth tiger.

The monster roared. But sound is not an illusion, it's a vibration, and my ears are getting the message.

It's only a rose.

The monster snarled. Tape cowered. It leaped. Tape dodged. Missed by an inch. Close shave.

You'd think the authorities'd have more sense than to put a

jumpy pattern like that in a sickroom. Must tell the admiral to change it.

Ringa ringa rosa . . . Ringa ringa rosa . . .

The little bird on the peach twig was singing. A black canary. Great voice.

Aw, stop it, squarehead. It's just my good old hi-fi belting out the last scene of *Wozzeck*. That's a human canary.

Ko-ko. Ko-ko.

But the bird on the curtain was definitely singing it and how could a goddamn bird know Berg?

Not I, sang the Sparrow, but your trusty old hi-fi.

But if it was, I could see that kid in the opera too young to dig death hopping around the stage on his horsy stick.

That's too stupid, you can't *see* hi-fi.

The music, well, just stopped, and Tape tried to decide what to play next. Maybe the Concord Sonata. A great loss to the world, the old redwoods and the new Schnabel.

But what play next? One hour to live, what play?

I'm Tape, think I'll just play myself. Joke. Old-Nick type. Hey, wonder what happened to Old Nick? Miss him.

The canary started to swell up, bigger, bigger . . . Tape tried to turn his face away but couldn't. The bird's downy stinking breast pressed against his mouth, his nose, suffo—

Andrew-Andy-Swede-Tape-Dad Alberg shit 'n died.

The bird burst like a balloon with a feathery *phthoop*.

He spat out the feathers "Pta. Pta."

Somebody was pouring gunky medicine over his tongue. Sonya. After the feathers it tasted clean, like whipped cream flavored with mouthwash.

He opened his eyes. The canary was back on the twig, a harmless design.

I may be stupid but I'm not crazy.

The thought relieved him enormously, and he relaxed for the first time in time.

Must tell the admiral the therapeutic logic of solid-color draperies in hospital rooms. Like most philosophical problems, it's one dealing with the difference between Ying and Yang . . .

210

Ahhhhhhhhhhhhhhhhhh!

The grapevine in the center was *writhing*.

This was no saber-toothed racial memory, no impossibly bal-looning sparrow, this was real. Real!

Real. Like that summer night he'd gone fishing on Willow Crick where it runs into West Fork, a great place for blue channel catfish, sometimes called Nebraska trout, if you're in Nebraska, or Kansas trout, if you're across the line.

And good old Grandpa Alberg was wading in the riffles downstream, while Andrew decided to sit on the bank, his bait dropped where the currents of the two streams met.

Andrew had a carbide light, relic of Grandpa's first days in America as a Pennsylvania coal miner. He set it in the mud between his legs and enjoyed its beautiful squirt of blue-rimmed orange flame.

He stuck the bamboo pole into the mud of the bank and adjusted the light so it shone on the shiny red-and-white cork bobbing out there in the current.

This was happiness.

The firm gray mud felt delicious on his bare heels. It was hot back in Grandpa's house, but perfect here. The riffles around the bend made gurgling water-music. Even the carbide gas stank good in the still sweet air.

Andrew located the Big Dipper, and thus the North Star, and felt like Columbus or Henry the Navigator or sumpin'.

Then he began to smell a peculiar smell, the kind that makes you look around uneasily, especially in the dark. It was like wet gunnysacks in a cellarful of potatoes. That kind of smell.

And there, just below his widespread feet and exactly between them, was the white mouth open, the flicking fangs, as the cold-eyed cottonmouth stared at the carbide lamp between his legs.

Even then, ten years old, Andrew knew you must not jump, or even twitch. Or they'd strike. The trick was to knock the head away first and jump second.

The mind knew all about the trick, but the body didn't, and he jumped first.

The snake got him in the fleshy part of his left calf.

211

Screaming, he somehow made it—he never remembered this part—up the steep muddy bank and onto the dry dirt road.

Grandpa Alberg came and set his carbide light down in the road and opened his jackknife and sharpened it on a flat stone and held the blade-edge in the flame of the lamp and *slashed.*

Grandpa spit. And spit again. Suck-spit, suck-spit. Suck-spit.

The Reservation was across the road and an old Indian about a hundred years old heard all the screaming and came and looked; then he disappeared and showed up again and this time he had a shotgun shell cut open. He wanted Grandpa to sprinkle gunpowder all over the wound and then light it with a match. He said it was good medicine, but Grandpa just snorted something in Swedish as he picked up Andrew, slung him across his shoulders and started down the road at a steady dogtrot.

A three-mile dogtrot that never slowed down to a walk until they were in the doctor's house at Beaver Crossing.

Old Grandpa, usually so shy, so very timid, never even knocked at the doctor's front door; he just impolitely kicked it open and dogtrotted inside, Andrew on his shoulders.

Oh, the pain in my armpits then, the exact same pain in my head now, this same weird world where thought is pain, sound is pain, color, shape, movement, all is pain. . . .

The grapevine writhed again. Now it was crawling out of the flowers and ferns which partially concealed it, and its head appeared for the first time, its white mouth open, its wet, gunnysack smell crawling off the drape, its black sickening body slithering, tail slipping through the poppies, the ferns, raised head weaving, cold eyes glittering . . .

and no mistake in its intention or destination—it was coming toward the bed.

"Darling," Sonya was saying, "please put your feet down, darling. And you mustn't jerk your arm, or the needle will pull out again. You wouldn't like that, would you, darling? Don't tremble, darling. Sonya's here. This is Sonya. Put your feet down, darling. Turn the other way. Please, Tape. Please."

She tried to straighten out his knees and he screamed, "No. No. No, Grandpa. I can't. I can't. Don't, Grandpa, please."

212

"Why can't you, darling?"

"The snake."

"No snakes here, darling." She turned on the overhead light and pulled down the covers and patted the lower half of the bed all over. "See. Nothing here. See."

"Snake."

"Tape, darling. You must put down those feet. It's not good to press your knees so hard against your sore stomach. No snakes, darling, see."

"Not snakes. Snake. Get it?"

It took her almost an hour to convince him that it was all right to straighten out his legs.

They were trembling with dread, so she rubbed them hard with alcohol, and as her fingers felt the mouth-shaped, mouth-sized scar on his left calf, she said, "Your snakebite was a long time ago, darling, remember? When you were just a little boy, remember? Visiting your grandfather. You were just a little-bitty boy then, remember?"

"Grapevines," he sneered, "are not bougainvillaea vines, sister. Get it?"

"There," she said covering him. "Anything else, darling?"

"Light."

She turned it off. "Better?"

"Headache."

And again she took up the hopeless vigil of the hand. Really hopeless now, because for the first time in all the time there was no faith to fight the fear, and she believed without any *Ifs*, *Ands*, or *Buts* that he was dying.

Whether from typhoid or some Unknown Virus no longer mattered. For eight days she'd believed in terramycin; chloromycin had held her trust for four more days; she'd put her faith in the heart for one of those days, too; and still the same fever, the same hand on the same head—nothing had changed except his mind, which was completely gone now.

She forced her eyes away from the hand and looked at the bottles lined against the wall. Sixteen failures.

All the doctors, failures. Including the admiral. Let him

worship the heart that plods so dutifully at its job, almost ignoring the burning body, the swollen belly, the racked lungs, the inflamed brain, the paralyzed bowels, the shredding bladder clouding his fiery urine with bits of skin and tissue.

All have betrayed us, failed us. We have lost the battle. We are done for. Done for.

Us?

We?

Us! . . . We!

The pronouns were like exploding stars lighting up the dark tunnel of her despair; the impregnable fortress in which the I-am had lived so long in almost total isolation suddenly collapsed, its walls and tunnels annihilated.

The sickroom filled up with beauty and terror; the beauty of Us–We and the terror of death, more than dark death, the death of a parent, but incandescent Us–We death, the death of Us, We dying.

There is no death like the death of the mate, for when the mate dies, where is there to go after, and what to do after, and for why?

My mate is leaving us. We have lost the battle. We are done for, done for.

At leisure is the soul that gets a staggering blow; the width of life before it spreads without a thing to do.

Sonya went to him. His eyes were closed. He slept. She bent over and studied the hand closely; the fingertips spanned the forehead and were doing all the work, the palm did not even touch the head. In the declivities at the temples, the little finger on one side and the thumb on the other pressed, even in sleep, powerfully enough to turn the hot pink skin paper-white; the middle three fingers spread across the hairline, pressing equally hard.

It begs you give it work, but just the placing pins—or humblest patchwork children, do, to help its vacant hands.

Finger by finger, she wrested the hand away from the head; it struggled to return to the head, but she held it tightly with one

214

hand, and with her other she did the exact reverse of what his hand had been doing.

It begs you give it work—she let go of his hand. It returned to the head. Finding another hand there, it dropped on his chest; the fingers waggled like those of well-trained Yugoslav schoolchildren waving at tourists.

The width of life before it spread, without a thing to do.

The width of death.

Oh, you bitch, why didn't you think of doing this ten days ago, with *your* vacant hands, instead of calling him *darling* and reciting sad little poems to yourself, you phony, do you think you fooled him with those cheap, ugly *darlings?* And once you even lied the greatest lie: I love you. Shame, shame, saying a thing like that to a dying man. Shame on you, bitch.

He stirred, mumbled.

"Yes?" she whispered.

"Harder," he said.

Her fingertips pressed into his skull, as hard as she could.

"Harder," he said.

She put her back into the job.

"Good," he said.

Seven minutes past five. Morning light. The dwarfish nurse peered in, saw her standing there, and dragged over a chair, but Sonya prefered to stand; she could exert more fingertip pressure standing, with the weight of her body back of it.

"Mom feeds me," he muttered. "Get it? The law educates me. Get it?"

Until now, my love, my mate, I have tended you with a powerful sense of fear, duty, sympathy of course, and guilt. Perhaps I overplayed the role through guilt, refusing sleep, food, rejecting all personal comforts, fighting your case with all those doctors. Perhaps even my fasting was a form of self-denying pleasure, perhaps to balance the scale for what I have done to you, said to you, not done to you, not said to you; perhaps, even, for what I did, and did not do, to my mother.

But no longer, my love. Do you remember that holier-than-thou sermon on love, back in California? The Perfect Love, said

I the smug preacher, must transcend the Ego. And look who was talking: Madame Ego in person.

Forgive me, mate. I promise, humbly promise, there'll be no more definitions of love from me. Just love.

Just . . . love. Just . . . death. Death is always the price of love, but must we pay so *soon?*

He groaned and said, "Gotta pee."

She brought the urinal, and the hand returned to the head after its carefree vacation. The fiery agony of micturation began . . . ended. She held the urine up to the light to see if the urine was less cloudy. No change. She put the bottle outside for the laboratory.

Then she replaced his hand with her hand.

"I love you," she said. "Tall boy, sick boy, I love you."

"Especially physically," he mumbled.

Too late. He couldn't believe her now. Too late.

When morning comes, I'll go to Split and phone Laney. Oh, if she can only get here in time for him to die in touch with love.

Not moving, for fear of lessening the pressure on his skull; not talking, for fear of antagonizing him, she stood there until seven-thirty, when the admiral came on his regular morning round.

The admiral bade her a cheerful good morning. She was indifferent; he was now to her like an employee you have decided to fire. Only, in this case, death was the employer who would hand the admiral his pink slip, regretfully informing him that his services would no longer be required.

So, with her mind on the phone call to Laney, she stepped back to permit the examination. Tape's hand went instantly back to his head.

"Now there's a heart," bragged the doctor, as if he personally had fathered it. "Are you awake, sir?"

"Headache," Tape said.

The doctor, feeling the spleen, said, "It's a beautiful morning. In my opinion, June is our best month in Split. You really must get out of this room and enjoy it, Madame."

Is this a trick to get rid of me, or is he really such a fool? Can he not recognize death's hand on death's head? Can he not see death's stare glazing the ceiling, or hear death's mouth sigh "Headache"?

"You may or may not know it, sir," the doctor said jovially to the patient, "but there are thirty-eight different types of typhoid. And you, my friend, have managed to catch the worst one of all. Congratulations."

Sonya came alive.

"You have the tests?"

"Yes. Beyond all doubt. Happily, it is only typhoid."

"Then why doesn't the chloromycin work? The fever has not changed all night. It's still one hundred and five."

"The chloromycin works, Madame. You are impatient. Soon we shall see the results. I guarantee it."

He patted her cheek, for she was crying. He led her out into the corridor.

"I think I can tell you now," the admiral said, "that your husband has been very sick. Too many days passed before the treatment was started. The terramycin reaction was . . . almost devastating. But now . . . you may stop your worries. Your devotion to your husband is beyond all belief—I have never seen its equal—but now the danger is over, so please go to your hotel. Sleep. Eat. Rest. Your face is still surpassingly beautiful, Madame, but it has on it the look of death. Beautiful death, I might say, but . . . life is better. Promise me you will go to the hotel at once."

"Not until his fever drops," Sonya said stubbornly. "When that happens, I promise you I will go."

And drop it did, that same afternoon. All the way down to 102.

Tensely, her hand on his head, she stood watch through the evening, for the fever had betrayed her once, but at eight o'clock, it was a glorious 101.

At midnight, it was 100.

Testing the hand, she left him and sat in her chair. The hand went to the head.

"Now you must go," the night doctor implored. "I have orders from the Chief to that effect."

"I'm going," Sonya lied. "In just a few minutes."

But she had no intention of leaving until that hand left that head. She decided not to hold the head with her hand, for there would be no way of telling.

At midnight, they removed the needle from the wrist and carried the rack which held the jar of fluid out of the room.

The sight of that departing contraption brought tears to her eyes.

At two, she helped the nurse turn him over for the injection, and when they put him on his back again, the hand did not return to the head.

But seeing was not believing. Perhaps he slept too deeply that moment . . . it just could not be.

With clenched fists and bitten lips, she kept intense watch on the limp hand, lying at his side.

Ten minutes, twenty minutes, a half-hour it stayed there, never once in all that immense stretch of time touching the head.

At three o'clock, she was convinced the miracle had actually happened, and she went to him and touched his forehead gently with her fingertips.

"How's the headache, sweetheart?" she whispered.

Tape turned his head and stared into her face . . . Sweetheart! She said sweetheart! My name for her.

It was beautiful hearing it from her lips. Beautiful.

"Headache?" he said weakly. "Why, it's o . . . kay."

Don't be foolish, don't be fooled. Her sweetheart is fifty per cent sympathy and the rest pity. Nothing else. *Nothing*.

He closed his eyes and saw the orange dress among the purple bougainvillaea, he heard her strange metallic voice saying "I suggest we go to Trieste . . . and part there."

Someone else.

"Yes, sweetheart?" she prompted, bending closer.

Fretfully he turned away.

"Hungry," he grumbled.

There was cornstarch pudding waiting for that miracle to happen and she spoonfed him joyously.

218

"This is the first food you've had since that soup back in the hotel," she complimented. "More than a week ago."

"Is it?"

He was almost asleep. She bent over him and whispered, "While you're sleeping I'll go back to Kastela and change these filthy clothes. Also, I'm going to write Laney, telling her you were very sick, but getting better now. Anything you want me to say to her?"

"No," he said.

CHAPTER 20

~~~~~~~~~~~~~~~~~~~~~~~~
~~~~~~~~~~~~~~~~~~~~~~~~
~~~~~~~~~~~~~~~~~~~~~~~~

The Herr Direktor himself was on night service, for some reason of no importance to Sonya, and he handed over her key without a glance.

She enjoyed his indifference, indeed was grateful to the hotel for its attitude toward clients; nobody, not even the old man, had bothered to inquire or comment; she was sure her many days of absence had never even been noticed. It was lovely to be ignored so completely.

Climbing the marble stairs made her realize how tired she was.

She bathed; she washed her hair; she put her dirty clothing to soak in the bidet.

And all the while, during these small chores, her mind sang small grateful hymns:

There was a hymn of Thanksgiving, for the survival of her mate . . .

And one to his hunger, sweet, precious hunger.

No more needles, no more headache, no more fever, her mind sang, as, in the crisp, sensuous luxury of a fresh nightgown, she climbed into bed.

But there was no sleep in her euphoria. An important some-

220

thing needed doing. Oh, yes, the letter to Laney. She got materials and wrote:

Dearest Laney,
Your father has been sick but is getting better and there's absolutely no danger, so please don't worry. It was typhoid and there was a lot of fever and so on; he got sick about two weeks ago, but I didn't write until I was able to tell you he is on the mend. Now please don't worry, Laney dear, it is all over, except of course for a longish period of convalescence. Typhoid plus an antibiotic reaction left his digestive system raw and tender, but it is nothing that proper diet and good care won't completely cure.
By the way, I am writing only to you, in case you wish to tell anybody else.
I promise you cross-my-heart that I shall take the best of care of your dad, Laney.
I'll keep you informed of course. Say hello to Bark for both of us.

Sonya went into a ten-minute sweat in search of exactly the right word to end on, finally choosing

Affectionately,
Sonya

She still was not in the slightest sleepy, so she went out on the terrace. A gibbous moon glorified the Adriatic and she sat down to enjoy it, feet on rail, considering the new world in which she now lived, the world of the Present Tense.

In the prime of his health and strength, he could not drag me out of the Past into the Present, though how very hard he tried and how doggedly he kept trying, but in sickness he succeeded where in health he had failed, and if my love was caused by that then I regret the typhoid but I welcome the irony.

Did I omit anything important in Laney's letter? Don't think so.

I must also write Togo—there's something about money and rich wives—buttering him up and . . . don't forget to tell him to keep our brush cherries watered.

221

Also Nelly Finch—whatever made Tape so bitter about his old pal Nelly?

And Katie-from-Chicago. And of course the Mayor. And . . .

This is the very first time I have ever bothered with his business. I like it . . . Wait! Great idea. We must start that partnership he suggested. Tape and Sonya Alberg, *décors* both exterior and interior.

And how arrogantly I rejected the same idea the night he . . .

She lit a cigarette and looked at the moon and somberly considered the dark side of the case:

Rejection. Now his of me, as once mine was of him.

She tried to find comfort and hope in his delirium.

He paid me back for all the shameful, rejecting things I said and did, including plenty right here in this hotel room—and who can blame him for that? Turn about. Another irony, most unwelcome.

But he has so obviously and sincerely adored me in my most loveless times—surely he will see, now that he is rational again, that my love for him is authentic, real. Not like the past. Oh, no, for the first time in time I am truly his mate. When he understands that, surely he'll . . .

If he understands that.

Don't say *if*. I must not doubt, as I for no reason doubted the chloromycin.

She went inside and took the Nembutal the doctor had given her, got into bed, and started a letter to Jack Hoover, figuring that a news item about Tape's illness would explain his absence to various prospects and clients until she got a chance to write each one separately.

But she had hardly finished the first sentence when:

Germans in full splash and cry outside; she looked at her watch. She had slept only two hours.

A young girl shrieked, a young boy laughed.

Yes, I who was not a mate have become one. And when your mate has children, it's always a problem, gloss it though we try. But if you are really his mate, you find some way of solving it to everybody's satisfaction, theirs, his, and mine.

222

Feeling she had just won another important victory, she tried to sleep some more, but she found herself hating sleep, because it would black out the happy knowledge that his fever no longer burned, his head no longer ached. But she realized how much she needed rest, so she settled down again and tried hard, but just could not drift off.

Lonesome.

The room was so lonely.

She got up and looked at his clothes, hanging in the closet. She collected his dirty underwear and socks, and washed them in the basin.

Lonesome.

And back at the hospital, those nurses would be spouting Serbo-Croatian all over the place, terrifying him; and he would be suffering bladder pains because he hated asking anyone but her for the urinal, and . . .

She went to the mirror and carefully made herself as glamorous as possible, lips, eyes, hair. She put on her finest underthings, her prettiest dress, as if for a celebration, or a date. Then, spraying herself liberally with Diorissimo—his favorite scent—she left for the hospital, his gift of cashmere from I. Magnin draped elegantly over her shoulders.

Lonesome.

In the hospital lobby, Doctor Nijaz, who was, as Sonya had already discovered, the Public Health Official of Split, stood talking with the admiral.

"Madame," the admiral said, "we have found the lair of the monster."

Doctor Nijaz referred to a paper in his hand. Handwritten in French. Sonya saw that it was the report she had prepared on all the places they had eaten since arriving in Yugoslavia.

"On April twenty," he said, "when you were in Sveti Stefan, you visited Bar and your husband ate a luncheon composed of oysters, bread, butter, wine, olives, fried red mullet, rice and fruit. Correct, Madame?"

"I'm almost sure," she said.

223

"And he first developed fever on May three."

"It takes the typhoid microbe twelve to fifteen days to strike," the admiral interposed. "We have traced the disease to the oysters he ate that day. It is a shoddy story, Madame. In that area there are still some religious superstitionists. Mostly old people, fortunately, so we shall soon be rid of them. And on one of their holy days, they are forbidden by their priests to eat anything but shellfish. Since there are never enough shellfish to supply this ridiculous demand, this year a band of unscrupulous fishermen began to collect oysters some weeks before the holy day. They were gathered in clean waters, but stored in nets submerged in the polluted water of the port. Your unfortunate husband, Madame, ate some of those oysters. Since it was some days before the . . ."

"Exactly nine days before the so-called holy day," Doctor Nijaz said, checking his report.

"So your husband had the honor of being the first victim."

"There are other cases?" asked Sonya.

"Seventy-three so far," the admiral reported. "Ten days ago, here in Split, our best doctors could not recognize typhoid. Down there in Bar today, any scrubwoman can diagnose it at one hundred meters. *Experienta docet,* Madame."

"Your husband will be avenged," Doctor Nijaz guaranteed in his earnest French. "Those capi— . . . those fascist fishermen will pay for this crime against the People."

"Please excuse me," she said. "I've been away from my husband far too long."

She ran up the stairs and entered the room, all dressed up and ready to . . .

When she bent over to kiss him, he turned pale, gagged, and broke out into a sweat.

It was the Diorissimo. And it was one way of learning that extreme hypersensitivity to strong odors is one of the temporary side effects of typhoid.

224

CHAPTER 21

~~~~~~~~~~~~~~~~~~~~
~~~~~~~~~~~~~~~~~~~~
~~~~~~~~~~~~~~~~~~~~

"Hi, Dad."

He opened his eyes and there was Laney, standing at the foot of his bed. He started to say "Hon—" then stopped. This was ridiculous. Impos—

"Hi, Dad," she chirped. She had a paper in her hand.

"Oh, stop it," he said. "Whatever you are, you're *not* Laney. I may be crazy but I'm not stupid."

"Really, Dad, I mean really," she said, smiling deliciously. "Who else could I be?"

"Oh, stop it," he was determined to resist her irresistible charm. "You are not Laney."

"But I brought proof," she persisted. "Look."

She held up the paper in her hand. The room was very dark, but he could see the Gothic printing on the paper as clearly as he could see Laney's dancing green eyes, flecked with honey-brown.

"I call you Honey, 'cause you got honey in your eyes."

The paper was some sort of document, with a red-wax seal trailing red ribbons, and he read:

<div align="center">

The Bearer is hereby certified to be

LANEY ALBERG

In proof hereof I set this seal.

</div>

It was signed, too, by a Sherman G Somebody.

"See, Dad," Laney said. "I came all this way just to tell you that I love you, as if you didn't know that."

She giggled Laney's irresistible giggle.

Resorting to cunning, he lied. "I can't read it. Too far away. Bring it closer."

"Oh, Dad," she protested. "You're such a pooklebrain, really. You know."

But obligingly she brought the document closer, moving teasingly up from the foot of the bed until . . .

Like a cat for a mouse, he grabbed for it, and his hand *passed right through* her arm *and* the paper.

And she disappeared, leaving not a single trace.

Tape became alarmed, not of the charming figment who had proclaimed herself Laney, but of whatever it was that had manufactured her in a mind cruising coolly along at a normal 98.8 degrees Fahrenheit.

The snake crawling off the drape had been delirium, but this was a colder turkey, hallucination, and there could be no other explanation, except . . .

Brain damage.

Half a brain for half a Hamlet.

Now there was a motorcycle wheel down there in the darkness. And two gloved hands gripping the gleaming chrome handlebars.

"Who's there?" Tape called. "Who is it?"

And of all people, Stan answered. "It's me, Dad. Good to see ya', man."

But no, the voice was too friendly for Stan. Tape said, "Oh, yeah? You're not *my* Stan."

"I sure am, Dad. I heard you got real sick, so I thought I'd gross you by hopping on my new bike and . . ."

"I can't see anything but your hands. Come closer."

"Take it easy, Dad."

"Stop calling me Dad. Whoever you are, you're too friendly to be *my* Stan. He doesn't like me."

"Aw, Dad, I like you. A lot. I was just kiddin', back there at school. That was just teen-age unsecurity. Honest."

"If you're Stan, let me see you. Come closer."

The wheel obligingly rolled closer, closer. Tape flailed out at the handlebars. His hand struck nothing but nothing.

The motorcycle melted, and he snarled bitterly, "The wish is father to the son."

"What?" Sonya said, waking up and sitting up. "What did you say?"

She was bending over him.

"Brain damage," he explained. "Those goddamned typhoid germs performed a frontal lobotomy on me."

"Your brain is perfect," she argued. "Don't you remember the admiral said you'd be disoriented for a few days?"

"I'm not disoriented, I'm dislocated. Not from the Present, like you, but from the Future. The order of tomorrow is scrambled brains without the eggs."

"But I'm no longer dislocated from the Present. Can't you see how much I love you, silly boy?"

But he could not accept that, no sir, and craftily he changed the subject.

"Not silly, crazy," he said. "Craziness is power, too. The roost is ruled by nuts like Nelly who puts Epsom salts in her swimming pool."

"The admiral expects you to be in the all-clear by tomorrow," Sonya encouraged. "And did I tell you, I wrote Nelly. And the Mayor. And Katie. To say you'll be back on the job soon."

For some reason this made Tape furious, and he shouted, "Why didn't you ask me first? To hell with that Epsom-salts queen."

Rejected, Sonya returned to her chair.

"Hi, Dad." It was Laney again, floating off the drape and waving her birth certificate.

"Brain damage," he muttered glumly, pulling the sheet over his head.

"What?" It was Sonya again, bending over him.

He decided to give her a riddle to chaw on.

"The Maize Goddess tends the bougainvillaea vine," he said enigmatically, "so who kicked the tail off the Tang horse?"

227

The next great event in Tape's life was hunger. Hunger was a new law that had been passed by the admiral and it sure as hell was being rigidly enforced by his trusty policewoman, Sonya, who had more interest in pouring salt into him, which he didn't want, than applesauce, which he definitely did want.

At first, they only permitted him rice gruel, applesauce, and cornstarch pudding, none of which so much as dented his ravenous appetite.

Then, as the days of starvation crept by, they added egg white, and sheep brain, and finally, breast of boiled chicken, all of which satisfied her and pleased the admiral, but not him.

Between meals, when he begged and sometimes even cried for food, the policewoman gave him camomile tea.

The admiral said, "They are all that way. When you get him home, Madame, you must lock the food box."

When who gets home? Tape thought but did not say, as his mouth was full of sheep brain at the time.

But the next great event in Sonya's life had not yet happened. She was waiting, not very patiently, for the first bowel movement. There had been nothing since laudanum had stopped the dysentery that first day in the hospital, and now it was all-important for the system to start back to work again.

"All these days and all that food and still no results," she complained to the admiral. "What are we going to do?"

"Nothing, Madame. Except wait another day and see."

"And then?"

"As the last resort, an enema."

But the urge possessed Tape that very night. Excitedly, Sonya ran to the nurse and asked for a bedpan, the name of which she had with foresight learned in Serbo-Croat, in anticipation of the great event.

But Tape wouldn't even try with the nurse in the room, so Sonya sent her out, helped him onto the bedpan and made him as comfortable as she could.

She found herself watching intently, eagerly, for the first sign.

228

"Try," she urged, cheering him on. "Try harder, sweetheart."

Like a baby he was. A suffering little baby. The longest tallest little baby in the whole world.

At last, success!

A pale-blond babylike stool emerged, the most beautiful little thing Sonya had ever seen.

More than success, triumph!

Proud of her man, she washed him with warm water.

"Ouch," he groaned. "Tender."

"Inside, you're nothing but yards and yards of tenderness," she said tenderly. "Good boy."

Proudly she bore the specimen to the laboratory, where she and the pathologist admired it together.

"And no enema," the pathologist marveled. "Now, there's a digestive tract. First class."

"Thank you," Sonya accepted the compliment as modestly as she could under the happy circumstances.

She hurried back to reward the Good Boy responsible with a first-class bath and massage.

During it, he noticed for the first time his emaciated body.

"Christ and Calvin," he exclaimed. "I'm less than half here."

More than once, Sonya had been reminded of those pitiful concentration-camp photos; Tape's great knobby knees were twice the circumference of his thighs, his ribs like a mountain over the valley of his abdomen, his arms mere birch sticks, and his neck-skin hung in wattles.

Thoughtfully he added, "I wouldn't be here at all if it weren't for you."

"But you're getting better by the hour," she cried happily. "And for dinner you're getting *half* a breast of a *whole* chicken."

The memorable day he was permitted to stand, Behka brought a scale. He'd lost forty-two pounds. Five minutes in the chair exhausted him, and Sonya helped him back into bed.

Later, when she was bathing him, she said, "It won't be long now—California is getting closer and closer."

And he actually *smiled*. Smiled and said, "I hope that lazy bastard Togo is tending to those brush cherries" . . . and she smiled back in joy at the beautiful event, but suddenly his face clouded and she was smiling into his frown.

He was wondering how she was explaining all this delay to . . . someone else.

Next day the Get-well-quick messages started to come in, from Jack Hoover, and Nelly Finch, and Katie-from-Chicago. And the day after, the Mayor cabled not to fret about unfinished business.

Tape accepted one and all with complete indifference, whether due to his weakened condition or to something more permanent Sonya could not tell.

In his apathy he seemed to be rejecting everything: his wife, his business, and his interest in life.

There was nothing to do but nurse him and hope for a change.

CHAPTER 22

The admiral called her to his office. "Putnik, the Tourist Bureau in Split, wants you," he said. "Something about your visa."

"Oh, it's expired," she said. "I've been intending to renew it, but . . . you've been so wonderfully hospitable, dear doctor, that I'd forgotten all about the perils of bureaucracy."

"Medicine has nothing to do with politics," he said graciously. He wrote a note which he gave to her. "They are demons of correctness, but this should quiet them. I am saying your husband will be able to travel in ten days' time."

Putnik provided Sonya with some money she had ordered by cable, and a girl interpreter, who escorted her to one office, for a form, and to another, for two forms, and finally to the police station.

On the way there, they met Petar, crossing a street. He needed a shave and his stubble was grizzly gray. The poor thing was getting old.

Their eyes met but neither spoke. Shhh.

A man in uniform heard her case, looked at the accumulation of papers, studied their passports, and sent for a file, which he opened and studied carefully.

Sonya instructed the interpreter to show him the doctor's note.

The man read it and made a telephone call. It was, at least from this end, an angry argumentative conversation.

He spoke to the interpreter, who said, "Your visas will be extended until forty-eight hours from this time; you must be across the frontier day after tomorrow at noon."

"But the doctor says my husband is still too weak to travel; the doctor himself asked for a ten-day extension."

The official was writing something on another form, and he wouldn't even permit the interpreter to finish; he stamped the paper, tossed the original on the desk in front of Sonya, opened the folder and put the carbon in it.

Sonya, angrily deciding they couldn't do that to her sick husband, was just getting ready to unleash her secret weapon, an insult in Russian, when two post cards slid out of the folder in the official's hands. One of the cards was message-side-up and she saw the signature on it:

Old Nick.

Frightened, she clammed up and picked up the forty-eight-hour visa and was relieved to be out in the street again, breathing the fresh, frightening air.

If they can do this to me, what do they do to their own people?

Old Nick wasn't funny here; later, across the border, he might be, but not here.

She thanked the interpreter, said goodbye, and drove to the hospital. It was just past noon, and they were 270 miles from Trieste, over slowish roads. Better avoid night driving and let Tape spend one more night at the hospital, leaving early tomorrow morning.

The admiral would be furious, of course, at having his orders countermanded. Probably he'd call the police and give them unholy . . .

She stopped at his office to discuss the problem. But even if he insisted on Tape's staying, she was by now determined to get him out of here. Unless of course . . .

232

Through the open door she could see the admiral at his desk. He was talking to a man in uniform. She waved at him, but he didn't wave back, although he definitely saw her.

She sat down. The buzzer buzzed, the assistant went into the doctor's office, then came out, this time closing the door behind her.

"The doctor says to wait, please."

The man in uniform left. Sonya rose and waited to be admitted, but nothing happened, so she sat down again.

In ten or fifteen minutes, the young resident came in, his hands full of various small packages and papers.

"You are checking out now," he said to Sonya.

"No. I plan to let my husband stay here one more night, and leave tomorrow, unless the Chief rules otherwise."

"No," he said. "That room is not available. You must check out now, please."

"But the Chief . . . may I see him?"

"I am afraid that is not possible, Madame. But he has instructed me to give you these."

He busied himself with the stuff in his hands, never once glancing at her, just like . . . another room clerk.

"These are suppositories, in case the anal fissions recur on the journey to Trieste. And these are more of the same pills he now takes. And here is the dietary regime. That is most important of all, please. Follow it carefully for at least four months. And here is your bill. Pay the cashier in the next office, please."

"May I see the Chief for just one moment to thank him for his . . . humanity and his skill?"

"I am afraid it is not possible, Madame."

Poor admiral. Old Nick's post cards had reduced him to a common sailor.

"I understand perfectly," she said.

Like it or not, they were getting kicked out, of both country and hospital. Since their things were still at Kastela, she decided the best plan would be to stay in the hotel for one last night of rest before making the forced journey.

I must not, I dare not, ask myself whether or not he is strong enough to make the trip, there is no other choice.

She went to the room and told Tape the plan, with no details whatever. Old Nick's story would have to wait until Trieste. She pretended the admiral had suddenly decided he was well enough to travel.

Tape of course was delighted; he'd been wheedling to get out for days, mainly to escape from his *bête noir,* the slippery rubber mat under his sheet.

Quickly she dressed him and helped him down the elevator and into the car.

How frail and *breakable* he looked, so thin he seemed nine feet tall.

She bedded him down in the back seat and drove cautiously to Kastela.

She sat him down in the lobby and went to the desk for the key. The old man was there, but he never looked at her or spoke, these days, not daring to risk even one peace-loving glance at such a dangerous warmonger as Old Nick's wife.

He handed her a cable.

She went out on the terrace, crowded with beer-drinkers, and picked the two most athletic young Germans there.

After the language had been agreed on, she said, "My husband is just out of the hospital, and our room is on the fifth floor, could you . . . ?"

They leapt toward the task and, cradling Tape in cleverly crisscrossed arms, bore him gently up the marble staircase, joking for the first three flights, panting the last two, and stood him up at his doorstep.

Our doorstep.

It could have been their own front door in Pobrecito, so intense was her joy, joy pushed so far it became almost a pain, the deep, clear, passionate joy of bringing her mate home *alive.*

Unlocking the door, she exclaimed, "Oh, I wish I'd had time to fill this room with flowers to welcome you back. Full, full, full of them, a wild celebration of flowers."

234

"Oh, that's all right," he said, entering. "Isn't this the same old room?"

"Of course. I never checked out. You must get right into bed."

"Yeah. I am a little tired, at that."

He sat on the bed and she knelt and removed his shoes and socks, thinking of the dreadful night he had fallen at this very spot, sobbing, "Done for. Done for!"

No tears, please. Not even tears of joy, please.

He was testing the floor with his bare foot.

"Same old room, same old sand," he said.

She helped him into pajamas and settled him in bed.

"No rubber sheet feels great," he said.

"There you are," she said. "Welcome home, sweetheart."

He closed his eyes and sighed.

"Would you mind not calling me sweetheart?" he said mildly, in his high, weak voice.

She went into the bathroom and washed the tears from her eyes.

Whatever he says, however I feel, no matter how it finally turns out, *I must get him home first.*

She pulled herself together and returned to the room. "Oh, I forgot the cable," she said.

It was from Laney. She read it aloud:

SHOCKED ABOUT DAD BUT TRUST YOUR REPORT THANKS SONYA
KNOW HES IN GOOD HANDS HEY DAD BARK WANTS WEDDING
THIS JULY FIRST DO YOU MIND CAN YOU COME LOVEYA GWQ
LANEY

"Isn't that wonderful news?" Sonya said. "I know you approve of Bark, and I'm sure you're very pleased."

"Yeah. Bark's a first-class boy."

"And a lucky one, to get a girl like Laney. I must shop in Trieste for a wedding present. And ship it from there, too. It'll be more impressive, coming direct from Europe, and . . ."

Sonya was struck with a really great idea, so really wonderful

235

that omnipresent problems were forgotten or at least ignored in present enthusiasm.

"Wait! Yes! I know exactly what we're going to send her."

She rummaged in her bag and brought out Madame Pompadour's jewel box.

"This."

"Oh, don't do that," Tape said. "It's too . . . priceless."

"It's exactly priceless enough for Laney"—she was very excited—"I'll put a note inside and send it immediately."

"But it's an heirloom, Sonya. From your mother. Calm down. It's too much."

But she was already writing the note:

Love and happiness to a wonderful couple, from
Sonya

She took the note to Tape.

"Write *and Dad* after my name," she ordered.

He pushed the pen away. "No. If you want to send it, from you, go ahead. It sure is a royal gift. And Laney will treasure it all her life. But if you don't mind I'd rather send something on my own."

Sonya put the note inside the box, locked it, and tied the key to one of its legs.

"I'll take it down to the porter right now and have him build a shipping case for it, and . . ."

Tape said, almost smiling, "Where do you think you are—the Paris Ritz, or maybe Claridge's in London?"

She hadn't thought of that.

"They order these things better in Italy," she said, recovering her good sense. "I'll get it cased and shipped in Trieste."

It was a disheartening anticlimax, putting the jewel box back into her valise, but she had no choice.

"You know how I am," she said. "When I get enthusiastic about doing something, I just hate to put it off."

But he was so engrossed in Laney's cable he didn't even hear

236

her, so she walked out on the terrace and looked at the sea, quiet as a millpond.

And asked herself a ruthless question:

Why am I sending that jewel box to Laney? Is it . . . something I must get rid of, on account of . . . ?

With a sturdiness that surprised her, and yes, pleased her, too, she confronted the question squarely, and . . .

All I see is Laney's face, her astonished, innocent child's face, unwrapping the surprise.

Are you sure? Then prove it. Say his name.

Werner. Werner Grunwald. Whom I once loved and who is dead and therefore a part of the ever-receding past.

Werner. Yes, Werner. *And who is Werner?*

Werner *was* the flute across the pond. Whispering me. Turning me toward memory. Fixing me entranced in its hypnotic melody.

You must be *sure*. Listen, listen. *Do you hear it now?*

Sonya listened.

The flute was silent. Its song had ended.

She re-entered the room. Tape put down Laney's cable.

"She said it exactly right," he said. "I certainly was in good hands. The admiral told me he'd never seen such nursing care as you gave me. I'll remember it with gratitude to my dying day. I want you to know how much I appreciate it, Sonya, how you took care of me. Now that I'm better, I understand how wonderful *you* were, and how difficult *I* was. I guess I'll keep on remembering it, more and more, as time goes by."

The speech, for all its sincerity, was so formal as to be embarrassing, and she countered with mock sternness:

"You're making this case sound finished, and I got news for you, Tall Boy. It's not. We've months of nursing ahead of us, when we get home. And we're not dawdling on the way there, either. Restaurant food is not for you. The minute we reach Trieste, I'm making our plane reservation."

He looked at the wall, cleared his throat, and said, "Oh, there's no need for you to go all the way to California with me.

After Trieste, I'll just go on by myself. I'm plenty okay to travel alone, really. But thanks anyway."

For days, she had been avoiding a confrontation, preferring later to sooner, as she didn't want to burden him with any extra tension.

But if I let this pass, he'll assume that I am accepting it.

Carefully, very carefully, she said, "Tape, I'm going home with you for, oh, lots of reasons. So, please, no more nonsense."

"Nonsense? Personally, I see no reason for changing the original plan."

"Exactly what original plan are you talking about, swee— darling?"

"Yours. Who else's? The Trieste plan."

"My Trieste plan? We simply decided to go there instead of Plitvice in order to get out of this awful country as fast as possible. Nothing else."

"Come now, Sonya. How can you say that after what you said, right here in this room, that morning I got sick? Typhoid didn't change anything, just postponed it, that's all. So let's not be . . . sentimental."

"Said what right in this room?"

"Oh, stop playing games," he said. "You told me that you were through because there was . . . someone else. You said we'd go to Trieste together, and part there. I accepted it then, and I accept it now. You needn't play nurse any longer. Except for driving me to Trieste, where we'll do as you planned. Of course."

"But Tape! I didn't say any such thing. Ever!"

"You've always compared my mind to a tape recorder," he said. "So let's just switch on the Playback, to refresh your memory. That morning, I didn't feel up to driving into Split to get the brakes fixed, remember? So you said you'd do it. You were wearing that gray canvas skirt and Madras blouse for the trip, and you went into the bathroom to change. I especially remember the dress you changed into, the orange one, because it was so bright it hurt my eyes. And then you walked over to the terrace, and stood in the doorway under the bougainvillaea, which also was so bright and purple it hurt my eyes, and you said, 'I'm sorry Tape, but I must leave you.' ''

"Wait a minute," she cried. "Please. I . . ."

"Please let me finish," he ordered, weak but severe. "And then you told me how you lied about going to Southampton that day I saw you in the train in Grand Central Station. You said you went to see . . . someone else. All that. Ending with 'I suggest we drive to Trieste and part there.' And then you walked out from under the bougainvillaea vine, crossed the room, and left saying, 'I didn't mean to tell you now, on account of your headache, but it just popped out.' So, like I said, let's be grown-up, and reasonable, and go back to your . . ."

"Popped out," Sonya repeated, almost stupidly. "Orange dress. Bougainvillaea."

Almost annoyed, he said, "Let's face facts, Sonya. Your plans were temporarily changed by my typhoid. Which brought out all your sympathy and compassion. And to ease my mind, you tried hard to make me feel you cared in . . . other ways. I appreciate everything you did. But, now that I'm better, what's the point in carrying pity, all that, into a future that was decided on right here in this very room, the morning I got sick?"

Trembling with exhaustion, he lay back with closed eyes. She bent over him. "Did you say bougainvillaea?"

"Please. Why press a detail that doesn't matter? You just happened to be standing in the bougainvillaea. So what?"

"I was standing where?"

He opened his eyes. "Over there, in the midst of all that . . ." He turned and pointed at the terrace door.

"Well," he said, astonished. "What happened to the bougain-villaea?"

"There never was any bougainvillaea there," she said. "Just that pathetic half-dead little rosebush. Don't you remember nursing it, the first night we got here?"

"Yeah," he still spoke in wonder. "Now that you mention it, I do. But . . . no bougainvillaea?"

"And no orange dress, either. I never even brought my orange dress; it's back in California, along with the bougainvillaea. And nothing just popped out of me, either. As a matter of fact, Tall Boy, you were sleeping deeply when I left and I tiptoed out without one word."

"Sleeping?"

"Sleeping and dreaming. Obviously. I may be a heartless, selfish bitch, but I never could say a thing like that to anybody as sick as you were."

"No bougainvillaea," he said, still staring at the terrace door.

She sat down on his bed and took his poor thin hand, almost a skeleton hand, and her fingers caressed the new scar on his wrist, a souvenir of that night when the Muir Woods burned down around him; it was a smaller, mouth-shaped replica of the snakebite scar on his calf. She felt the pebbly ridges along the vein where the needles had been buried.

"Now it's my turn," she said firmly. "Turn about. And not one word out of you, mind. You're too weak for backtalk. So relax."

She fussed around him, putting an extra pillow under his right hip, which was still giving him trouble from all the injections.

"Now just you listen to me," she ordered. "When we met in Verona, I was trying, not very successfully, to recover from a desperate love affair I'd had with a man named Werner Grunwald."

"Not the pianist?"

"Shhh. Yes. And he . . ."

"Tough act to follow," he muttered, closing his eyes.

"Shhh. And he had a wife, and because of me his wife committed suicide, and . . ."

On and on she talked, including everything she could think of that was important: The Concord Sonata and Madame Pompadour's jewel box; her sudden flight from Pobrecito; death and grief and incompatibility—

And the undiscussable flaw which had stained and discolored

240

her attitude to everything else, including the discussable flaw. And Laney and Stan. She even revealed her ugly thoughts as she had watched Werner's wife place the blood-orange azalea on his grave.

"In my mind *she* was the interloper," Sonya said. "And I still owned him and was owned by him, even in death. And his widow had betrayed me because she too must have made that same trip to Charleston, sharing his passion for the azaleas. Imagine such immaturity, such cheap romanticism, masquerading as sensitivity! I could not understand that Werner belonged to her, and that of course they had shared the azaleas, and that I to him could only exist as a form of memory, a kind of *pastness* . . ."

She paused, watching Tape for a reaction but getting none. His eyes were still closed, his face passive. She could not even tell if he was listening.

Hopelessly, she added, "And that's the way I was. All our years together, until . . . the night before your fever broke. I'd lost faith in medicine and I *knew* you were going to die. And only then, only then, did I recognize my mate, lying there, dying, with no one he loved there to comfort him, and no way to convince him that, suddenly, suddenly, like an explosion, I had become his mate. And even when my mate recovered, still, I couldn't convince him that I was his mate. Oh," she cried in passion and despair, "I learn the hard way. It's probably too late, but still I learn."

He opened his eyes. "Learn what?" he asked.

"I learn about Time," she said sadly. "And the three tenses of love. The Past can never be anything but a dried heap of flowers mixed with weeds; the Future is nothing but seeds of unknown species, flowers and weeds. And the only tense capable of bloom is the Present. And that's the one I neglected, failed to take loving care of, the only tense capable of blooming, of bearing fruit. The Present."

She bent over and looked deeply into his face, but his eyes were so indifferent that she became almost embarrassed at all the intimacies she had confided.

She drew back and looked away.

He turned again on his side and studied the terrace door, still in wonder. "No bougainvillaea," he said. "And how could there be, this far north? We're in wisteria country."

"I've worn you out," she apologized. "I intended to save it until you were stronger, but . . ."

The medical instructions were on the bedside table, and she picked up the pages on diet. She recognized the admiral's painstaking hand, like miniature Japanese brush-writing. Poor thing, all that time she'd waited, he'd been hiding in his office, preparing this, and too ashamed, or frightened—or both—to face her.

At the bottom of the last page he had written in the tiniest letters:

> *Important! No soft bread at all.*
> *Rusks only. Good luck, please!*

And the same to you, dear admiral, sir.

Tape was still looking at the terrace door, as if expecting that bougainvillaea vine to explode into existence any moment now . . .

"For all these years," he said, in his thin, quavering voice, a half-octave higher than normal, "I've been waiting for you to call me something like that, and then, when you finally did, I . . ."

His weak voice drifted off into silence, and she said, "Something like what?"

"Like 'sweetheart.' All these years of waiting for it, and then, when it finally came, I . . . I ordered you to stop it."

He began to cry, really cry, like a . . .

His tears were a glorious release to both of them, and she knelt and wived him tenderly.

"And I ordered you to stop it," he repeated, brokenly.

"Sweetheart," she said, ecstatically fulfilled and, yes, proud of herself, too, for clinging to her faith through all those fragile, breakable moments when everything could have been smashed to

242

pieces. "You did fine, sweetheart. It's about time somebody told me off. About time."

Oh, these delicate lives of ours, so safe and yet so insufferable when lived alone, but so dangerous when paired with another life, exposed to every passing sound and sight and thought and word and feeling and wordless action, forever exposed, the dangerous pairing. Each of us afflicted from birth in some way or the other, merging our afflictions into one dangerous pairing.

Helpless victim of every passing train and oyster and swimsuit and motel cheap or dear, and, yes, the Concord Sonata and Madame Pompadour's jewel box.

Our dangerous pairing was almost destroyed by a bougainvillaea that wasn't there; perhaps it survives only because a Communist bureaucrat decided Old Nick must go at once, or why would I have brought him back to this room, to see with his own eyes the bougainvillaea that never was?

And we are merely one pair of millions such, millions on millions of dangerous pairs, most of them poisoned or half-poisoned by lights and shadows and snakes creeping off curtains and lurking Unknown Viruses real and unreal.

And glaring orange dresses amid the dazzling purple blossoms.

All the millions on millions of us dangerous pairs with no exceptions—we need nursing through our crises, and nurselike watching every minute, every second—each nursing the other and the self with tender care lest each kill the other and the self.

We are a dangerous pair. Watch out. We must handle and be handled with care.

She lightly spread her fingertips across his forehead, where once . . .

She stroked his sunken, wasted cheek.

"We need a shave," she said.

"I need *you*."

She took his hand again, lightly kissed the new scar on his wrist, and said, "You want to know something, sweetheart? I think we made it."

He nodded.

We. More joyous than Mozart, the music of your *We.* And I in typhoid's grandeur becoming the Lord of Rejection, and—shame on me—enjoying my petty role.

We. Walking on hummingbirds' eggs. *We.*

"Yes," he said. "By Jesus and Joseph and Martin Luther, I guess we finally made it, didn't we?"

ABOUT THE AUTHOR

When Frederic Wakeman's first novel came out in 1944, *The Nation* called it "the spiritual parallel, from this war, to Ernest Hemingway's version of World War I"—and *Shore Leave* was dramatized on Broadway, filmed in Hollywood, and eventually sold more than a million and a half copies in a dozen languages.

Next came the novel about which Russell Maloney wrote in *The New York Times:* "The only other author capable of writing *The Hucksters* is Charles Dickens." But in his *Book of the Month* essay, Clifton Fadiman found his analogy in Sinclair Lewis.

Ten novels later, the comparisons extended from Chaucer and Boccaccio (*DeLuxe Tour*) to Joseph Conrad (*Free Agent*)—all of them proving that it is impossible to pin Wakeman down.

The author's work can be traced in his life, for both have followed winding but parallel paths, literally leading all over the world.

Born in Scranton, Kansas, in 1909—educated at Park College in Missouri—Madison-avenued in the Thirties—then the War years. He wrote *Shore Leave* while still in the U.S. Navy, returned to New York, quickly "retired" from advertising to write *The Hucksters,* settled first in Mexico, then—during 1946–1958—in Bermuda, California, Cuba, England, Florida, France, and Spain.

These past seven years he has lived in Greece with his second wife, the famed Athenian actress Ellie Lambetti. There are three children by a previous marriage, and two grandchildren.

Recently the Wakemans left Athens to take up residence—"This one is permanent," he says—in Riverdale, New York.

The Flute Across the Pond is his "new" look—and a piercing one it is—at the American scene after the years of wandering.